Letters to Erik

The Ghost's Love Story

An Wallace

Outskirts Press, Inc.
Denver, Colorado

Letters to Erik
The Ghost's Love Story
All Rights Reserved.
Copyright © 2008 An Wallace
V2.0

Outskirts Press, Inc.
http://www.outskirtspress.com

ISBN: 978-1-4327-1354-6

Outskirts Press and the "OP" logo are trademarks belonging to Outskirts Press, Inc.

PRINTED IN THE UNITED STATES OF AMERICA

Dedication

This is dedicated with much gratitude to my beloved husband, whose name means "gift from God."

I have always found it most fitting.

Acknowledgements

This book cannot be published without my expressing my extreme gratitude to the following people:

- My brother Bruce, who inadvertently introduced me to <u>The Phantom of the Opera</u> when I was a teenager
- My sister-in-law Krista, whose love for Erik proved wonderfully contagious
- Marjorie Loze, who helped me with the French, illustrated some of my favorite scenes, and sang Faust with me at the Paris Opera
- Stefanie Bean, who assisted with several of the historical details
- Angela Taratuta, the wonderful artist who drew the cover for me

- Nellie Clay, who very generously provided editing and comments
- Naomi Poe, whose late-night critiques and conversations were more helpful to me than she knows
- Whittney Olsen and Ashley Peck for providing suggestions and criticism when necessary
- Leatha Ann Betts, whose extensive genealogical research on the real-life "Changy" family inspired an essential plot point

Preface

The Opera Ghost really existed.

With these words, Gaston Leroux begins his 1910 novel, *Le Fantôme de l'Opèra*, a classic tale of madness, horror, true love, and sacrifice.

It is the story of Erik, a musical and architectural genius cursed with a deformed face and skeletal appearance. He lives in the lowest cellar of the Paris Opera House on the far side of a subterranean lake. Erik helped to build the Opera, *le palais Garnier*, and filled it with innumerable trapdoors, hollow walls, and secret passages. When he moves into the lowest cellar, the opera folk begin to hear footsteps and see movement in the shadows. They start believing the Opera is haunted.

Christine Daaé is a young Swedish soprano who sings secondary roles at the opera. Christine is a naïve and honorable girl, an orphan who lives alone with her foster-mother. Before her father died, he promised to send her the Angel of Music, which is the spirit that touches child prodigies and other great musical talents. Erik becomes intrigued with Christine and takes advantage of her innocent belief. Afraid to reveal his face to her, he deceives Christine into believing that he is the angel that had been promised. He gives her voice lessons through the walls of her dressing room without her seeing him. She comes to care for "The Voice" and to depend upon his support and tutelage.

No one is prouder than Erik when Christine makes her debut as Marguerite in Faust, and astounds the audience with the beauty of her singing.

What he doesn't count on is Raoul de Chagny's presence in the audience that night. Raoul is a viscount, a childhood friend of Christine's, who is in love with her.

Erik has fallen in love with Christine himself, and has demanded that she never entertain any suitors. She must keep herself only for her "angel." When she begins to show interest in Raoul, Erik is threatened. He masks his face, kidnaps Christine, and takes her on horseback down to his house in the cellars.

Christine is heartbroken to discover that her "angel of music" is really a man, and worse, that he is the feared opera ghost! He comforts her enough to sing with him, but during the song she takes off his mask, and he goes into a fury. He tells her that since she has seen his face, she will have to stay there with him forever! She is badly frightened by his face but more so by his temper. His music comforts her again, though, and she collects herself enough to lie to him about her horror at his appearance. She convinces him to let her leave by promising she will visit him again. Looking as he does, he knows he dare not hope for more. He agrees. Encouraged by her repeated visits, he continues to build up his hopes for her love and their eventual marriage.

Christine is horrified by Erik and intensely drawn to him at the same time. She is frightened by how compelling she finds him. He scares and comforts her at the same time, and his music enraptures and enthralls her. Confused and not knowing what else to do, Christine confides the whole story to Raoul on the roof of the opera house. The two make plans to escape together after the performance the following night. Unbeknownst to them, the heartbroken Erik overhears the entire conversation and kidnaps Christine right from the stage during the final act.

In a panic, Raoul accepts the help of a Persian police officer from Erik's past, and the two of them make their way down through the labyrinth of tunnels in the cellars looking for Erik's house. The Persian brings him to what he thinks is Erik's door, and they drop down into the house. Unfortunately, it is an entrance that Erik has booby-trapped, and the two men are nearly killed in his "torture chamber." While trying to escape from the chamber, they discover barrels and barrels of gunpowder that Erik has stored below his house.

Meanwhile Erik has lost his mind and is violently out of control. He drowns Raoul's older brother Philippe, who has come looking for Raoul. Then, clothes still dripping, Erik returns and offers Christine a choice: either she marries him or he uses the gunpowder to blow up the entire opera house. Terrified, betrayed by her trusted teacher, Christine chooses to save the people in the opera—and the two men in the torture chamber—by marrying Erik.

Erik releases the two men and takes care of

them, and then returns to Christine.

Christine shows her true compassion and tender affection for Erik by weeping with him and letting him kiss her forehead—he, who had never been allowed to kiss anyone before, not even his own mother. Transported with happiness, Erik comes to his senses. He realizes that Christine truly loves the viscount, and would be unhappy staying there with Erik. Having reached his pinnacle of bliss, weeping, he sacrifices his love. He releases her and sends her away to marry Raoul. He only asks her one thing: since he expects to die soon, he requests that she come back to bury him with the gold wedding ring he had given her.

The story ends with an advertisement placed in *l'Epoch* by the Persian policeman, stating, "Erik is dead." Directly after this, Christine and Raoul board a train to take them back to Sweden, where they are quietly married.

This horrifying but beautiful story may even have some basis in fact; many of the details correspond with real events and people, and some say that even on his deathbed, Leroux continued to maintain that *the Opera Ghost really existed.*

Chapter 1
The Prodigal's Return

1884

*D*ear Erik,
   I am writing this from my hotel room in Copenhagen. Mamma Valérius, Raoul, and I were able to catch the last train heading north, and plan to be back in my beloved homeland very soon. It will be good to breathe the air, see the mountains, and speak my own language again.

   Raoul and I are planning to be married in a small church in my hometown. I almost wish you could be there—but it would be cruel of me to wish that upon you, wouldn't it? All the same, it will be one of the happiest days of my life, and I do wish it were possible to share it with the people who have been dearest to me.

Yes, Erik, you are one of them. If I were to write from now until doomsday I could not express enough regret for how I hurt you. I only wish I could have told you while you were still alive, that you changed my life. It was your touch upon me that gave me any greatness whatsoever. Without you, I would have been nothing... and without your influence I would not have become a star, and Raoul would never have noticed me again.

I wager that's the part you probably regret the most!

My dear Erik, I rather miss singing with you. Raoul doesn't like me to sing for anyone but him; and while I love singing for him, I must confess that I do miss the public acclaim I used to get. Does that make me vain? I miss you as well, my friend: I miss sitting with you in the evenings, reading with you, singing with you, talking with you. You know such a great deal about so many things—I'm still at a loss to see what you could have seen in a timid little songbird like me. I've tried to hide my grief

from Raoul. He never understood what you and I shared; even though it wasn't what you wished it could be, it was still far more than I ever hoped for or deserved.
Rest in peace, my friend.

With love,

Your Christine

With a faraway look, Christine blew on the ink to dry it. She emptied her reticule on the dressing table and poked around the scraps and objects there until she found what she was looking for. It was a very tiny key, strung on a loop of black velvet ribbon. She inserted it into what looked like solid wood in the front of her jewelry box, and opened the hidden bottom drawer. She lifted out an oval of black silk, very finely shaped and hemmed—even the two narrow eyeholes.

The full-face mask had a long piece of black ribbon that would have tied behind the head of its wearer. Christine sat for a few minutes, just holding the mask. She fingered the silk thoughtfully, lifting it up to feel its smoothness with her lips. Erik had removed it during their final moments together, when they had clung together and cried like children. They had mingled their tears and exchanged tender kisses, before Erik had sent her away with her beloved Raoul. She hadn't realized that his mask was still clutched in her hand, but now she found a poignant sort of comfort in keeping it. Knowing that she had abandoned Erik to die alone still grieved her more than her sunny-faced fiancé could possibly guess.

She folded the now-dry letter and slipped it into the hidden drawer, placing the silk mask on top of it. She heard her fiancé call her name, and she quickly locked up the little box and put it back into the drawer of her dressing table. "Coming, my love," she called, and turned down the lights as she left the room with a sad smile.

# # #

My dear Erik,

I know it is sad and even rather disturbing that even though you're gone I still feel this compulsion to tell you about my day! Is writing letters to the dead a sign of mental imbalance, do you think? For that matter though, you may very well be the last person I should be asking about mental imbalances! Oh, my poor Erik — how things might have been different for you, had you been treated differently! You might have been the sanest and wisest of men!

Or is it simply that old habits are difficult to break? It is ironic that when I used to spend my time with you, I used to write letters to Raoul (that he never received). Now that I am married to him, I end up writing letters to you (that you likewise will never receive).

We arrived in my hometown today, and you would be amazed at how many people remembered "Little Stina," as I was called here. Christine was only my French name—here, I was Stina Daaé, the violinist's daughter. It was so nice to hear my old name again today, and my own language! Raoul was quite lost, I'm afraid. The poor dear, how confused he looked when I introduced him to all of my father's old friends—and he couldn't understand a word of the introduction! I was tempted to laugh, but it would have hurt his feelings. I fear that he saw my amusement anyway; he became rather sulky for the rest of the day.

We have bought a palatial house on the outskirts of my old village. I had wanted to move closer to Gothenburg, where I would have been able to continue my musical education, but Raoul insisted that we stay here in my old village near Upsala. I tried to explain that I didn't know many people here; Papa and I left for the city while I was still young. But Raoul insists that a small village is what we want, because no one will be able to find us.

Personally, I don't think we'll be that hard to find in a house this large, but I held my tongue. I didn't want to get involved in an argument so soon before we marry. I do wish that I could go on studying music and singing, though; it doesn't look as if I shall have that chance if we remain here.

We arranged for my old priest to marry us next week. But now, hear the best part! When he heard about who I had been in Paris, Father Fisk now wants me to come and sing in church on Sundays! Not even Raoul could object to that, I'm sure! I am so excited—and now I really do wish you could come and hear me. I know my voice is rusty from being out of practice, and I know you would be cross with me if you heard me now. I shall have to start practicing; he wants me to begin the Sunday after our wedding. I cannot wait!

I just re-read that last paragraph, Erik, and it sounds as if I'm more excited to be singing again than I am about my own wedding. I assure you, I'm quite excited about both. I am! Honestly!

I'm just not that eager to live in Upsala again.

I still miss you more than I can say. I could never wish for a better companion than you were. Raoul loves me, but he has no great love for music. My father, God rest his soul, loved music as much as you do, but was never much for reading. Mama Valérius loves reading, but (God bless her) lacks the intelligence to make good, sparkling conversation. You, on the other hand, satisfied my need for companionship on nearly every level. Your death has left a giant hole in my heart that nothing else seems to fill, no matter how hard I try.

My dearest Erik, why did you not keep your promise to me? I read your death-notice in l'Epoche, *but when I went back to your house I found only the Persian, who informed me he had already taken care of your body. I would have been honored to do that for you, Erik— why didn't you make him wait for me?*

Listen to my foolishness, asking a dead man

why he didn't make the living do one thing or another! Still, it was a disappointment. I do appreciate that he gave me back your ring to keep, though. It gives me something tangible to remember you by, for when my voice fades into insignificance.

Speaking of which, I had better get practicing if I'm to sing in public in two weeks! I shall simply pretend that you're here with me, teaching me, and I should do fine.

I wish you really were here with me, my dear.

Ever your loving

Christine

Christine folded this letter up with the other, and locked them into her jewelry box. She had no idea why she felt like writing to Erik every so often, but as long as Raoul never found out about it, it should be fine. Erik had been a huge part of her life after all, and his passing had left her feeling empty. It's just until I get through my grief, she told herself. Raoul wouldn't understand about my grief, so I simply won't burden him with it. I'll pour my feelings out on paper, where they'll harm no one, and if the dead really do haunt the living sometimes, then Erik will know I'm thinking of him.

# # #

Dear Erik,
Dear Mamma Valérius is very ill. I am worried about her. She has not been well since shortly after our wedding. I hate to see her suffering; she has been so good to me through the years, staying in Paris with me even though she longed to see her homeland again. Like my father. I wish he could have lived to return here with us; to think of him just wasting away in Paris, pining for his native land, just breaks my heart.

Truth to tell, it also makes me a little angry that Sweden meant more to him than I did. He could have become accustomed to Paris if he'd wanted to, and continued to teach me my music, but instead he just stayed locked up in his room playing his old country folk songs all the time. I miss him greatly, and I've never stopped loving him, but I am old enough now to realize that he was not infallible as I used to think. I wish he had chosen to engage himself with the world around him, instead of always looking backward to what might have been!

I can ruefully acknowledge that there is a certain irony to my writing those words to a dead man.

Am I growing up, Erik? Or am I just becoming discontent?

Your loving

Christine

# # #

Dear Erik,
This morning I sang in the church for the first time. It was beautiful, with the sun coming in the windows and the lovely acoustics in the church. It reminded me of that time you made me sing in the rotunda, so I could hear my voice bouncing off all those rounded stone walls! Father Fisk thanked me, and several others complimented me and said I must have had a very great teacher! I told them I had, but that he'd died recently, and I was still mourning him. They offered their condolences, but Raoul hurried me out of there soon after that. It

*was strange. I hadn't thought it possible for
him to be jealous of a dead man, but so he
seems.*

*I asked him about it in the carriage: I
wanted to know what the harm was in even referring to you, and he made some half-hearted
excuse about not wanting the outside world to
know who we were.*

*Who were we, I asked, a little bit angry—
these are my own people, after all! —and he
said we were now the Count and Countess de
Chagny. Since Philippe died without legitimate
issue, Raoul inherited the title of Count de
Chagny. It's so strange, Erik—I don't feel
much like a countess, even though we got married a week ago. I just feel like little Stina, finally come home.*

*It still seems odd to think that little Stina got
married a week ago. The wedding was lovely,
with many of my parents' old friends in atten-
dance. It was not comfortable; the dress that
Raoul insisted I be married in was really a bit
much for such a small community. Our
neighbors seemed ill at ease, as if they didn't
know what to do or how to talk to me. I tried to
put them at ease as much as I could, but
Raoul's not being able to speak any Swedish*

made it difficult to introduce him and interact with all of my family's old friends.

It's all so strange, to live with a man, to be married to him. I thought married people always shared a bed, but Raoul tells me this is not the case; only the lower classes share a bed once they're married. Men and women of his rank keep their own separate bedrooms. This seems odd to me, for the husband to merely visit his wife for their—ah, but there I cannot talk of something so private, even in a letter— and then return to his own room afterwards.

If I had married you as you had wished, dear Erik, would you have still made me sleep alone? But there, I'm being ungrateful again. Raoul has given up a great deal to marry me, and I am sure I'll become accustomed to the customs of the nobility soon enough. I mustn't think of you in that way in any case, as I'm now married to someone else whom I love quite deeply.

All the same, my dear, you never left me when I asked you to stay.

Your Christine

Christine locked up the letter and stood up,

shivering. She reached up and turned off the gaslight, and then hurried over to her bed by the moonlight that came in the window. She took off her dressing gown and laid it carefully over the bed—she could use the extra warmth—and crawled in between the covers. The last lingering bit of heat from the young *comte's* body had dissipated, and Christine steeled herself to shove her already-chilly bare feet down to the bottom of the bed where the sheets were still icy.

Swedish winters were something she hadn't missed much, in Paris.

She lay still, shivering, knowing it would be a long time before she warmed up enough to fall asleep. She wished Raoul had stayed—to provide some extra warmth, if nothing else!

# # #

Dear Erik,

I haven't needed to write to you for a while, which I had hoped was a good sign that I was getting over my grief over your death. I am beginning to fear, though, that you were right when you told me I could never, ever leave you—you seem to be present with me all the time in my mind. You were all I could think of when I sang in church last week. You would be proud of me, though, because I managed to re-member to keep my chin down when hitting the high notes. I still remember with fond amuse-ment, the time you demonstrated the difference in sound between hitting them properly, and "trying to reach for them with your chin." It was such an awful sound that I was afraid the corps de ballet *would come running to stop me from killing some poor cat! That was in my dressing-room before you ever showed yourself to me, and I remember wondering if angels, as beings of spirit, even* have *chins? It was no wonder that little Giry and little Jammes were always bleating about being afraid of the ghost, if that is how you haunted them! And while I think of it, did you really have to frighten them so? I know it must have amused you, but my dear, they were so shrill!*

I must apologize, Erik, for the way I reacted when I discovered that you really were not an angel from heaven. How silly I was, to think you might have been! I do think, though, that you could have been a bit more honest with me back then and spared me the pain of my disillu-sionment! I do sometimes wonder what might

*have happened if you had told me from the be-
ginning that you were a man, and had taught
me anyway. Perhaps things could have been
different.*

*Certainly I would not have been treated as
coldly after I sang as Raoul has been treating
me. The silly boy—he knew I loved to sing.
Why, then, must he act so cold and distant toward me every Sunday when we're driving
home from church? He has never asked me not
to sing in church; he has merely forbidden me
from going on stage anywhere. So why is he so
aloof? He doesn't thaw out until mid-week, but
by then I'm anticipating another chilly Sunday
after church so I can't really enjoy the time he
spends with me when he isn't being cool or
reprimanding me.*

*I knew it would be cold in Sweden, but I
thought it would be warm in my own home.*

*He spoke to me quite sharply the other day
about my being too "familiar" with the house
staff. I was only chatting with one of the maids
a little, because she had asked where we were
from and was very excited to hear that we'd
been in Paris for the last several years. It was
quite innocent, honestly, but Raoul overheard
us and called me into his study to speak to me*

about it. He reminded me that I am a countess now, and that I'm required to keep a certain distance between myself and the servants; it wouldn't do to treat them as equals, because then they'd start putting on airs and thinking they were entitled to special privileges. I wasn't treating her as an equal (though, as the daughter of a peasant, I really am); all I was doing was treating her as a person. But Raoul didn't see it that way.

And in truth, I might not have been quite so inclined to chat with her and keep her from her work, if I had any other friends to talk with. But no one comes to see me here, and when I go to see them they are very uncomfortable with a countess in their midst. Sometimes I wish that Raoul were nothing but a peasant, like them! Like me. He has changed from the sweet boy I used to know; as a man, he has a much more commanding presence. I just wish he would save his commands for the navy, and not apply them to his own wife. I know that he loves me, but when the only time he spends much time with me is to scold me for not upholding his noble honor well enough, the love gets harder to see.

Raoul's two sisters, with whom he used to

live, came up to visit. I use the term "visit" extremely loosely, as it was not an enjoyable time for any of them. For me it was neutral; as soon as I saw how they were going to be, I withdrew to my room. I don't think I spent more than five or ten minutes with them, and so emerged unscathed. Poor Raoul had to host them for nearly an hour of being shouted at, berated, and threatened with the loss of his inheritance. Luckily this is an empty threat; Raoul has told me that both Clémence and Martine willingly signed over all of their inheritance to Philippe when their father died. With Philippe gone as well, Raoul is the one in charge of the family fortunes.

They shouted dreadful things about me, though, and about Raoul for marrying me. I could hear them all the way up the stairs and through my closed door. Raoul says they are going home tomorrow, and I am glad. I don't want them around long enough for him to really pay attention to what they tell him about me; he might start to believe them.

I am sorry, my dear, for coming to cry to you about my marital woes. Raoul really does treat me like a queen most of the time. When he's with me at all, I mean. He does love me, and I am grateful that he does allow me to sing on Sundays at least (even though he does get short-tempered about it). He is so sweet to me by mid-week that I can certainly forgive him being a bit snappish on Sunday afternoons, and when he catches me acting in a way that isn't befitting my rank.

Heaven knows you were certainly irritated with me much more often than that, my friend! But I am so empty without you that I even miss that. Not to mention that your irritation was usually because I'd done something silly that might damage my voice.

I must go and try to placate my dear husband. I feel better for having written; I think you do me good, Erik, even from the grave.

I think you must have influenced me toward morbidity, my dear, with all your talk of death and sleeping in coffins and such.

Your loving friend,

Christine

Christine locked the letter up and stood, straightening out her skirts. It was almost time for dinner, and this time she was determined to talk to Raoul about his Sunday afternoon be-havior. It was time for this coldness to stop. He had been that way ever since the first Sunday she had sung, when people had complimented her voice and condoled with her over the death of her teacher. She had had enough.

Unfortunately, her discussion did not go as planned, and she and Raoul retired to their re-spective rooms that evening in a state of cold reserve.

Chapter 2
A Promise of Hope

*D*ear Erik,
     What do you think? This is one of the most amazing things that has ever happened to me! And for once I'm glad that you won't be reading these letters, because I know I could never talk about this with you if you were alive. I would be much too self-conscious.

Raoul and I are going to have a baby.

I am so excited! And Raoul has been very sweet to me even though I have been ill very often (almost every day). The doctor tells me that I should start feeling better soon; I do hope he's right! He says that women like me shouldn't have children, because we don't have the hips for it. He is a shocking and dreadful little man, and Raoul was very curt with him as he showed him out.

So now we get the delightful privilege of choosing names for our child. I hope it's a boy. Raoul says he hopes we get a little blonde-haired girl who looks like me, but personally I'm hoping for a boy so I can name him after my father. Blond hair is quite likely in any case, considering how fair we both are.

The down side of this news is that Raoul doesn't even "visit" me in my room anymore, and I get lonely especially at night. I get lonely during the day as well. It seems that few of my old friends feel comfortable paying calls to a countess, nor do they wish me to visit them because they're ashamed of their small and dingy houses.

Oh, Erik, if only they could remember my father and me, sleeping in haystacks all over Sweden, they might not be so conscious of the differences between us! I miss my old friends at the Opera as well, and I miss the excitement there. It was a whole different world, and a whole different life shared only by those people who lived and performed within those walls. No one from the outside can really understand it. I have very few friends here, and Raoul is now so careful and solicitous of my health that he makes me go to bed early every night and refuses to accompany me.

It is boring. I don't need that much sleep, and I usually end up reading. You remember how late I used to stay up all the time, Erik—I recall many, many times, the two of us in your sitting room, reading together until well after midnight. But Raoul rises with the lark, and he wishes me to be more like him, so I go to bed at eight every night, and then lie awake until one or two.

Ah, but there I go complaining about him again. He is really very sweet, and it is kind of him to care for me so well. It isn't his fault that my body still keeps theatre hours. Perhaps being a mother will cure me of that.

I know you would not be happy to hear my news, Erik, but I can wish you would have cared for my own happiness about it at least. Raoul and I are thrilled to be having a child together.

Perhaps this is another of those times when it's a good thing you won't be reading these letters.

Ever your friend,

Christine

Christine blew on the ink to dry it, and locked up the letter as she always did. Not for the first time, she wished that Erik were still alive for her to talk to. There was something about him, some spark of understanding that had been between them, that she had never shared with Raoul. After she had gotten used to Erik's face, and had spent more time with him, they'd enjoyed long evenings of conversation during her visits. He was a good listener and a clever conversationalist, and for much of the time she was able to forget that he was deformed, skeletal, and mentally unbalanced. It was as if her friend the "Voice" from her dressing room were still there with her.

She smiled sadly, remembering her close friendship with the "Voice," and later how it transformed into her friendship with Erik. Because Erik's irrational behavior had frightened her so badly, she had never spoken much to Raoul about the good times, the non-frightening times, the times when she had thought seriously about accepting Erik's proposal. She had tried to tell Raoul once or twice, just so that her husband would not think Erik more of a monster than he was, but it only served to anger him.

No, she must accept it: Raoul would never understand the relationship she had shared with Erik, nor how much she missed him.

# # #

Dear Erik,

Mama Valérius is dead. She lived long enough to see her homeland again, and to see me and Raoul married, but then she took a chill and her health declined rapidly. So now she won't be able to see our child born, nor will she be able to keep me company and help me during the pregnancy which, for some reason, makes me even lonelier.

This morning I sang in church, for her funeral. I had not wanted to sing on so sad an occasion, but as it was at Mamma Valérius' urging that I accepted lessons from you in the first place, it seemed only fitting.

I sometimes wonder about her mental capacity in that regard. I know that I was frightfully naïve, almost simpleminded in my gullibility – but, then, I was a mere child. At the risk of sounding ungrateful to her (which I am not), what was <u>her</u> excuse?

Am I sounding childish, dearest Erik? Or

*simply disillusioned? For I am definitely disil-
lusioned. None of my hopes and plans from
childhood have ever come to fruition except for
when I was with you. I had always dreamed of
singing the opera leads, and you made that
possible! But my father abandoned me in favor
of his memories of home; Raoul abandons me
to my lonely room at night; my old friends here
have abandoned me because of my rank
(strange, I don't feel like a countess! I still feel
like little Stina, but no one treats me like that
anymore), and most recently Mamma Valérius
has abandoned me in death. She was the closest
thing to a mother that I can ever remember
having, and although she was a simple woman,
she had a kind and generous heart. I am sure
she would have loved you, if she had ever met
you. Certainly that night that Raoul came to
call without warning, she defended my right to
love you without even knowing who you were.*

*Erik, I am so lonely, so lonely! I know I
should feel grateful, for how many other "opera wenches" have married counts and get to
live in a huge, beautiful house, surrounded by
luxury? But I don't feel grateful; I just feel sad
that I have no one to share it with, and despair
that I shall always be alone.*

During my last weeks with you, when you were acting so strangely and scaring me so much, I confess I went to Raoul for comfort. He seemed like a pillar of strength to me, terrified and anguished as I was, and I clung to him. I may even have fallen in love with him then, simply because he was so calm and sane, so different from you. But my dear, I think he has trouble coping with the day-to-day hardships of being a man. When he doesn't have some grand, noble quest to save the damsel from the madman, it seems that he doesn't quite know what to do with himself—or even with the damsel in question! Our dinner conversations are polite and stilted, and that is the only time we ever spend together. He passes most of his time in his study. He seems to have lost his direction, and is probably regretting his decision to marry me.

I shall be glad when our child is born. Perhaps then Raoul might discover a new purpose in life. I only wish that my foster-mother could still be alive to see our child.

My dearest Erik, why does everyone I love die?

Your grieving friend,

Christine

Christine locked up the letter and took a moment to admire the jewelry box itself. She had never told Raoul, but it was one that Erik had made for her. True to his mischievous nature, he had made it full of secret compartments and tiny trap-doors, hidden levers and switches. She turned it over and pressed the side, and a small drawer popped open. She reached inside with two fingers and pulled out a plain gold ring. She held it up to the light and looked at the inscription on the inside: "C.D." it said on one side, and on the other, "Erik."

Slowly, not knowing quite why, she slipped her wedding ring off her finger and put Erik's ring on instead. It sparkled in the dim gaslights, and she looked at it with a sad smile before putting it back into its secret compartment and putting her wedding ring back on.

She wondered if she could ever have born children for Erik, if they had married.

Scolding herself for the thought, she quickly put away the box, put the key around her neck, and crawled into bed. Too restless to sleep so early, she picked up a book and started reading.

# # #

Dear Erik,

Yesterday I was out with Raoul, and our carriage broke. It was one of those rare times that he wanted to spend time with me outside of mealtimes, and I was so happy! But then the carriage wheel broke and we could go no further. He unharnessed the horse and swung up on it, to ride it back to the house. He wanted to help me up, to ride pillion behind him. I was startled; I had thought that when a man and a woman rode double, the woman was always in front. You see, I was remembering you and me riding double on César, the night the chandelier fell and you brought me through the mirror in my dressing room.

Raoul was bewildered and suspicious, wanting to know when I had ridden double before, and with whom, and—Erik, I am ashamed to say this, but I found myself lying to him! I told him I'd done it with my father, when I was little.

He seemed to accept this and laughed, saying that children did indeed ride in front, but that grown-up people ride pillion. He humored me, though, and brought me up to ride before him.

I am sorry for lying like I did. I assure you, it is not because I am ashamed of you, or of anything that we did when we were together! It is just that Raoul gets so jealous if I even mention your name, that it is just easier to avoid it altogether.

Erik, I hope you don't mind a personal question, something I have been wondering about ever since that ride with Raoul. What was it like for you, that time we rode together on César? Because I think you had me drugged, and I don't really remember much about it. With Raoul, though, we found we were pressed together rather closely on the moving horse, and Raoul became quite amorous—and then when we reached the house he didn't immediately go find a wheelwright; instead, he came in and followed me right up to my room! In daylight!

He kept saying what a good idea I had had, to ride in front, and now that I know his meaning, I am afraid to tell him that it was you who did it first, in order to keep me on the horse after you'd drugged me!

I know that you must have drugged me, for the scent of chloroform clung to your skin and clothes. Ever since I was a little girl watching M. Valérius perform experiments, I have always thought that must be what death smells like: that musty, sweetish scent that weighs down your lungs and makes your gorge rise. It frightened me very much, especially when combined with your emaciated appearance and chilly hands. I know now that none of that was your fault, but at the time you terrified me.

For a long time, I thought that if you had only spoken the truth to me from the beginning, then your betrayal would not have been so painful. If you had told me from the start that you were a man, albeit a deformed one, who wanted to give me music lessons—but no, you're right. I would not have accepted it. Imagine, some unknown, deformed man showing up in my dressing room every morning? As it was, Raoul gave me enough trouble over having just a man's voice *in my dressing room. Imagine how much more my reputation might have suffered had I had the whole man himself in there with me?*

It was probably best that you did what you did; but all the same, I wish you had foregone the chloroform!

Always your

Christine

Christine stowed her letter in the jewelry box, blessing Erik for the way he had made the drawer look so small, yet be so capacious. Even with all the letters she had written so far, the drawer was only half full. She leaned down for just a moment, and sniffed the inside of it.

It smelled of ink and beeswax, and just the faintest tinge of mustiness, and Christine leaned back and smiled. She remembered that Erik had smelled much the same, when he hadn't been near any chloroform. Oddly comforted by the fact that whenever she wanted to, she could open the tiny drawer and breathe in the scent of her teacher, she closed the box and put it away.

# # #

Dear Erik,

I have been thinking lately about your face. I know it is a strange object of contemplation, for even your dearest friends could never have said you were handsome. How many friends did you have, Erik, dear or otherwise? It strikes me that there is so much about you I don't know. Your stories about your travels in Persia and other places always filled me with such fascination, and yet I know that you never shared even half of them.

I sometimes wish I could have traveled with you.

But I was speaking of your face. I happened to mention to the doctor (who really isn't that bad a man, now that I've gotten to know him better) that I used to know someone with a birth defect of the face, and he told me it's more common than many people realize. He told me of a man he knew in his youth, who had been born without any nose—he just had a hole where there should have been a nose. And my doctor's mentor fashioned a false nose for the man to wear, that looked like any other nose.

I know your deformity came with a certain... well, cadaverous aspect (that was only made worse by your thinness—Erik, I should have done your cooking for you, all those times I was your guest! I could have fattened you up a little!) that took some getting used to, but it saddens me that there may have been some hope for you to enjoy normal society, and that you never found it.

And I must confess to an unworthy thought. If you and I had married, would your deformity have transferred to our children? I mentioned this (hypothetically, of course!) to my doctor, and he thinks not. He says that this sort of thing tends to be a one-time occurrence, and not nec-essarily passed on to the children. Which eases my mind somewhat, though I have no idea why.

Although why I should be thinking of other people's beauty or ugliness when I resemble a beached whale myself, I really don't know. The doctor says I am about two-thirds of the way through my pregnancy. What joy. I am miser-able: my back aches, I am bloated, my shoes no longer fit, and I resemble a great pink walrus in shape. If you could see me now, you would not think me beautiful any longer! I also don't know how I'm going to survive the next three months if I'm this big already!

Your unhappily huge

Christine

Christine locked up the letter and stood, stretching to ease her back. She wondered if she really was supposed to be so big when she still had three months to go, but the doctor as-sured her that some women did, and that it was all right. She rang for her maid, Anneke, to help her undress.

It was odd, for someone who had grown up

poor and self-sufficient as Christine had, to have to employ a maid to help her dress and undress. She had gotten used to it at the opera but she still preferred the simpler fashions that she had worn as a girl, which did not have as many hooks and laces. With her body the shape it was in, though, she literally couldn't reach her fastenings these days. Anneke came in to help her undress and get into her nightgown. Then the girl had to brace herself firmly against the bed-frame in order to help Christine lie down in bed. Christine had lost all of her natural grace, and hated the fact that she couldn't even get into bed by herself.

"Shall I lower the lights, my lady?" Anneke asked.

Christine thought a minute. It was much too early for sleep; she'd rather read, but then she would either have to get up and turn off the lights herself, or make her maid stay awake until she was ready to sleep. Out of consideration for the young woman, she nodded. "Yes, please, and then you may retire. I shan't need you again this evening."

The maid gave her a grateful curtsey and lowered the lights as she left. Christine sighed and lay back, prepared for several hours of sleeplessness. As was her wont, she slipped into a daydream as she lay there. She thought of Erik, and what it might have been like if she had chosen him out of love, and married him. She admitted to herself that if Erik's face had not been so ugly, and if Raoul hadn't happened on the scene when he did, it was a valid possibility. Certainly she had never been able to give Raoul an honest answer, that time on the rooftop when he had asked if she would still love him if this Erik were a handsome man? She had asked him why he wanted to know things that were so hard to answer, that she preferred to hide in the bottom of her soul "like sins"—and then had changed the subject. Now, though, lying in the dark with nothing to do but think for the next several hours, she was forced to confess to the empty air that yes, she would have loved Erik if he'd been handsome.

Blushing in shame at her own shallowness, she carefully rolled onto her side and sniffled. It was disgraceful that she had allowed her feelings to be swayed so much by someone's outward appearance. Suddenly she remembered a Bible passage that Father Fisk had spoken about a few weeks ago: man looks on the outward appearance, but God looks on the heart.

Christine was quite devout, and was ashamed that she had proven herself no better or closer to God than anyone else who had abused Erik throughout his life.

Without her realizing it, her tears came as she lay there thinking about him. Her pregnancy had made her emotional, and this was no exception. She thought of what her life had been like, as opposed to what it might have been like with Erik, and she wept unashamedly.

As she slipped into sleep, she dreamed of him.

#

Dear Erik,

Ever since Mamma Valérius' death, I have been thinking of you a great deal. Since she was the first one who ever put the idea into my head of the mysterious voice in my dressing room belonging to the Angel of Music, thoughts of her have invariably led to thoughts of you. It's quite odd, though, the extent to which you have invaded my mind. I do usually think of you quite often, but this has been bordering on obsession! You have even appeared in my dreams on an almost nightly basis.

I had been starting to be concerned for my mental health, because my dreams have been so vivid that the waking world had begun to seem dreamlike to me. I have been reassured on that count, I am happy to say. My maid, Anneke, had her married sister come to visit yesterday. Her name is Charlotta, and I was amused to hear Anneke calling her "Lotte." It reminded me of the old folktale that my father used to tell me and Raoul when we were children. Lotte has three children, though, and when she heard that I was expecting, she was able to reassure me on a number of points— including the fact that pregnant women frequently have exceedingly vivid recurring dreams.

Raoul would scold me if he knew that I had a lovely visit with my maid's sister. He thinks I am not keeping to my place as a countess well enough. He does not understand, though, how badly I need other women to talk to about some of these things. If I complain of something, he just sends for the doctor. But so much of what is wrong with me is actually normal for a pregnant woman that I hate to have to keep calling the doctor when twenty minutes conversation with another woman would set my mind at ease!

But I was speaking of my dreams. Usually they are just memory dreams, remembering various things we did together—singing, carriage rides, reading—but this one was of the night we first met in person. It was different, though; in my dream, you and I had been married somehow, up in my dressing room before you brought me through the mirror. When you held me up there in front of you on César, it was as my husband—and when you kissed me, you were kissing your wife. You were unmasked, but it didn't seem to matter to me.

There are details that I blush to even think about, much less write to you. Suffice it to say that we behaved very much as husband and wife in my dream. Afterwards, though, you wept and told me that it was wonderful but it wasn't real.

Upon waking and discovering that you were right, I could not ward off my own tears.

Indeed, the dream had been so full of vivid and passionate detail, that waking up in my cold, lonely house with no music was more like waking into a nightmare. I had to remind myself of what had really happened: that you kidnapped me, frightened me, and drugged me, and that our ride through the cellars was fraught with terror for me, rather than romance. Even so, I kept feeling as if my dream was really the way things should have happened between us instead of what really did happen. I have not been able to keep from revisiting my dream, and so have been making myself unhappy for much of the day.

I shall be glad when this child is born, and I can have my mind to myself again.

Ever your

Christine

Christine folded this letter and put it away in the tiny box. There were some parts of the dream that she hadn't mentioned to Erik in the letter that still caused her to wake up gasping. In her dream, her sensations of riding César with Erik behind her, holding her close to his sinewy body, were extremely real and intense. At the time of the ride, she had been nearly senseless—but now, in her dream, her senses had been on overload. She had felt every inch of his lean body pressed against hers, his wiry arm around her waist holding her steady against the slight rocking motion of César's walk.

Ducking her head, she blushed even redder when she remembered some further details that she would never, ever divulge—no, not even in a letter to a dead man.

And then in the morning, when she had awakened to find it had only been a dream, she had not been able to stop the flow of tears. It was past lunchtime before she had stopped crying.

She was morose at supper, and when Raoul asked what her problem was, she snapped at him. When he came to her room that night, she turned him away. It felt like a betrayal of Erik, to have Raoul in her room.

It took a long time for her to feel normal again.

# # #

Dear Erik,

Raoul is a rat and a bloody bastard and I wish I had never married him! Here I am, still a month away from delivering his child, and he has the nerve to call me irrational and to talk down to me! All I wanted was some strawberries—was that too much to ask?—and not only did he refuse to get them for me, but he took it upon himself to lecture me about seasonal agriculture!

I told him he was certainly rich enough to buy his wife some out-of-season strawberries, since he seems to be able to afford everything else he has a whim for. He became quite cross with me, and stormed out. I was still angry and wanted to stalk around, yell, and break things—but instead all I could do was cry, and it infuriated me even more that I couldn't indulge my temper as I wished!

I am sorry, Erik. I have been so dreadfully cranky and cross lately that I don't know myself. The doctor tells me it's not my fault; it's the fault of the baby. He says many expectant women "go crazy," as he somewhat insensitively put it. It's not Raoul's fault, either; he's been nothing but accommodating to most of my (admittedly) irrational demands.

But oh my goodness, won't I be glad when this child is born and I can go back to normal! It kicks and squirms, you know, Erik: I can feel it moving about, within me. I never knew babies could do that. And I wish Mama Valérius or some other women were still around, for me to talk to. I miss having women friends.

I miss having friends.

I miss you most of all. I pray daily for your soul, my dear, that our Father in Heaven would have mercy on you and admit you to paradise in spite of your sins. If I cannot enjoy your company here on earth anymore, then perhaps He may yet allow it on the other shore.

I have heard it said that one can achieve sanctification through martyrdom. If that is the case, my dear friend, then you certainly qualify.

I am just sorry it came to that. I am certainly not worth anyone's life.

Your Christine

Christine took a deep, calming breath. She really had been a bit over the top with poor Raoul! She rang for a servant to let her know the instant he returned; she had to apologize to him for some things she had said in the heat of her anger. Smiling a little ruefully at her own foolishness, she folded the letter and put it into the jewelry box with the others, and put the box away in her dressing table drawer.

Chapter 3
Hopes Dashed

*O*h, Erik,
It is a tragedy worse than any other I have ever experienced.

Our child has died.

He was born a full month early, and something about him wasn't quite right. Apparently, my child had a defect before he was even born!

Oh, but Erik, he looked so perfect! I got to hold him for a few minutes, and he looked up at me with eyes the color of the sky. He had a shock of blond hair, too, and a dimpled chin such as Raoul tells me his older brother Philippe used to have.

Raoul demanded that we name him after

Philippe, and we did so.

But Erik, I so wanted to name him after you! It would have been one way that you could have lived on somehow... but of course Raoul wouldn't hear of it, and demanded we name the baby after Philippe instead.

And now our dear, beautiful little Philippe is gone. He only lasted a day and a half, because he couldn't take any nutrition. He couldn't swallow, the doctor said, which led to my getting so large, so early in the pregnancy. I don't understand it completely, but we could not get him to swallow any milk at all, and so he died.

I don't know how I'm going to be able to get through this, Erik. Raoul is just as devastated as I am—at least he says he is, but he didn't carry little Philippe beneath his heart for most of a year, and then give birth in screaming agony, so I don't see how it could be comparable. But he is my husband and I must believe him.

Oh, the birth was dreadful, Erik. I never thought the human body was capable of feeling pain like that and surviving. Although in truth, I almost didn't. The doctor swears he won't tell Raoul what a close thing it was for me, although I suspect Raoul knows already. I just lay there, limp and bloody, unable to move, for days.

It wasn't until I was finally able to get up, that Raoul told me of our little son's death. He says it is because he was afraid I would not recover if he had told me right away, but I think it was somehow crueler to wait until I was recovered and eager to hold my baby before he told me that little Philippe had died a few days before.

I worry a little, Erik, because I'm not feeling grief; at least, not the same sort of grief I felt when my father died, or when you did. I just feel sort of empty: hollow and brittle, as if I would shatter into a million pieces if I fell. Raoul has not spoken with me since he told me about Philippe, three days ago. I haven't left my room.

I remember how, whenever anything was bothering me, you used to make me sing it out with you. You'd pick something passionate or despairing, and you'd sing it all out with me, and it was a sort of catharsis; I always felt better afterwards, even if the problem was still there.

If any time I needed you to make me sing it out, Erik, it is now. Somehow, the Kyries and Hosannas that I'm allowed to sing in church just aren't enough for me. I need catharsis: I need feeling and passion, grief and despair, joy and rage in my singing. I need something to make me feel again.

I need opera, my dearest Erik.

I need you.

Christine

Christine carefully put away the letter and locked up the box. She rang for her maid to help her dress and do her hair, and for once she was glad of the help. She just didn't have the energy to do it herself.

"Tell my husband I've gone out for a walk," she directed, and the maid nodded as she helped Christine on with her wrap.

While she was gone, Raoul came quietly to the door. He knocked lightly and entered. "Christine?" When he glanced around the room and didn't see her, he sighed and was about to leave when Christine's jewelry box caught his eye. It was beautiful: several inches tall and intricately carved, with a Persian peacock on the top. He didn't remember ever having seen it before; frowning with puzzlement, he went over and opened the top.

Christine's pieces of jewelry that he had

given her himself lay innocently in the main compartment. He took them out, one by one, and examined them, smiling. He remembered how like a queen she had looked, with the diamond necklace about her neck when they had married. He wondered why she didn't wear it more often, or the ruby earrings either, or any of the other pieces he had given her. He put them back into the main compartment and tried to open the tiny drawer below.

It was locked. He frowned, leaning down to examine it. Yes, there was an actual keyhole there, even though the drawer was so small he could hardly see the edges. He glanced around for the key, but didn't find it.

He wondered briefly why Christine would leave the main compartment unlocked, which held all the valuable pieces, and what was so valuable in comparison that she had to lock it up in the tiny drawer? Any of the maids could simply reach in and take something from the main compartment if they were of a mind to; surely that's the one that ought to be locked, rather than the little one below it. Ah, well. When he found her, he'd ask her.

Chapter 4
Longing and Desertion

*D*ear Erik,
        I don't think Raoul is very happy here: not in Sweden, not in our house, and not with me. I don't know how to help him, because he won't tell me what his problem is. When I ask, he tells me he is fine. But the Sunday afternoon coldness has now extended to cover the rest of the week as well, and I haven't even sung at all since we lost little Philippe. Raoul spends most of his time alone in his study, and I spend most of mine alone in my room. He complains that he has no friends here because he doesn't speak Swedish; well, I could teach him if he wished (he doesn't), but it wouldn't help. He

*doesn't realize that I have no friends here ei-
ther. None of my old friends are comfortable
consorting with a countess.*

*I haven't sung in church for almost a year,
not since before we lost our child. I try to sing
now, and my throat closes up. I'm sure you
would be angry with me, Erik, if you could hear
my poor pathetic warblings now. I feel that
somehow I've failed you—even more than
usual, I mean. I know I failed to return your
love while you were alive, but for some reason,
my losing my voice seems like a much worse
failure. I am sorry, Erik: sorry for everything. I
wish I had it in my power to go back in time
and change a few things.*

*I am starting to wonder if I would change
my decision to marry Raoul? Certainly our
marriage, and our life here, is nothing like I
had envisioned. Perhaps it would be better if
we had another child, but I hardly see how that
is to happen since he hasn't visited me in my
room for months. We have dinner together, we
make some polite conversation, and then he returns to his study and I, to my sitting room. The
only conversation of note that we have had
since Philippe died, was when Raoul asked me
about the jewel box that you gave me, where I*

store these letters. He asked what on earth I kept in the locked compartment, that was worth so much more than my (unlocked) jewels that he had given me. I told him that compartment contained my past, and that it was private. He seemed satisfied, or at least was happy to change the subject.

He was certainly not best pleased with me, after I read your notice in the paper and returned to the opera to bury you! I think he only wanted to take me away and make me forget all about you. I could never do that, my dearest teacher and friend. You were too large a part of my life, for too long a time, and Raoul only ever chose to see the bad aspects of our relationship.

I used to wonder whether my feelings toward you have changed over the years since your death because my mind has unconsciously forgotten the frightening aspects of our interaction and only concentrated on the nice things? Perhaps it is because I have been taught from childhood that it is not polite to speak ill of the dead? Even if the deceased was a murdering, kidnapping madman? Forgive me my bluntness, but you cannot deny that you did seem such, at least for a little while.

Were you really mad, Erik? At times you seemed so sane and quiet, that it was not even a chore to think of living there with you, keeping house as your wife. But other times you seemed positively unhinged, threatening to blow every-one up with that foolish grasshopper. I wish I could understand you, but I suspect that in or-der to do so I would have to descend deeper into the darkness that filled you. I have no de-sire to do that; rather, I wish I could have brought you up into the light with me.

I don't think that my feelings have changed because I have forgotten the not-so-nice as-pects of our relationship. I have come to be-lieve that it is simply that I have grown up. I was so young and childlike when you knew me; I had no idea what much of your conversation alluded to, and all of the hidden nuances of your actions and gestures escaped me. I re-member most of them, though, and as I have matured I have come to understand the more subtle significance behind many of them.

You were a very complex man, Erik!

I can just see you now, lifting one shoulder in a small shrug, and letting me know, with that dry tone of amusement in your voice, that you already knew that.

Erik, I am sorry, but I must ask—why did you kill those people? I can understand some measure of self-protection, and I can understand the amusement of playing tricks on the managers and the corps de ballet. *But what of the torture chamber? Why did you kill Joseph Buquet? Or even Philippe de Chagny? When we heard that he'd been found dead on the banks of your lake, I remembered your going to answer the door and then coming back all wet. It seems so pointless, my dear, unless you really were deranged.*

Even now, more than two years later, I still think about you, Erik. You're still haunting me, even though you're not "le fantôme*" any longer. Are you a real ghost now, my dear? I can think of worse people to be haunted by. Perhaps you're a guardian angel now.*

It is a nice thought.

Ever your

Christine

Christine heard footsteps in the corridor and quickly locked up the letter. She didn't have a chance to put away the box this time, though, before Raoul's knock sounded gently on the door. He pushed it open and stuck his head in. "May I come in?"

She nodded, surreptitiously tucking the key on its black velvet ribbon back inside her bodice.

Raoul came in and sat down on the edge of her bed. He sighed. "Christine, I have decided to make a change," he said.

"What kind of a change?"

"I have got word that there is going to be another expedition through the far North, perhaps even as far as the North Pole again. Anyway, I am going to rejoin the navy and go with them this time." He did not meet her gaze.

"Raoul! I thought you were finished with the navy! The North Pole? It will be so dangerous!"

He seemed to explode then, like a coiled spring suddenly let go. He jumped to his feet and began pacing around the room in tiny, constrained circles. "Maybe it's time for a bit of danger, then! Certainly our present existence is a little too 'safe' for my tastes! I cannot go on like this, being a stranger in a strange land, and even a stranger in my own house!"

"I hope I have never made you a stranger,"

Christine said, her heart pounding. She had never seen Raoul like this before.

He scoffed. "It's nothing you could help, Christine, but it's there all the same. I've always felt as if I've been competing for your attention, that you're equally divided between me and your dearly departed."

Christine went pale. Did he mean Erik?

He went on talking, slightly calmer now, as he sank down on her bed again. "I know you loved your father—I loved him, too—but you cannot go through your life with your whole outlook being influenced by a dead man."

"You should talk!" Christine exclaimed. "Your own outlook has been poisoned by the jealousy of a dead man: Erik! Or else, why don't you like to hear me sing anymore?"

Raoul stiffened. "I thought that was only part of your life with *him*—I hadn't realized you would be dragging it along into *our* life as well!"

"What, music? Raoul, music is as much a part of me as my hands or my face. You thought I could leave it behind when I married you? When my singing is what made you notice me in the first place?"

"Your singing was something you shared

with him first," Raoul said through gritted teeth.

"And with my father before that. What of it?" Christine's lips were tight with anger.

Raoul sighed. "Never mind. Believe it or not, I didn't come here to argue with you, but to tell you that I'm rejoining the navy."

"When?"

"I leave next week."

# # #

Dear Erik,

Well, Raoul has gone. We had a big argument before he left, of which I shall spare you the details. Suffice it to say that he feels I have driven him away by my devotion to my father. I still miss my father, it's true, but he is no longer the guiding light in my life. You took over that mantle quite admirably when we met, and even now I still miss you in a way that I never felt for my father.

Raoul did come to my room once more before he left. Honestly, I don't know why he bothered. He had hardly spoken to me or touched me for the better part of a year, but suddenly the night before he left, that's when he decided to indulge his "amour."

We even had a fight that night, in fact. In-stead of calling for my maid to help me un-dress, as he has always done in the past, this time he chose to act as my lady's maid himself. It was very strange and uncomfortable, espe-cially afterwards when he saw my jewelry box key lying on my dressing table.

He remembered that I had been wearing it around my neck, and demanded to know whether that was the key to the secret com-partment, and then when I said it was, he went and got the box.

"Don't open that, please; it's private," I told him. He only raised an eyebrow and in-serted the key. "Raoul, please! It's none of your concern!" I tried to take the box out of his hands, telling him the only thing I could think of, that had ever made him do what I wanted him to do. "In the name of our love, Raoul, do not open the box."

This only made him stop and stare at me a moment in disbelief. Then he just scoffed at me and opened the compartment before I could stop him. He looked at the stack of letters with rather a puzzled air, and asked what they were.

"Letters," I told him, "To the dead."

He picked one up and began to unfold it, but I snatched it out of his hand and returned it to the box. "You shall not read them, Raoul," I told him. "They are not your concern. I have given up everything else for you, and you will respect my privacy in this."

He snorted. "How about everything I have given up for you, my dear?" His voice made the endearment sound like an insult, but he did put the box down. "I don't know why I'd want to read a young girl's maudlin ramblings to her dead father anyway," he muttered. It seemed quite cruel, especially after what we had just shared.

For just an instant I was tempted to tell him who the letters were really addressed to, but common sense won over pride and I held my tongue. The news would not have gone over well, and he would have insisted on reading them.

But now he is gone, and will be gone for at least a year. And I am even more alone in this house than I was when he was here. And he scoffed at me when I mentioned our love! He is very much changed from my childhood play-mate, the eager, gentle boy I fell in love with.

I have been thinking lately of the possibility

of returning to Paris, at least while Raoul is gone. It is plain that this, the town in which I was born, is no longer my home. Oh, wouldn't it be wonderful, to see the opera again, and all my old friends!

I only wish I could see you there as well, my dearest. Perhaps I shall hunt down the Persian, and discover the location of your grave, so that I can visit it.

Maybe Raoul is right, and I really am obsessed with the dead!

No matter. Alive or dead, I still miss you desperately.

The bright side, though, is that since Raoul's departure, I have been able to sing a little. Only a little, but it's a start.

Your loving but out-of-tune little songbird,

Christine

Christine put away the letter and rang for her maid. "Anneke, send for my husband's solicitor. I wish to discuss a temporary relocation."

"Yes, my lady," the maid answered.

"Anneke… have you ever wanted to travel? If, for example, I were to have a sojourn in France until my husband returns, would you wish to continue in my employ even there?"

"Oh, yes, my lady!" the maid replied, eyes shining.

Christine smiled. "Very well, then. Send for the solicitor, and I shall make some arrangements."

Chapter 5
Hope Renewed

*D*earest Erik,
 It is so good to be home again! I
know, I know; I've said that to you before,
when we first arrived in Sweden. But now I
know that my true home is the city where I
knew you, and where I had the happiest times
of my life.

 I had such a good time this afternoon! I visited the opera and saw all my old friends (and
a few old enemies; would you believe they have
re-hired La Carlotta?) and visited all my old
haunts. It was wonderful, wonderful! I hummed
to myself as I walked through the rotunda,
enjoying the sound of the acoustics in that
room. I remember how you once compared it to

remember how you once compared it to singing in a tiny cathedral; but now that I have done so, I must say the rotunda is better.

I had almost forgotten how beautiful the building is! Everything about it is graceful and elegant—did you really help build it, Erik? You're a genius! I already knew you were a musical genius, but I had not realized that you were an architectural one as well. It took a few years away from it, for my jaded eyes to see the splendor of that building properly.

I did not go onto the roof, or into the cellars. The memory of the rooftop is tainted with Raoul, and the cellars are redolent of your presence. I could not bear to descend to your house and not see you there.

Having immersed myself in music and opera all afternoon, I have reclaimed at least part of what I've been missing for these past few years with Raoul. I hadn't realized how much music had permeated my being—or how much losing it had dried me out—until I spent the afternoon surrounded by it once again. I am so happy that I came home to my new flat afterwards, and actually did a little bit of singing!

My voice croaked worse than Carlotta's ever did, even when you were playing your ven-

triloquist's tricks on her—but I could hear the potential there, if I can only get it into shape again. I shall pretend you are still with me, cracking the figurative whip over my head and making me practice, use good technique, etc. My technique has become very sloppy of late. I was ashamed of how I sounded—but for once, my shame is motivating me to practice, rather than depressing me into silence as usual.

I am so glad to be back, my Erik!

Your happy little Swedish Parisienne,

Christine

# # #

Dear Erik,

Isn't this just the most ironic thing you ever heard? Raoul came to me in my room one single time in the whole last year, and now I think I'm with child again. It is rather frightening to contemplate, as this time I shall be completely alone. Raoul wrote me briefly, to say that he had gained a promotion even in the short time he's been away, and that he didn't expect to be home for at least a year. I shall wait to make sure of my news before writing to him about it.

At least if he isn't around for the child's birth, he shan't be able to tell me what to name it this time.

It would seem that I'm in rather an odd position in Paris. I'm officially a member of the titled nobility, but without Raoul's being with me, I have taken a flat that is much more the sort of thing I'm used to. Our grand house in Sweden dwarfed the rest of the houses in the town, and now that I am back in Paris I would rather blend in than be ostentatious. I have made some friends here, some of them former opera people. It's quite shocking, really, because some of my new friends aren't quite the sorts of people that members of the titled nobility should really be associating with.

Sorelli, for example. Remember Sorelli, the prima ballerina, who had an affair with Philippe de Chagny? She just finished celebrating five years of marriage to a respectable, well-heeled young man named Henri Picard. They live at Louve-ciennes, where Sorelli retired. Coincidentally, she has a six-year old son who strongly resembles Philippe. If our little Philippe had lived, I suspect he and Michel Sorelli Picard would have been cousins—by blood, if not by law. Sorelli is much nicer than she used to be.

And do you remember Mme. Giry, your box-keeper? The lady who was good enough to bring me a footstool, one of those times when you took me to your box to see the opera? She and her daughter Meg (who has taken Sorelli's place as the prima ballerina) have become friends of mine as well. She is so wonderfully earthy; she's a delight to be around after my association with all of Raoul's stuffy, titled friends.

If Raoul does return and wants to move back to Sweden, I shall be so disappointed. I feel as if I'm finally back where I belong. I am back in Paris; I am back among opera people; the only thing missing is you, my dearest.

I don't think I shall ever stop missing you.

Your loving

Christine

Christine blew on the letter to dry the ink, and then placed it into the box with the others. There was a knock on the door, and the maid, Anneke, stuck her head in. "Mlle. Giry is here to see you, my lady."

Christine smiled. She locked up the box and put it away, saying, "Oh, do show her in, Anneke!"

"Little Meg" Giry had not changed much, only grown taller. Still slim and olive-skinned, with a wealth of straight, shiny black hair that could never stay coiffed for long, she came darting into the room as if she were running onto the stage.

"Hello, Meg!" Christine greeted. She turned to the maid. "Anneke, have some tea and biscuits brought up."

Meg greeted her with a smile, her teeth showing brightly in her dark little face. "Oh, Christine, just wait till you hear the news!"

Christine smiled. This was what she had been missing. Having friends over, listening to theatre gossip—it was the next best thing to being a part of the opera herself. She settled in to hear Meg's tale of what the director had said to Carlotta during rehearsals that day.

"...and then Carlotta stormed off, swearing in Spanish," Meg finished with a broad grin. "So what is new with you?"

Christine chuckled at Meg's story, and then sobered. "Well..." she said, debating whether to tell anyone or not. Oh, why not? "I think I am going to have another baby," she said.

Meg gasped, and then squealed and ran to embrace her. Christine laughed in delight, excited about her new pregnancy for the first time since realizing it.

# # #

Dear Erik,

It is official: I really am going to have another baby. And this time I won't be alone like I thought I would be. Sorelli and Mme. Giry have both promised to help, and to stay with me. Sorelli is even sending over one of her servants, who is also a midwife, to stay with me for the entire year. Mme. Giry tells me that she has a friend who is a nurse, and who may be looking for work about the same time this child is born. So things are actually working out well in that area.

I have written to Raoul about it, but I have no idea how long it will take to reach him. I hope he is pleased; maybe this will give him some motivation to stay home for a while, but I doubt it. I have received two letters from him so far, and though brief, they both emphasize how happy he is now that he has returned to his old life.

That is a sentiment I can certainly understand, as I feel the same way myself.

You'll be pleased to know that I have made

some good progress in reclaiming my voice! I am now probably as good as I was when we first met. I am tired all the time now, though, because of the child. Still, most of my waking hours are spent singing. My voice has finally become more used to the demands I've been making on it. I think I have become almost as harsh a taskmaster as you used to be, my dear! Give me some more time, and I think I might be able to get my voice back to where the sound of it pleased your discriminating ears.

Will I ever stop missing you, my dearest of teachers? It has been several years now, and I still feel the pain of your loss almost as much as in the beginning. It's true that I am much happier here in Paris than I was at our house in my village, but that is partly due to the fact that this city is full of so many good memories—most of which involved you.

I went for a carriage ride last evening, and I remembered the time you took me out and we encountered Raoul. This time was uneventful, and I wished you had been with me to enjoy the cool, quiet summer evening together.

I fear that one of these days I shall get so lost in my memories of you that I shan't want to return to my real life. It is a constant tempta-

tion, and a legitimate concern. It's good that I have people around me now, to distract me from my memories and remind me that I'm still a living person. Somehow I doubt you would have wanted me to follow you into the grave, my dear.

Though at least there we could be together.

Your loving friend,
Christine

Chapter 6
Betrayal

*D*ear Madame de Chagny:
   It is with great sadness that I inform you that your husband, Raoul de Chagny, was lost at sea on the 23rd of November. The ship encountered an iceberg in the North Atlantic, and your husband was thrown overboard upon impact. We lost several other good men as well.

   I offer my sincere condolences. I also enclose M. de Chagny's personal effects that he had wished sent home to you. If I can be of any further service to you, madame, please let me know.

                                        Yours truly,
                              Capt. Etienne desJardins

Christine read the letter over again, ashamed that the initial feeling that swept over her was one of shocked relief. It soon gave way to grief, and then to tears, which she gulped back as she folded the letter up. In a sort of mechanical action, she opened up her jewelry box and placed it in among her letters to Erik before putting that box aside and reaching for the carton of Raoul's things that had accompanied the letter.

Raoul had not brought very many personal effects with him. Christine picked up an old opera program and a handful of pressed violets fell out; tears came to her eyes as she remembered their lunches of wine and biscuits—with a vase full of violets on the table—that summer they had pretended to be engaged. Raoul had kept some of the violets.

Raoul's captain had also sent her Raoul's dress uniform, several books, a hair ribbon, some folded papers, and his last letter to his wife. With her heart in her throat, Christine opened his letter.

Dear Christine,
Thank you for your letter containing your news. It helped me to open my eyes and see more clearly where my duty lies.

I know now that it was the right thing to do, for me to rejoin the navy. Certainly I could not have stayed in Sweden with you, with things between us the way they were. I married you, knowing I loved you and thinking that you loved me; but after so much time spent in the same house with you, I am convinced that I am not enough to make you happy.

I am sorry to have failed you.

And I confess that I eventually became jealous of your devotion to the dead, as it seemed to exclude the living. Now it seems, though, as if you have found someone living to devote yourself to. I hope he is worth the loss of your reputation, since I know that our one single encounter before I left would not have been enough to get you with child.

I hope that whomever you have found to be your new companion will be enough to make you happy, and I wish you joy in your new life with your new child. I would not have thought you the kind of woman to seek a replacement in her husband's absence, but when I thought about it I realized that it would be only natural considering you had much of your moral instruction and example from the world of opera. I forgive you, and I hope you will confess your sin and seek forgiveness from God as well. If you take the opera as your model, then I hope you will cast yourself into the arms of the angels, as Marguerite did, and be shown mercy.

I hope you will eventually repent of your transgression, even though you shall have life-long consequences of it in the form of a bastard child. I hope that you will eventually return to the goodness of heart that your father instilled in you as a child; when that happens, may I suggest that you speak to Father Arnaud, our family's priest, about it, and make your confession to him. My solicitor should know how to contact him.

In any case, know that you have my love, forgiveness, and best wishes for your health and happiness.

I shall not be home again.

Your old childhood friend,

Raoul

Christine gasped at the audacity of the letter and burst into fresh tears of grief—and anger. Not only was she a widow now, but her husband had died believing her faithless!

She bristled at the injustice of his assumptions as she got her jewelry box back out and put the letter in. The nerve of him, offering her forgiveness because of his own ignorance! She knew that one marital encounter was quite enough to result in a child if the conditions were right; her dumpy little Swedish doctor, who had delivered Philippe, had told her so! She wished he had informed Raoul similarly. How could her husband possibly believe that she had been with another man? She had only ever loved two men in her life, and now they were both dead.

#

Dear Erik,

Oh, I am so angry! Since receiving Raoul's last letter, and the one from his captain informing me of his death, I have been angry and sad by turns. How could he possibly believe it of me? I am bereft of him and betrayed by him, both at the same time. My love, I wish you were here to say all the things about him that I am too ladylike to utter—and at the same time, I am glad you're not, because it is not right to speak ill of the dead.

Oh, hang propriety! I shall speak ill of him

for as long as it takes me to recover from his accusations of infidelity, and then I shall go to confession and be forgiven. He claims that he loved me, but if he did then why did he ignore me so much when we were together in my homeland? Why did he desert me for the navy again? And why, oh, why, did he not believe that the child I carry is his? He thinks me nothing better than an opera tramp, with morals learned from the operas I performed. Raoul, who grew up with me, and who lived with me as my husband for three years, thinks this of me! Erik, how could he? Especially when you, his only true rival, died before we were even married.

And now he is gone, and gone with him is any opportunity I might have had of proving my faithfulness.

Oh, Erik, if you happen to see him wherever it is you have gone, be sure and give him a good thrashing for me. I did not deserve this. He should have known me better than that.

On a happier note, though, this pregnancy is progressing at a much more natural rate than the last one. I'm getting large, but certainly not like I was by this point last time! My French doctor tells me everything is normal, and has started teaching me some things I can do to lessen the pain a bit, when the time comes. I told him about my last experience, with little Philippe. He thinks that the amount of pain I had then was unnatural, resulting from Philippe's birth defects, and that this birth will likely be much more normal. This is a relief, as I had been dreading a similar experience.

I am even looking forward to having a baby, though it will be without a father. It is very odd to be a widow, Erik. In some ways it is exactly the same as when Raoul was only away in the navy, but in other respects it is completely different. As long as some thought that he might be coming back to me, I was welcome in the houses of his titled peers. As his widow and a former opera star, however, many of those doors are now closed to me.

It doesn't matter. I have a few good friends; I am no longer burdened with an absent husband who thinks I betrayed him; and in just a few more weeks, I shall have a baby.

The only negative aspect to having this baby is that (again, forgive me for sharing such personal details with you, dear Erik—you know I would never dare to, if you were still alive) it presses on my lungs and diaphragm, and I find it hard to take a good, deep breath. I have gone on singing as much as I can, but it is difficult to hold a note for long when there is no space left inside for my lungs to fill! My breath support is, alas, a thing of the past.

Well, after it is born, I shall have my lungs back to myself again, and I look forward to being able to sing to my child.

I wish I could still sing for you, my dearest.

Christine

Christine blew on the ink in a contemplative manner. She had received the news of Raoul's death, and his letter, more than a week ago and she still didn't know how to feel about it. She missed Raoul in an abstract way; but the thing was, he had already become absent for the last year they'd lived in Sweden. Physically present in the house, but very distant from her. His leaving for the navy did not affect her much at all, except in facilitating her move back to Paris—and she was so much happier here that Raoul's physical absence hardly signified.

She still burned inwardly, though, over his assumption of her infidelity. "Foolish, foolish man," she muttered to herself as she folded and stored her latest letter to Erik. "Thinking those sorts of things about me, when the only other man I loved is long dead."

# # #

Dear Erik,

It is with great pleasure I inform you that I have been delivered of a son. The labor was dreadfully painful, but nothing like it was last time. And joy of joys, the baby is quite well! The midwife (Heaven bless Sorelli for sending her to work for me!) examined him most thoroughly, and she tells me the boy is fine and healthy. I was worried, because of little Philippe, but this baby has no problem swallowing or eating. The problem is getting him to stop!

He has blue eyes of course—most babies have blue eyes when they're born, I'm told— but his hair is darker than Philippe's was. Darker than mine or Raoul's, and more like my mother's. Wouldn't it be lovely if he turned out dark-haired? It could happen; Philippe de Chagny had much darker hair than Raoul's, which means it runs in both our families.

And this should please you, my dearest: I have named him after you.

I hope you're not offended that I have given a Chagny baby your name, but if you are then you can just assume along with everyone else that I chose "Erik" because it is Scandinavian. But really, little Erik-Daaé de Chagny is named after you. That shall have to be our secret, though I am quite sure not many people ever knew that "le fantôme de l'opèra" even had a name, much less knew what it was.

Raoul's two sisters came to visit shortly after my baby was born. It was the first time I had seen them since their brief visit to us in Sweden just after Raoul and I were married. They were frostily polite to him and barely civil to me during the ten minutes or so that we were in the same room. It wasn't until after I left that the shouting began!

This time, though, they called and stayed almost a half an hour! Martine seemed to have thawed the slightest bit, but Clémence was still just as cool as ever. They did coo very gratifyingly over Erik-Daaé, even though they didn't approve of his name. It seems they had an Uncle Erik whom they did not like, and as for Daaé—well, why would they be happy about the newborn Comte de Chagny being named after a Swedish peasant (even if he was the greatest violinist in the world, save you)?

It was a much nicer visit than last time, but I was still glad to see them go. I shall never fit in with the Chagny family, and don't want to.

I have been in Paris for a year now, and still have never ventured into the cellars beneath the opera. Every time I visit there I am tempted to go, but do not dare. If I stay above, then I can still pretend that you're down there somewhere, and the thought comforts and warms me. If I were to dare to go alone I know the sight of your empty, dusty house would just hammer home the fact that I shall never see you alive, and it would be like losing you all over again.

And part of it is simply a practical matter, too: if I were to slip and fall, and hurt myself three cellars down, it would be months and months before I was found! Your legend lives on: I hear the little ballet girls whispering about the opera ghost every time someone falls, or loses her glove. The scene-shifters are still afraid to go into the cellars by themselves, even years after your death! They go in stealthy pairs, whispering to each other with wide eyes, and jumping every time they hear a noise. I find it most amusing. I just want to go in there and shout out, "The ghost is dead, everyone! He's been dead for five years!" but I know it wouldn't do any good. People are people, and they must have their little superstitions.

I am keeping busy with opera affairs (I have been able to subsidize them a little, with what Raoul left me in his will), visits from friends (such a welcome change from my loneliness in Sweden), and of course with little Erik-Daaé. He is such a darling! I wish you could see him. And he will be a great singer, too; I can tell already. I swear, even his cry is musical. It certainly sounds no worse than when La Carlotta sings Desdemona.

It is amusing, after performing for so long, to sit in the audience and just listen to an opera. Once, when Mme. Giry was bringing me a fan in my box, she caught me laughing during the tearful scene at the beginning of "Orphée et Eurydice." When she asked what was so funny, I pointed out that the props men had given Amore the wrong bow and arrows. Mme Giry just smiled and said she was sure none of the other members of the audience would ever notice such a thing. She told Meg about it, and the

*next time Meg visited me she teased me merci-
lessly about noticing the error. "You can take
the singer out of the theatre," she said, "But
you cannot take the theatre out of the singer!"*

*It is true, I fear. I love theatre and singing.
Every time I go to an opera, I cannot help but
wish I were back upon that stage. I wish it were
more proper for a countess to sing in public—
oh, I miss it so!*

*All the same, I wonder how anyone could
have missed it! Instead of Amore's tiny bow
and arrows with which he shoots his lovers, it
was very funny to see him prancing around
with Ulisse's massive war bow and arrows
from* Il Ritorno d'Ulisse in Patria! *I doubt even
you could have refrained from laughing at such
a gaffe! Especially when you consider the symbolism of Ulisse's bow, that his "widow"
would only marry the man who could bend it—
and the only man who could bend it was Ulisse
in disguise. I had to wonder whether even the
god of love could have bent it; certainly Fonta
is getting rather scrawny as he ages.*

*Except for not being able to perform, and
missing you, I find myself quite content here in
Paris with my friends and my little son.*

Perhaps some day I shall have the strength

to descend and see your old house. But not yet, my dear, not yet; I still miss you far too much.

Your devoted

Christine

# # #

Dear Erik,

It seems the older I get, the more time flies by without my noticing. Little Erik-Daaé is almost a year old now. His hair has darkened just as I'd hoped, but his eyes are still blue. Not pale blue like Raoul's, though; a dark, midnight blue like my father's. He is a handsome little boy, and I was right about his being musical! He still cannot carry a tune, but I hear his voice going up and down to at least follow the melody a little bit as I sing to him.

I am singing again, my love. Not in public yet—oh, no!—but I am planning to! I finally decided that I've had enough audience-sitting to last a lifetime. I am going to audition for the chorus at the opera. I have given up on propriety and keeping my "position" in society. None of the rest of the titled peers respect me anyway *because of my past, so I have decided to make it my future as well. I have nothing to lose, and it is something that I love.*

I don't think my voice is quite up to its old quality yet, but it's at least as good as it was before I debuted as Marguerite. I think I should be able to get into the chorus without any trouble. The only problem will be putting up with Carlotta's crowing over seeing me relegated to the chorus again! Well, if I can get back into opera again, it will be worth it.

And honestly, without your tutelage, I doubt my voice will ever soar to the heights that it did before. For a couple of years now I have looked for voice teachers, but have been disappointed in every one. I could almost hear your scornful voice dismissing them as mediocre at best, and actively harmful to me at worst. One of them even went so far as to recommend that I "not breathe so deeply" or open my mouth so wide. In truth, I think he was too distracted by staring at my décolletage during all those deep breaths to know what he was saying. Fear not: I sent him packing not two minutes after that. Another recommended that I curl my tongue in such a way that the tone was almost guaranteed to be flat. Faugh! I shudder to think of how their students sound, with teachers like this.

Perhaps I shall begin some vocal instruction myself. Even if all I teach them is the little I remember from our lessons, it is bound to be better than the instruction they're getting now! And it will give me something to do. Little Erik-Daaé is enchanting and delightful, but he's still just a child. I fear my brain is going to atrophy from lack of use (a fate that I suspect has already happened to most of the other titled women in this city).

I know how little you respected foolish women, who are only concerned with being seen in their new hats, and with spreading gossip. I have no wish to become one of them.

You see, my love? You're influencing me, even from the grave. And speaking of graves, I wish I knew where yours was. The Persian never told me, when I met him in the cellar that time. I would like to visit it, and perhaps leave you some flowers to show the world that at least one person in France is sad that the Opera Ghost is dead.

Actually, though, I'm not the only one! I overheard MM. Moncharmin and Richard complaining the other day about how dull things were. "Every season, the same old thing," Moncharmin was saying. "I don't know why we bother to rehearse. Even I know these operas by heart now, and I'm not known as the musical one!"

To which M. Richard replied, if you can believe it, "I sometimes wonder if it wasn't actually worth twenty-thousand francs a month, just to keep things interesting around here! At least in the days of the ghost there was always something going on."

...To which M. Moncharmin replied with a shudder and a forceful change of topic. And I just walked away laughing to myself, thinking that I'm not the only one who misses you!

You livened up the world considerably, my dearest Erik.

Christine

Chapter 7
Paying her Respects

*D*ear Erik,
   *I saw him! I finally found the Persian!
He was in the audience at the opera last night
(They're doing "Norma" now, with La Carlotta
in the title role—most uninspired) and he remembered me. During intermission I even got a
chance to talk to him for a few minutes. I realized to my shame that I had never known his
name! All of Paris used to refer to him as just
"The Persian," so when I confessed this to him,
he very kindly introduced himself: Kaveh Tallis, former daroga of Mazenderan. I told M.
Tallis I wanted to talk with him about you, and*

he agreed to meet me here at the opera today after my last lesson.

I am waiting for my last student now, Erik. You see, until my voice is good enough for me to audition for a leading role, I decided not to bother with the chorus. You didn't spend all that time and effort on me, getting me out of the chorus only for me to get back in. So I am working privately to improve my voice, and in the meantime I did decide to start teaching singing. I have found enough students right here at the opera to keep me busy for a long time to come. But, oh, I wish I hadn't found this one, because if it weren't for her, I could be meeting with M. Tallis right now! I am so eager to speak with him that my hands are literally shaking! It is well that you won't be reading this, as I'm sure my handwriting suffers. It will be good to speak of you, with the only other person of my acquaintance who really knew you.

It is evening now. I did see M. Tallis this afternoon. It was very strange; he seemed even more nervous than I was! He told me that he has been living in Provence for the last several years, for the sake of his health. That explains why I had not seen him in Paris lately. He only came back for a brief visit, on business. I am so glad I happened to see him last night!

We spoke of you a little... and of me a great deal, which surprised me. He asked many questions about me, my life, what I had been doing, what happened to my husband—in truth, some of them were a little impertinent, but he was so very polite that I felt I had to answer them anyway.

He seemed especially interested in hearing about my son, and he got the strangest smile when I told him Erik-Daaé's name. He murmured something about how flattered you would have been, and I told him I doubted it, since the child was a Chagny! That made him laugh.

The strangest thing, though, was when I asked him to show me the location of your grave, and he pretended not to know what I was talking about. I reminded him of our last meeting on the banks of the cellar lake, when he told me that he had taken care of your body already. I asked him where he had buried you, as I wanted to visit your grave and pay my respects, and he would not tell me. He made me promise to meet him there again tomorrow, and he would tell me then.

I am baffled. What could possibly be so se-cret about it? The only thing I can think of is that he may have buried you illegally—in hal-lowed ground when you weren't a confirmed Catholic, or some such thing.

Were you a confirmed Catholic, Erik? I know your faith had... let us say, "lapsed," for the sake of understatement, but I never knew how you stood in relation to the Almighty and the Church. Surely He would have forgiven your masquerading (forgive the pun) as an an-gel for me. After all, I did.

So I shall meet with M. Tallis again tomor-row, and discover the big mystery of your gravesite.

Honestly, Erik—even in death you contrive to complicate things for me!

I would expect nothing less, my love.

Your somewhat exasperated

Christine

Christine put the letter away, laughing qui-etly to herself. It had cheered her immensely, to talk with *Monsieur* Tallis that day. Just to be able to mention the name "Erik," and have him know exactly whom she referred to, was wonderful. They had shared a rather chummy laugh when Christine had mentioned Erik's temper; M. Tallis had agreed that he, too, had seen that temper displayed on countless occasions. "And I was the chief of police, *madame,* and not easily frightened—but Erik's flashing eyes made me want to flee!" Christine had nodded, knowing exactly what he was talking about.

He had been keenly interested in what had befallen her since she'd left Paris, and had asked her many questions. Christine recalled how his jade-green eyes had lit up and sparkled when she told him she'd named her second son after Erik, and the sound of his laughter at her self-deprecating comment about the Chagny bloodline had rung out loudly in the little café where they had gone.

The Persian had posed her a question, just before they parted. It was a personal question, and he apologized for it as such, but he asked it anyway.

Had she ever loved Erik? If Raoul had never entered the picture, did she think she could have been happy with the Opera Ghost?

Christine sobered now, thinking of it. She

had gone pale and quiet when he asked the question, and all the hustle and bustle of the street had seemed to still as she contemplated it. M. Tallis had said nothing; merely awaited her answer quietly, his brilliant eyes fixed steadily on hers.

"Yes," she had finally managed to choke out. Then, as if she couldn't bear to stop the flow of words, she had continued, "I was too young and naïve, *Monsieur* Tallis, to realize what Erik was offering me—and what Raoul was planning to take away. I loved my husband, *monsieur*, but we were both so very, very young! And my life without music was not worth living. I know I was a selfish, diffident little creature—I did love Erik, but did not have the capacity to appreciate him during his life. But since his death he has become much dearer. I hold Erik's memory as close to my heart as I hold music itself."

Kaveh Tallis' face had lit up at those words, and it was with a genuine smile that he had thanked her for her sincerity, said goodbye with a bow, and strode whistling up the street.

Christine had watched him go, with tears in her eyes from all the long-buried emotions his words had stirred up.

Chapter 8
The Resurrection of Lazarus

*D*ear Erik,
You'll remember I warned you that I might see Mme. de Chagny if I went to the opera last night? Sure enough, she accosted me during the intermission, and begged me to meet her again today in order to talk about you. She had some extraordinary things to tell me about her own situation, which I know will interest you greatly.

Erik, she asked me to disclose the location of your gravesite, so she could pay her respects. Be a good boy, won't you, and think of something for me to tell her when I see her again tomorrow? I managed to put her off for a day, but she is a singularly determined young woman. When last we met, I told her that I had taken care of your body already, myself; but as you know, I neglected to tell her that it was still living at the time.

If you can dignify the state you were in by calling it life, I mean.

Yes, I know, I know: "My state of health is my own affair, daroga!" You don't have to tell me again. Just as I don't have to tell you that your health is my affair as well, whether you like it or not.

Unless I get delayed, I should be home around eight. Kindly refrain from strangling any of the servants in your impatience.

The cleaner-up of your dirty work and resident liar-for-your-sake,

Kaveh

The Persian folded and sealed the note, and handed it to his manservant. "Bring this back to Erik at top speed, would you, Darius?" A somewhat evil smile came to his face as he went on, "The sooner it's delivered, the longer he'll have to climb the walls until I get home.

Do hurry, won't you?"

With a grin, his manservant took the note and was gone. Kaveh watched him go and then started to laugh. Erik would be going crazy with impatience by the time Kaveh returned to their flat.

# # #

"Tell me again why we're doing this?" Kaveh asked his companion wryly as the two men grunted with the effort of hauling a flat square of marble out from the boat.

His slender fellow laborer grunted. "If she wants to leave flowers at my grave, it would be impolite of us to not even have a stone there." Stronger than his foreign comrade, he picked up the stone and held it over the hole he had dug to hold it. "Here, Kaveh—you keep it steady while I lower it."

With matching groans of exertion, the two men carefully lowered the stone into the hole. It fit perfectly, like a puzzle piece. Without speaking, the men gathered soil and fitted it around the stone, tamping it down solidly.

Kaveh stood back and held up his lantern to illuminate the face of it. "ERIK" was all it said, in large, block letters. "I still think you should have put something more on it," he told his friend. "Just the name by itself seems a little... terse."

"Ah, yes, and I'm such a chatty fellow myself," Erik said, sarcasm dripping from his voice as he wandered around the cavern brushing dust onto a sheet of paper. "What else could I have said? 'Erik, beloved Opera Ghost'? Or perhaps, 'Erik, cherished madman, trusted murderer'?"

"How about 'Erik: musician, architect, trusted friend, devoted lover'?"

Erik scoffed. "Trusted friend? You're the only friend I've ever had, Kaveh, and you still don't trust me after twenty years. And 'lover' seems to imply a certain reciprocity that didn't exist." He brought the paper full of dust over to the new stone and tapped on the paper carefully to strategically scatter the dust.

"How do you know it didn't, Erik? Why wouldn't you let me tell you her news, anyway?"

"There's no sense in digging up the past, my friend. What could she have said, that she didn't already say to me five years ago?"

Kaveh threw up his hands in frustration.

"You'd be surprised! You should give her another chance!"

Erik finished sprinkling dust on the gravestone and crumpled up the paper. "I am giving
her another chance. I want to hear what she
tells me herself, when she pays her little visit to
my grave here today. Just on the off chance she
has something new to say, I'd prefer to hear it
from her lips instead of yours." He shoved the
paper into his pocket and leaned his head back
against the wall of the cavern. With a grin that
was just barely visible beneath the bottom edge
of his mask, he said, "You have to admit, her
lips are much prettier than yours, *daroga*."

Kaveh groaned. "You are so exasperating,
Erik! I purposely stayed out late last night, just
to make you sweat, wondering what she had
told me—and then when I finally got home you
didn't even want to know! This is just another
way to irritate me, isn't it, because you know
how much I want to tell you?"

Erik's reply was a hearty chuckle of confirmation. "And it's working beautifully!"

Kaveh went on griping. "And then you drag
me out of bed in the wee hours of the morning
to come and set up your gravestone, which
you've stayed up all night to carve—and I

don't even want to know where you got it from in the middle of the night, Erik, I truly don't—but when in God's name do you sleep, man?"

Erik made a dismissive gesture. "Oh, you know I've never needed that much sleep. Come now, we must get cleaned up for our visitor." Unthinking, he turned in the direction of his old house.

His companion shuddered. "Uh, Erik... if you don't mind, I think I shall retire to our own flat for that. You have no way of knowing whether your plumbing is still in order, or whether the rats have taken over your house, or—oh, and don't forget that she might wish to see the house while she's down here. It would confuse her to see any evidence of use in it."

Erik nodded. "Good point." He stretched, his arms high over his head, and rolled his shoulders. "Living in Provence has softened me, I think; I no longer feel the desire to bathe in the icy lake."

Kaveh studied him as Erik stretched his tired muscles. "Provence has been good for you," he said, noticing that his friend no longer resembled a walking skeleton. Erik still wore a mask, but it was white silk now instead of black, and his forearms were muscular and lightly tanned where his sleeves were rolled up to work. "Instead of looking cadaverous, you now look merely hideous," he teased.

"We must be thankful for even the smallest of improvements," Erik said dryly, picking up the lantern. "Come, let us be on our way. What time are you supposed to meet Mme. de Chagny, to bring her here?"

"Three, after her last lesson."

"Lesson?" Erik stopped, and then held up his hand. "Never mind, don't tell me. I shall find out for myself, soon enough." They continued in silence for a time, and then he said thoughtfully, "If she won't be here until three, that should give me time to prepare."

"Prepare what?" Kaveh demanded.

Erik laughed. "Always so suspicious, *daroga*! I only meant preparing myself to see Mme. de Chagny again!" To himself he mused, "I wonder whether I should shave again yet. It wouldn't do to have an unshaven chin, even what little of it shows."

Kaveh sighed. "Erik, if you're not planning to show yourself, promise me that you won't do anything just to scare her. She... she is quite a different woman from the frightened young girl you knew five years ago."

Erik chuckled, a soft snort. "Kaveh, you know I could promise things all day long and never fulfil them. Why do you always extract promises when you know I never keep my oaths?"

Kavah smiled grimly in the dark. "Ah, and you said I didn't trust you. You're wrong, my friend; not keeping your promises is the one thing I can always count on you to do!"

The next morning, Christine wrote her final letter to Erik and sighed as she capped her ink-pot. She felt confused and unaccountably emotional. She wanted to stay there and ponder her feelings about Erik, that the Persian had dredged up from deep within her heart. It was time she was leaving for the opera, though, to teach her lessons. She folded up the last letter and stuffed it into her jewelry box on top of the others, and then carefully placed her jewelry box into her music bag. She sighed again, wondering how she was going to make it through the day.

Her students found her rather distracted that day.

Promptly at three, M. Tallis showed up just as Christine's last student was leaving.

"Are you ready, *madame*?"

"Yes, *monsieur*. Just let me get my things." Christine threw on her wrap, gathered up her music, and picked up a small wooden box. It had a hand-carved lid and several hidden little drawers. Kaveh had seen one like it, long ago in Persia, and he smiled a little to himself. He hadn't known that Erik had made another and given it to Christine.

"His grave is in a small, hidden cavern beside the lake, *madame*," Kaveh told her, leading her up the long, empty hallway toward her old dressing room. "It seemed best to me not to bother a priest with his burial since I did not know the state of his soul."

"He had no funeral mass?" Christine asked, a little shocked.

Kaveh shook his head sadly. "He had requested none, and I as a Musselman was unqualified in any case."

"I shall sing for him, then," Christine decided. They had reached her dressing room, and she tried the door. It was locked. She looked a question at her companion, who shook his head.

"It is not in use, *madame*. People say it is haunted."

Christine nodded, with an amused look.

"Perhaps it is."

She turned the handle halfway, lifted the door a little, and struck it with her hip. It swung open. She turned to smile at M. Tallis, pleased that she still remembered the trick. He grinned.

Erik's inventions were excellent, Kaveh thought as he pressed the button for the mirror to open. The mechanism still worked in smooth, flawless silence. He and Christine stepped through onto the Communards' Road. He lit one of his two lanterns for them and Christine closed the mirror.

The lantern cast a fitful light onto the road, but it was enough for two people who knew the way so well. They did not speak as they descended through all four cellars until they got to the lowest one. Kaveh was a little surprised that Christine did not shriek or faint when they saw the rats. She just tightened her lips and swished her skirts a little more, to scare them off.

Kaveh brought her down past Erik's house. Not wanting to use the boat in case she might notice it had been used earlier, he brought her over the rocks and half-tumbled-down walls to the small natural cavern that Erik had chosen to be his final resting place—and where they had placed his stone only that morning.

"Here it is, *madame*." Kaveh held the lantern aloft, finally setting it down on top of the gravestone.

Christine went forward slowly, and placed a hand on top of the stone. She knelt and traced the large block letters with her fingers, reading them aloud. "Erik." She smiled sadly. "It even looks like his handwriting."

Behind her, Kaveh shot a nervous glance into the gloom at the back of the cavern where he knew Erik was hiding.

Christine looked around at M. Tallis. "*Monsieur*, would you mind giving me a few minutes alone?"

"Of course, *madame*." He lit his second lantern and withdrew from the cave.

Christine turned back to the stone. She knelt down and carefully placed her jewelry box at the base of it. Her voice sounded small and quiet in the gloom as she spoke.

"Erik, my love… what can I possibly say to you that I haven't already said in my letters? Here, I give them into your care. Keep them safe for me, dear. Don't let anyone else read them, will you?"

In the shadowed arch of the cavern, Erik

shook his head solemnly. She had written him letters?

Christine leaned forward and pressed her cheek to the cool marble, and then her lips. And then the tears came. She wept for several minutes; and Erik, watching from his hiding place, was hard-pressed not to go to her. Had she really called him her love? Had she really just kissed his gravestone? That was rather a morbid gesture, especially for her, but he appreciated it.

Finally she calmed down, and rose. Wiping her face with a handkerchief, she backed up a few steps and began to sing. Erik recognized it as the *"Valedicto,"* the last part of the requiem mass.

In paradisum deducant te Angeli:
in tuo adventu suscipiant te Martyres,
et perducant te in civitatem sanctam Jerusalem.
Chrous Angelorum te suscipiant,
et cum Lazaro quondam paupere
aeternam habeas requiem. [1]

Her voice rang out like a bell, echoing in the

---

[1] Into Paradise may the Angel lead you:
At your approach may the Martyrs receive you,
And conduct you into the holy city Jerusalem.
May the Choir of Angels receive you,
and with Lazarus, who was once poor,
may you have eternal rest.

vast, empty caverns. Her technique was basically still good, Erik noted clinically, but her range had suffered from her lack of practice. Notes that she used to soar up to and land on as gently as a dove now sounded just the merest trifle strained. He doubted anyone else would notice, but it made him itch to step back into his teaching role and train her out of it. Two or three good lessons ought to do it, he knew.

He was a heartbeat away from speaking when Christine suddenly smiled. His heart leaped at the beauty of her smile. She put her hand on the stone like a caress, and murmured, "Goodbye, my love."

Then she turned and walked away, calling for M. Tallis.

She was barely even out of sight before Erik had snatched up the box and cradled it in his arms.

Kaveh and Christine did not speak on the long trip back up the Communards' Road. They passed quietly by the little well where Erik had once brought Christine and bathed her temples while she was fainting. Christine wanted to stop there for a moment, and Kaveh took advantage of her reverie to take a few steps away and see if the skeleton was still there.

When he and Darius had brought a dying Erik out of the opera five years before, Erik had demanded that there be a body left somewhere in the cellars to be found. "If I am not dead," he had said, "then they will continue searching for me, and may perhaps find my house, *daroga*. I beg you: make sure they find a body, will you?"

Kaveh and Darius had brought back the corpse of a recently-dead man that they had found in an alley, and had left it there by the well. The man had obviously been homeless and destitute, and in a moment of macabre irony, Kaveh had placed one of Erik's old rings onto the corpse's finger. It was one that Erik had prepared for Christine that had turned out to be too big; now it fit nicely over the deceased's knuckle bones and announced to the world that "C.D.'s" sweetheart was pining for her no longer. Kaveh found a grim satisfaction in the fact that this beggar had found such wealth in death that he had likely never seen when he was alive.

The skeleton was still there; apparently no one but the rats had ever found it. Kaveh grimaced at the sight of the gnawed bones. He heard Christine sniffle, and, recalled to his duty, made his way back over to her. "*Madame*?" he said gently. "Shall we go?"

She nodded and Kaveh led her back up the Communards' Road before she could catch sight of the skeleton.

When they arrived at the place that used to be her dressing room, he touched her arm to stop her. "*Madame*, if I may ask..." He hesitated.

Christine made an amused noise. "Well, *monsieur*, you haven't scrupled to ask me anything else—why stop now?"

"I am curious as to what was in the box, *madame*."

Christine shrugged. "Letters." She reached for the lever to open the mirror for her to step through.

"Letters?"

"Letters to Erik, that I have written over the years. Why?"

Kaveh's face took on an expression of alarm. "What—what did the letters say?"

Christine frowned at him. "Ah, now, *monsieur*, that is going too far. Those letters are private, in a locked box five cellars down, in a hidden cavern, sitting on a grave. I have the only key to the box. No one else can ever find them, so why must you know what they say?"

His Parisian manners already sliding into place over his Persian curiosity, Kaveh bowed. "As you say, *madame*. That was rude of me. My apologies."

Christine nodded, and they stepped through the mirror together into the unused dressing room. Back in the lobby, Christine gave him her hand. "Thank you, *monsieur*. Thank you so much for the kindness that you have shown—both to me, and to Erik as well. I know you were very dear to him."

Kaveh nodded. "He had more than a passing fondness for you, as well, *madame*."

Christine laughed. "And I for him. Alas that I realized it too late. Well, *monsieur, adieu*." She headed out into the late afternoon sunlight.

"*Au revoir, madame*," Kaveh muttered to her departing back. He somehow had the feeling that he hadn't seen the last of her. It depended on those letters, though. What sorts of things had she written to Erik over the years? For a moment he was tempted to head back down, but he caught himself in time. Either Erik would decide to leave the box alone, or else he would not appreciate being interrupted as he read all that Christine had written to him over the last five years.

He sighed and hailed a cab back to his flat. He would know soon enough.

Chapter 9
The Delayed Post Finally Arrives

In the cellars, Erik cradled Christine's box in his hands as if it were a baby. Not bothering to light a lantern, he brought it back to his old house and opened the front door. A whiff of musty air drifted past him, and he went in and turned on the gaslights. He was chuffed with himself to see that they still worked. He sat down in his old chair, put his feet up, and opened the box.

Christine had retained the key, but the box knew the touch of its maker. He pressed the hidden release and the drawer full of letters popped open. He took the first one on the stack;

it was still new and crisp, and when he unfolded it he noted that it had been written only
that morning.

My dearest Erik,
I am confused, tired, and weepy this morn-
ing. Yesterday afternoon, M. Tallis asked me
some rather pointed questions about my feel-
ings for you, and in the process of dredging up
my answers I have come to some disquieting
conclusions.

My heart is yours. That is no surprise to me,
although I suspect it might be to you if you
knew. It always has been, and always will be.
Raoul had a good portion of it for a while, but
little by little you wrested it away from him
even from the grave until now you own the
whole thing. I love you, Erik, totally and com-
pletely.

I love others as well. My son Erik-Daaé is
my pride and joy in this life, and the Girys,
Sorelli, and her husband and children are quite
dear to me—but if I am to move on and succeed
in my life and my new career, I must let you go.
I cannot truly live while my heart is buried with
you.

I will always think of you and I doubt I will

ever stop loving you or missing you—but Erik, I must say goodbye to your memory. I am going to stop writing these letters (which is wise, because now there are so many they barely fit into the jewelry box you made for me!) and I am going to concentrate on my singing, and on raising my son.

M. Tallis tells me that today he will take me to visit your graveside, and I intend to leave the whole box of letters there with you. I know you will keep them safe, and I know that without the key, no one else will ever be able to find them— thus my privacy will be protected. I thought about burning them altogether, but I cannot make myself do it. Leaving them locked up in a secret box, in the custody of the dead, is the next best thing I can think of.

Take care of them, my dearest.

If you see the Angel of Music there in paradise (for I no longer have any doubts as to where you must have gone), give him my thanks for sending you to me. If you see Raoul, tell him I have forgiven his misapprehension, and if you see my father, tell him of his grandson, who is named for you and for him.

I hope for a long and happy life, my Erik, and I hope to be with you at the end of it. That will be the sweetest happiness I could ever wish.

Yours always,

Christine

Erik's heart nearly stopped. His mouth fell open and hung that way as he went back and read the letter again, and then a third time. Christine loved him? When had that happened? He quickly perused the other details, about her husband's misapprehension (*what* misapprehension?), the existence of her son (whom she had named after *him*!), and (he smiled; this part was delicious) the way he had "wrested" her heart away from Raoul de Chagny even from the grave. He shook his head. What on *earth* had led her to this conclusion?

Seeing that the letters had been placed into the drawer in chronological order, Erik pulled out the whole stack. He flipped it over and started from the beginning: her first letter, written from the hotel in Denmark before they had even arrived in Sweden.

He smiled sadly at Christine's assertion that she missed him and regretted what had happened between them, but he soon began frowning when she talked of Raoul's wanting to live in a place where Christine would have no access to music or companionship. "Not near Upsala, you young fool," he muttered to the ghost of Chagny as if the man could hear him. "She'll never have any friends if you're the only noble in a peasant village!"

Sure enough, as he progressed through the letters, Christine's loneliness was made plain. Her brief flare of happiness when she spoke of her expected child was short-lived, and was soon drowned out by her discontent and loneliness when her foster-mother died.

He scowled when he read of her horse ride with Raoul, and his subsequent "amorousness." That was the biggest drawback to her having been so forthright in these letters; he had to put up with reading details about her life with Raoul that he had been happier not knowing. Remembering his own horse ride with Christine, though, he really couldn't blame the man. He himself had been hard-pressed to maintain his composure during that ride.

When he got to the letter about the dream she'd had about him, his eyes widened. She dreamed of his kissing her! She had dreamed of being married to him! He blinked a few times in total disbelief when he read the next part: she had even dreamed of them "behaving as husband and wife." Erik recognized the euphemism; indeed, he had dreamed of the same sort of thing more times than he could count. What touched him the most, though, was when she told of waking to her cold, lonely house, realizing that she was in a cold, lonely marriage, and wishing she could have her dream back. Erik swallowed hard and shifted uncomfortably.

If only he had known! But it would not have made any difference. There would have been no respectable way for them to be together with Raoul still living, and Christine's honor meant almost as much to him as she did herself.

After that came the letter telling about the death of her child. His heart broke for her when he read the letter that reminisced about how he would make her "sing it out" whenever she was distressed. That was the one that made him break into weeping. It stressed how much she had needed him to help her sing through her grief. If only he had known that his beloved was in such pain! He took off his mask and draped it over his knee to keep it dry, finally indulging his overflowing heart and crying unashamedly.

When he had composed himself, he dried his face but left his mask off. He picked up the next letter and began again.

His temper rose as he read about her husband accusing her of infidelity, and he could easily envision his gentle Christine turning into a vengeful harpy in her righteous outrage. "*Salaud!*" he growled in Raoul's vague direction. "*Bâtard! Quel connard!*" As if Christine could ever be unfaithful! What a git the little fellow had turned into!

His wrath receded only when he read the brief note from Raoul's captain, informing Christine of her husband's death. For some reason, Christine had got those two letters out of order. "*'A moi la vengeance, à moi la rétribution,' dit le Seigneur,*" [2] Erik quoted with great satisfaction. "Drowned in the North Sea, which was probably almost as cold as the bastard's heart!"

After she recovered from her anger at her husband, the tone of her letters lightened. They made him smile and wish he had been there to help her establish herself when she returned to Paris—but she had managed quite nicely. The fact that the Paris letters were fewer and less

---

[2] "Vengeance and retribution belong to me," says the Lord.

frequent told him how much happier she had been in Paris than in her childhood homeland. With amusement he read of her defiance in naming Raoul's child after Erik, and about her attending the opera and noticing the prop mistake in *Orphée et Eurydice* that no one who had not trod those boards would have been likely to notice. Ah, but she was an opera star, he thought with some degree of triumph. She may be a countess in rank, but in her heart, she is an opera diva! Smiling, he returned to the letters.

Now that he was familiar with the way her life had been since he had last seen her, he could begin to see the progression of her feelings for him. She loved him! He still marveled at the thought, even as he continued on to her last few letters. He laughed outright at her tale of having overheard the managers talking about him. So, Richard missed his livening things up, did he? He might have to sneak in and play a trick or two on the managers, just for old times' sake, before he went home.

Suddenly reminded of home, Erik glanced at his watch. He had been there all evening and all night, reading the letters, weeping, reminiscing, and then reading the letters all over again. It was almost time for Kaveh to wake up. Erik gathered up all the letters and put them carefully back into the box, and put on his mask again. He wanted to share his happiness with someone, and Kaveh was his only friend. Still smiling, he made his way up to the street, where the sun was rising on Erik's newfound hope.

Chapter 10
Music Hath Charms

I t was a changed Erik who came in while Kaveh was about to sit down to breakfast that morning. His manner had gentled considerably since they had moved to sunny southern France, but this morning the last cynical edge had melted away. His yellow eyes did not blaze, but merely glowed with happiness. "Good morning, Kaveh!" he greeted. His mask was smudged and his clothes bore evidence of his sojourn in the cellars.

Kaveh stopped short. "Those letters must have been good," he remarked.

Erik smiled; Kaveh could barely see the

curve of his lips at the bottom of his mask. "She told you about the letters?"

"She mentioned their existence, not their content." Kaveh was a bit unnerved by this exhilarated Erik. Suspicious.

Erik buttered his toast quickly and motioned to a chair. "Sit down, *daroga*; I am happy, yes, but no one has been hurt this time. Did you know that Mme. de Chagny was a widow?"

Kaveh nodded.

"Did you know that she has a baby son?"

Another nod.

Erik put down his toast and leaned back, folding his hands behind his head expansively. "Did you know that she'd named the poor little blighter after me?"

Kaveh nodded again, beginning to smile at this strange, euphoric version of his acerbic and cynical friend.

"So tell me, my friend: how could you have known all these things and not told me?" Erik asked him quite innocently, just as if he hadn't stubbornly refused to listen to Kaveh's news the day before.

Kaveh stopped, seriously tempted for one moment to fling the butter dish at Erik's head. He wisely refrained, though, and contented himself with breathing in deeply and counting to ten in Farsi. He purposely did it aloud, for Erik's sake.

Erik grinned. Kaveh could tell by the glint in his eye that Erik was enjoying this hugely.

"You're laughing at me," he accused him. "Don't try to hide it, Erik: you're laughing at me under that mask!"

At that, Erik threw back his head and laughed aloud this time. "The angels in heaven are laughing today, *daroga*. Why should I not share in their joy and mirth? Christine loves me. She loves me!"

"Yes, I know," Kaveh told him quietly. "What will you do about it?"

"Do? Why, I have to go to her."

"And frighten her into a fainting fit?" Kaveh asked pointedly. "She has just said her final goodbye to you, at your gravestone. How do you plan to inform her that you're not actually dead?"

Erik frowned. Lost in his elation, he hadn't thought that far ahead. "In writing?"

Kaveh shook his head. "Let me tell her," he suggested. "I am the one who lied to her in the first place, five years ago. Let me be the one she gets angry at, not you." He rang for Darius.

"I shall send her a message, saying that I have more to tell her about you and asking her to come here this afternoon. I shall tell her the truth, and if she is not too shocked, then you shall come into the room."

"And you shall leave," Erik said pointedly.

Kaveh smiled. "As you wish. After I have made sure that *Madame* de Chagny is in no danger of a fainting fit."

Erik smiled as he rose and shook out his napkin. "Fear not. If she faints, I shall be the one to catch her." He pushed his chair in and left the room, singing.

"I do not doubt it," Kaveh replied to the empty room. "All that practice..." he let the sentence trail off as he took a sip of his morning coffee. From what he remembered, Christine had been a vaporish kind of girl.

After breakfast, he wrote his letter to Christine.

Dear Mme. de Chagny,
In my musing over our conversations recently regarding a certain mutual friend, I have a confession to make to you. I regret that I was not completely honest with you, the last time we met below the opera five years ago. Forgive

me; at the time, I only thought to protect you from some unhappy knowledge. The one lie then called for another, and so it went. Believe me, I was only thinking of what would be best for both you and he.

If you would care to come to my house this afternoon after your lesson, I will tell you the complete truth. Please send an acknowledgement with my servant, and I look forward to seeing you.

Regretfully yours,

Kaveh Tallis

He sent the letter in person with Darius, who brought back her reply in less than a half an hour. It read:

Dear M. Tallis:
Yes, I will come. I do desire to hear the true story, even if it is an unhappy one. I shall be there shortly after three.

Yours truly,

Christine Daaé de Chagny

At ten minutes after three, Christine alighted

from her cab and rang the bell at the address M. Tallis had given her. Darius showed her in and brought some tea, and then Kaveh entered the room alone.

He looked worried as he took a seat, and he kept glancing nervously over Christine's shoulder. "*Madame*, thank you for coming. And I apologize in advance for my not having been honest with you."

"What was it that you were not honest about?" Christine asked. She was mildly irked with him, but he looked so unhappy and guilty that she couldn't condemn him any further.

"Well… everything," he admitted. "I am sorry, *madame*. Let me start from the beginning."

He told her about receiving Erik's message, five years ago, that Erik expected to die in the next couple of days. He put Erik's death-notice into the paper, but instead of waiting, he went to Erik right away. Sure enough, the man was almost gone—but seeing him lying there like a living corpse and remembering all their years of history together, he couldn't bring himself to walk away and leave him there to die. He and his manservant had waited until dark and then brought Erik's near-comatose body back to his flat. He had called a doctor, who examined Erik and said he was suffering from advanced consumption and an illness of the brain more than he was from a broken heart. He treated Erik as well as he could, but recommended his immediate removal to a warmer and sunnier clime. A calm, quiet environment such as the seaside would be ideal, he told them, for Erik to be able to regain his mental and physical health.

Kaveh was tired of Paris, and with Erik in his care, there was no further need for him to stay in the city to keep an eye on the "opera ghost's" activities. He immediately commissioned Darius to find them a small but comfortable house in the south of France, preferably private and near the shore.

He returned to Erik's house to gather his things, and that was when he had met Christine. Knowing Erik wished her to think him dead, he explained that he had taken charge of Erik's body himself, and wished her *bonne chance* [3]in her new life.

Darius returned two weeks later with the deed for an elegant seaside cottage just outside Sète, in a remote area of Provence. Erik was conscious by that time, furious with Kaveh for

---

[3] Good luck

saving his life, but was still too weak to resist when Kaveh forcibly relocated him to Provence.

"And that is the story, *madame*," Kaveh finished his narration. "Again, I apologize for being untruthful, but it was what Erik wished."

Christine sat for several moments, frowning. "But—the gravesite we visited. There was a stone. What about that?"

Kaveh pursed his lips. "It was placed there yesterday morning. It marks no real grave."

"So where is he buried?" Christine pressed.

Kaveh raised his eyebrows. "He is not buried, *madame*. That is what I am trying to tell you. Erik is alive."

Christine's eyes widened, and she gasped. "Erik is—he is alive?"

Kaveh nodded, shooting another glance over her shoulder. "He is, *madame*. Would you like to see him?"

Christine's expression was answer enough, and Kaveh nodded toward the window behind Christine. She turned, shading her eyes from the afternoon sunlight.

A man stood silhouetted against the window. He was elegantly dressed, tall and slender, but not quite the wraith-like thinness she remembered. Christine stood up and went over to him. She raised a timid hand and pressed it against his chest. The man inhaled sharply. She looked up at his face.

He wore a white mask made of silk, which extended down almost to his chin. She could see just the suggestion of a lower lip. She moved her hand to his shoulder, and stroked her other hand down his torso and over his ribs. The man's hands, held clenched at his sides, began to tremble.

Kaveh was just beginning to wonder whether he should leave, when Christine abruptly removed her hands from the man's body and turned back to him angrily. "This is an unkind jest, *monsieur*," she spat. "This man is not Erik."

Kaveh met Erik's startled gaze and blinked. This was not an outcome they had planned!

"Christine," Erik said softly.

She whirled around and narrowed her eyes. "You have done very well, M. Tallis," she said coldly. "He even sounds a bit like Erik. But this is not Erik's figure; nor it is, I suspect, Erik's face."

A low chuckle issued from behind the white mask. "Unfortunately it is," Erik told her with wry humor.

Christine ignored him, turning back to the Persian. "M. Tallis, this man has not Erik's build—no, not in the slightest. How could you have overlooked such a detail? He is much more solidly built than Erik was—and with the mask on, his face tells me nothing."

"*Madame,*" Kaveh tried to explain. "When you first met Erik, he had already been seriously ill for several years with no treatment. He is recovered now, and would naturally cut a more robust figure than he did then."

Christine frowned again, turning to study the masked man. She approached him. "*Monsieur,* if you are Erik, then prove it. Let me see your face." She raised one eyebrow in challenge.

The man stiffened. Christine stood there with her arms crossed and chin raised, waiting expectantly. Slowly, the man reached behind his head to untie the mask. He shot a warning glance at his friend. "You may turn around if you wish, *daroga.* I know you've seen me before."

Kaveh could not have moved a muscle if his life depended on it. His jade-colored eyes were glued to the scene before him.

Erik shrugged, turned his attention back to Christine, and let the mask flutter to the floor.

It was Erik. Ugliness such as his could not have been faked. His gruesome, corpse-like face was exactly the same as she remembered: his jutting brow shadowed his two piercing yellow eyes; his skin stretched tight across his cheekbones; his nose was almost nonexistent, little more than two large nostril-holes in the center of his face. He had a little more hair than he used to, but it was still quite thin and sparse.

Christine took a deep, rapturous breath at the sight of his beloved hideousness, and fainted into his arms.

"Good catch," Kaveh muttered under his breath, but Erik heard him and chuckled.

"I told you I would, didn't I?" he retorted, picking Christine up and laying her carefully on the divan. "And yet you say I'm not to be trusted."

When Christine awoke, she was lying on the divan, with Kaveh hovering in the background and Erik kneeling next to her. He had put the mask back on, but was holding her hand tightly. When her eyelids fluttered open, he tried to pull his hand away, but she held on.

His skin was warm now when it used to be so cold, and no longer had that dank and musty smell that she associated with death. She clutched his hand and gazed up at him with a bewildered expression. "Is it really you?" she whispered.

In answer, he opened his mouth and sang. Christine recognized the line as one of the opening songs from the prison scene in "Faust." Erik skipped the lines about feeling tortured, and went right to Faust's exclamation at seeing his beloved imprisoned.

"C'est elle, la voici, la douce creature!" he sang. He left out the next few lines and called, *"Marguerite! Marguerite!"*

Right on cue, Christine sat up and sang, *"Ah! c'est la voix du bien aimé! A son appel mon cœur s'est ranimé!"*

Across the room, Kaveh recognized the recitative and nodded to himself with satisfaction. It was only fitting, he thought, for those two to make their confessions of love through opera. Not just any opera, either; it had been "Faust" in which Christine had made her stunning debut, and "Faust" from which Erik had mysteriously captured her from the stage just as she had invoked the aid of the angels. And it was "Faust" that they sang from now.

"Marguerite!" Erik sang.

Christine felt her eyes welling up at the familiar sound of his spellbinding voice. She sang the response, in which Marguerite recognizes her beloved's voice. *"Sa main, sa douce main m'attire!"* Christine sang. *"Je suis libre! il est là! Je l'entends, je le vois!"* As she sang "I see him," she reached up and pulled the mask from Erik's face so that she could see his expression as she sang the next lines.

Holding his gaze steadily, and with tears running down her face, she sang of her love for him, *"Oui, c'est toi, je t'aime, oui, c'est toi, je t'aime."* She closed her eyes as Erik reached down with a trembling hand and wiped her tears away. Voice shaking, she finished the next lines. *"Tu m'as retrouvée...C'est toi, je suis sur ton cœur!"*

Erik hesitated a moment before taking a deep breath and singing his and Faust's reply. *"Oui, c'est moi, je t'aime, oui, c'est moi, je t'aime, malgré l'effort même du démon moqueur."* When he sang the line about the mocking demon, Erik couldn't help himself. He pointedly cut his eyes toward the Persian. Kaveh got the message and left the room grinning, closing the door behind him.

Erik went on singing tenderly, *"Je t'ai retrouvée, C'est moi, viens, viens sur mon cœur!"* [4] By the time he finished the line, Christine had risen from the divan and flung herself into his arms.

Kaveh stopped outside the door, where Darius had just happened to be dusting the furniture in the hallway. They could still hear the singing. When it came to an abrupt stop, Kaveh glanced at Darius, and the two shared a knowing smile. With one accord, they made their way downstairs, where they couldn't hear anything more.

They would not have heard anything anyway, because for a long time there was no sound but that of weeping: gasps of breath, choked sobs, and a few hoarse, broken words spoken in a half-whisper as the two clung together desperately.

"Can it be true?" Erik asked hoarsely, tears

---

[4] Faust: It is she; she is there, the sweet creature! Marguerite! Marguerite!

Marguerite: Oh, that is the voice of my love. At his call, my heart started beating again.
His hand, his sweet hand draws me near
I am free—he is there. I hear him, I see him.
Yes, it's you—I love you. Yes, it's you—I love you.
You have found me again… It is you; I am in your heart.

Faust: Yes, it is I—I love you; yes, it is I—I love you,
even in spite of the efforts of the mocking demon.
I have found you again. It is I; come, come to my heart.

running freely down his skull-like visage. "Is this real? Oh, Christine! *Can* you love me?" He buried his face in her hair, trembling.

Christine laid her smooth, soft cheek against his ridged, bony one and held him tighter. "Erik! Oh, Erik, my love. Are you truly alive, my darling?" She cried openly, pressing her rosy lips to his ravaged cheek, and his tears started afresh as she kissed him all over his horrific face.

A long time later, when the tears had finally stopped flowing and the emotion had dwindled into sniffles and an occasional hiccup, Erik escorted Christine back to the divan and sat down next to her. He started to reach for her hand, but drew back.

Not as shy, Christine took his hand and held it firmly in hers. The look he gave her made her blush and look away. The silence began to be uncomfortable after their strong emotions of a few minutes before.

Erik stepped easily back into his teacher role. "You have done well, getting your voice back after it had gone unused for so long," he said. "Your tone is excellent; only your range seems to have suffered, and that is easily regained."

"It was difficult to come even as far as I

have, without your instruction," Christine admitted.

"Would—would you like me to begin teaching you again?" Erik asked tentatively. What, exactly, would be the parameters of their renewed acquaintance?

"If you were willing to, my dearest, I would be exceedingly grateful," Christine said, brightening a little.

Erik closed his eyes and breathed in deeply. He opened them again, to see Christine staring at him and looking puzzled. "Is something wrong?" she asked, stroking his hand.

"Forgive me," Erik said. "I am just... unused to endearments. When you call me 'love' or 'dearest,' it quite takes my breath away." He gave her a shy smile and looked away.

Christine reached up and caressed his face, running gentle fingers over his taut, pallid skin. He closed his eyes and unconsciously swayed toward her.

"You'll probably get tired of hearing them before I get tired of using them, my love," she said. "If you only knew how much I missed you, thinking you were dead, then you'd understand."

"I wonder if it was as much as I missed you,

thinking you were happy with your little *vicomte*. Pardon me, *comte*." Erik mused, putting a tentative arm around her. When she did not protest, he drew her closer to lean against his chest.

She raised her head sharply. "How—how did you know I was unhappy with him?"

"You told me."

"I? How could I have told you?"

"You wrote me five years' worth of letters, Christine. My heart ached for you as I read them."

She gasped. "You read—you read all my letters? Erik, those were private!"

He shrugged, a hint of an impish grin quirking one corner of his misshapen mouth. "My dear, you addressed them to me, you brought them to me, you left them with me in one of my own boxes—of course I read them! I found them most, ah, enlightening."

Christine groaned and buried her face in his shoulder. "But some of them were so personal!" she wailed, mortified.

"Those were the most enlightening ones," he replied, deadpan. He pressed a kiss to the top of her head where it rested on his shoulder. "Come, Christine, *mon coeur*[5], don't be upset.

[5] My heart

You should know by now that there is nothing about you that I don't adore."

Christine raised her face to his, moved by his statement. "I feel the same way about you, Erik."

Her face was mere inches from his, and tilted up toward him. She had wept with him, sung with him, and confessed that she adored him. There was only one response that Erik could possibly make to her, and he made it.

Erik lowered his face to hers, and for the first time in his long, violent, and eventful life, he kissed the lips of the woman he loved.

The kiss started out tender, just a gentle press of the lips before he withdrew to stare at her, eyes wide. She had let him kiss her! She had let him kiss her like a lover, and she did not die! She did not even faint.

She had even, he realized, kissed him back.

Even as these thoughts came to him, Christine reached for him again and barely touched her lips to his. The kiss grew in ardor until their mouths were fused together hungrily. Her fingers snaked through his sparse black hair and curved around the back of his head, to hold him closer as she filled her senses with Erik. It had been so long since she had been kissed by a man who loved her—and she had never been kissed like *this* before in her life. Erik's kisses were untutored, but the mere fact that it was *him* touched her, moved her, and made her feel things that Raoul's kisses never had.

Erik felt as if he were drowning, but didn't even think of breathing. Inside he was reeling from the force of all these new sensations: within the course of a single day, he had experienced things he'd never thought he would. He had loved before, but to be loved in return was a new and ecstatic feeling. He had once dreamed of someday being able to kiss Christine, but had never expected her to allow it. Now, not only was he kissing her, but she was kissing him back, kissing him with a keen longing as though if she stopped she would die.

He felt the same way. He could not sit upright any longer; Christine was making his head spin. He leaned back on the divan, drawing her after him so that she lay halfway across his chest. He tore his mouth away from hers so he could breathe, but with the skin of her neck so invitingly close he couldn't stop himself from nuzzling his face into it. He inhaled the scent of her skin, tasted it on his tongue, and felt a rush of power when Christine made an inarticulate noise and arched herself against him. Yet another new sensation made itself known to him—now he knew what it was like to be desired.

This discovery, that Christine wanted him, was almost too much for the remnants of his self-control. He was a breath away from pulling her fully on top of him and reaching for the hooks of her dress... but at the last minute he loosened his grip and turned his head away.

Christine seemed to sense his change of mood, and put her head back down on his chest, to catch her breath. He kept his arms around her, stroking her hair until they had both calmed down. He helped her to sit up, taking her hand in his and pressing it to his lips with a tender smile. At least, he hoped it looked tender. With the mask, he hadn't had to worry about his expressions in so long that he hoped he didn't look grim and menacing when all he felt was vulnerable and loving. The astonishing intimacy of what he had just shared with Christine left him feeling even more naked than being maskless did.

Christine held his hand, smiling, and pressed it against her cheek. She gazed up into his glowing golden eyes. "Oh, my," was all she could say. She blushed a little. "I—I've… I've never felt quite like that before."

"Nor have I," Erik said quietly. "I think I have tasted all the happiness the world has to offer, just in this one afternoon."

Christine gave him an arch look. "Not yet, you haven't," was all she said.

Then the clock on the mantle chimed six, and she gasped. "Oh, no!" She pulled her hand away and stood up, smoothing her wrinkled skirts and reaching up to tidy her hair where Erik's passionate fingers had pulled it out of the loose chignon she wore. "My love, I hate to leave you, but I've stayed too long."

Erik's heart sank. He knew he had no right to, but he had been hoping that the events of this afternoon weren't a one-time occurrence. He swallowed his disappointment. "I understand," he said. He stood up, keeping his distance from her, and put his mask back on. "I thank you, Christine, with all my heart, for what you did for me here today."

She laughed, not quite catching his new, somber mood. "Believe me, my dear, I'm every bit as grateful to you!"

This emboldened him to catch her hand and ask, "May I see you again?"

She went over to him, boldly lifted his mask and gave him one more lingering kiss. "If you don't come to see me, it will break my heart all over again, Erik. You simply must visit."

"When?"

"Tomorrow, if you please. I shall have to go to the opera and teach in the morning, but I shall be in soon after three. Will you come then? And stay for supper?"

Erik hesitated an instant before nodding. "Tomorrow, then." He raised her hand to his lips once more, and then she was gone.

Christine hurried home and apologized to her maid and her cook for being tardy. "I met up with an old friend and we spent the afternoon catching up with each other," she explained. "Where is my little Erik-Daaé?"

"He's in the nursery, my lady," Anneke said.

Christine nodded. "I'll dine with him there this evening, then," she said. She felt slightly guilty for not having spent any time with him that afternoon as usual, but she was so eager to tell him about Erik that she didn't want to wait until the next day.

The maid raised her eyebrows at the unusual request, but nodded and said nothing.

Christine hurried upstairs to the nursery. She

eased open the door and looked at her tiny son, wondering what Erik would think of him when they met. Would he look too much like a Chagny? Would Erik be uncomfortable with this living reminder of her marriage to Raoul?

Erik-Daaé de Chagny was small for his age and slight, with a mop of dark brown, wavy hair shadowing a pair of intense, dark blue eyes. He had always reminded Christine much more of her father than of Raoul, and for once she was selfishly glad of that fact. Just past two, he was sweet-natured and happy—as long as he got his own way. He was also determinedly and stubbornly shy, refusing to speak to new people at all until after he'd known them for weeks.

He was perfectly affectionate, however, with people he did know. He looked up from his blocks and saw her. "*Maman!*" he cried, jumping to his feet to throw his arms around her legs. "Where were you?"

"I'm sorry, darling," Christine told him as she picked him up and gave him a hug. "I missed our afternoon playtime, didn't I? Never mind, though; Nurse is going to bring our supper in here tonight, and while we're eating I have a wonderful story to tell you!" She nodded a quick dismissal to the nurse.

That was promising enough to distract the little boy from his complaint about her absence, and the company of his mother for supper in the nursery was a rare treat. The boy was content.

"You said you had a story," the child prompted, sitting down to his light supper of soup and biscuits.

"I once knew a man," Christine began. "A clever man and a great teacher. He taught me how to sing like an angel, at the opera. He was my good friend and I loved him very much, but he was sick. He thought he was dying, and so he sent me away to marry your Papa."

"And did he die?" the boy asked, blue eyes wide.

"I thought he did," Christine told him. "I thought he was dead, and even though I was happy to be with your Papa, I was still sad because I missed my teacher very much. But you know what happened?"

"What?"

"He hadn't died after all, and I saw him again today. That's where I was when I didn't come home after my lesson—with him. And he's coming here tomorrow, and you'll get to meet him."

"Oh." Young Erik-Daaé seemed downcast.

Christine thought she knew why: meeting someone new was always scary to him. She leaned down with a smile and whispered, "My friend can do magic, you know."

"Magic?"

She nodded. "Magic. He can do magic with his voice; just you wait and see. And he has a very special secret. And I have a secret to tell you, too, my little one. Would you like to know his name?"

Erik-Daaé nodded.

"His name is Erik, just like yours. You see, when you were born I loved you so much that I decided to name you after my friend and teacher, whom I also loved very much. He's my favorite big person in the whole world. Just like you're my favorite small person."

"And we're both named Erik," the boy said with satisfaction.

"That's right. And maybe someday, if you're a very good boy and don't tease Nurse so much, Erik might teach you how to sing like an angel, too. Would you like to meet *Monsieur* Erik tomorrow?"

The boy nodded eagerly, and spooned some more soup. Suddenly he thought of something, and stopped with his spoon halfway to his mouth. "You said the big Erik had a secret."

"Yes, he does," Christine said. "But it's something that you must not tell anyone else. I will tell you tomorrow. Come on, let's get you ready for bed."

Christine enjoyed the novelty of getting her son ready for bed; usually the nurse did it, and presented her with a fed, washed, and sleepy toddler to kiss goodnight. Tonight, though, she did all of the feeding and washing, and she tucked the sleepy toddler into bed herself.

Young Erik-Daaé was precocious in his speech, but still very much a baby in all other ways. He looked rather like a doll, lying there in his cot with his big blue eyes and untidy mess of hair. "*Maman*, will you sing to me?"

"What would you like to hear?"

He dimpled. "Sing the bullfighting song!"

Christine laughed. "All right, my blood-thirsty little son." She always hoped to instill in her son a love of her own favorite opera, "Faust," but he vastly preferred the excitement of the matador life from "Carmen." She sang it quietly and at a much slower tempo than it was usually performed, in hopes of lulling the boy to sleep.

"Toréador, en garde! Toréador! Toréador!
Et songe bien, oui, songe en combattant,
qu'un oeil noir te regarde,
et que l'amour t'attend, Toréador,
l'amour, l'amour t'attend!"[6]

Almost asleep, Erik opened one blue eye a crack. "Faster tomorrow, *Maman*," he requested.

Christine chuckled. She hadn't fooled him. "Yes, *cheri*; I'll sing it faster tomorrow. Good night."

Christine was so joyful and animated the next day at the opera house that Mme. Giry gave her an appraising glance as she bustled past the practice room while Christine was warming up. She stuck her head in. "And what makes you so happy today, *Madame* de Chagny?" she asked with a teasing and toothless smile.

"I've just caught up with an old friend, *Madame* Giry," Christine told her. "Someone I had thought was long gone has returned, and we

<hr>

[6] Toreador, be on your guard,
Toreador, Toreador.
And think of this, yes, remember while you fight
One black eye is watching you!
And love is waiting for you, Toreador,
Love, love awaits you

had a nice visit yesterday."

"Oh? And who is that, *madame*?" Mme. Giry asked, her curiosity plain to see—she had known Christine for almost the whole two years she'd been back in Paris, and knew of no "old friends" that the girl claimed to have.

Christine opened her mouth to answer (though what she was going to say, she had no idea), but was interrupted by three taps.

She frowned. Mme. Giry looked around suspiciously. "Is anyone in here with you, *madame*?" she asked.

"Not that I know of," Christine answered.

Mme. Giry chuckled. "It must have been the dancers. For just a moment I was reminded of the Opera Ghost! He used to tap on the door of his box just that way, when he wanted something."

"Did he," Christine said weakly. Was Erik hiding in the opera somewhere? "I wonder if he has returned, to play some tricks just for old times' sake? I wouldn't put it past him, knowing the Opera Ghost."

Mme. Giry chuckled. "No, indeed! He was always up for some mischief, that one. Why, I recall..." Then she stopped and stared at Christine, who was staring at her.

"You know the Opera Ghost?" they each said at the same time.

"To be sure, I do. Was I not his box-keeper for all the years he haunted this opera house?" Mme. Giry said. "Did I not bring him a footstool for his lady, all those years ago? How do you know the Opera Ghost, *madame*?"

Blushing, Christine asked, "Can you keep a secret, *Madame* Giry? Even from the managers?"

Mme. Giry nodded. "Of course, *madame*. It would not be the first time."

"I was the Ghost's lady."

"Ah, now, I knew it!" the old woman gave a delighted smile. "I thought all along that it was you; especially when you went away with *Monsieur le Vicomte*, and the Ghost disappeared at the same time. Did you take him with you, *madame*?"

Christine shook her head. "No; I thought the Ghost was gone forever, but I just had a visit from him yesterday."

"Ah, that's why you're so happy today, then," the woman correctly surmised.

Christine blushed. "It is, yes—but please, you mustn't tell anyone, *madame*. Not even little Meg."

Mme. Giry made a dismissive gesture. "The things I know about this place, that my daughter doesn't, could fill a book. You may depend upon me to keep your secret, *madame*, just as I've been keeping the Ghost's secrets for years."

"Thank you, *madame*."

Mme. Giry went out, and Christine had a few moments of privacy before her student was scheduled to arrive. She put out her music and was about to go on warming up, but just then she heard another tap. She stopped abruptly and glanced up at the ceiling. "Are you in here, my dear?" she asked, smiling. "Did you come to eavesdrop on my lessons?"

Erik's voice, light and amused, sounded as if it came from under the piano. "I could not resist the urge to come and watch you try to teach those little toads everything I taught you."

Smiling at his ventriloquism, Christine ducked her head to glance under the piano. Of course no one was there. Erik's voice now issued from her music bag. "Of course, if you'd rather teach in privacy, I could always find other areas of the opera to haunt."

Christine laughed. "No, no, that's all right! I had better keep you with me, and make sure you don't start terrorizing the managers again!"

"They deserve it," observed Erik, whose voice now came from behind Christine. She turned reflexively, but saw no one. "They continue to overlook the natural talent under their noses in favor of singers so overtrained they have little of their natural voices left. Singers like La Carlotta and Carolus Fonta have only their reputations left to recommend them. The managers would rather get a famous singer to play the leads rather than someone who can actually sing." He sounded disgusted.

Christine nodded. "Some of my students have been showing some promise," she said. "Especially this one I have first. I'm glad you're here, Erik; I'd like your opinion on him. He seems to have stalled and I don't know how to get him to the next level."

"I am at your service, my dear, in this as in everything," Erik's silky voice sounded right next to her left ear. Christine turned quickly, and there he was. He took her hand and bowed over it, pressing it to his lips.

She let out a startled laugh, putting her hand to her thumping heart. "Now you're being naughty," she accused him, "startling me like that."

Masked, he merely cocked his head and

nodded toward the door. Christine turned to the door and saw no one, and when she turned back Erik had vanished.

"Very naughty," she muttered, smiling.

"*Madame* de Chagny?" asked her student from the doorway. "Did you say something?"

"Uh, no, Jean-Michel. Come on in."

The lesson went on as normal, but Christine could sense Jean-Michel's frustration at not having made much progress since last time. She had tried all the tricks she could remember from her own lessons, both from her father and from Erik, but Jean-Michel's weak areas were different from her own and she did not know how to help him past his plateau.

Sighing, she sent him down to the chorus-master for some different music, and while he was gone she spoke to the silent walls. "Well? You can see the problem. Any suggestions?"

"Yes," said Erik, his voice coming from her bag again. "Take the rope out of here."

Rope? She hadn't any rope in her bag. Frowning, she reached in.

She pulled out the short piece of rope and sighed, shaking her head in mock aggravation. "When did you put—oh, never mind. So what do I do with the rope?" It was only about two and a half feet long, with the ends tied together so that it formed a circle.

"Have him pull on it in opposite directions while he sings," Erik suggested from the piano.

There was no one at the piano when she turned to see, but just then Jean-Michel reappeared in the doorway. She instructed him on what to do with the rope, and then started playing one of the new pieces he had brought.

The difference was amazing. Where before his voice had had a good tone but was still too light, now it practically boomed. Pleased with his teacher and his lesson, Jean-Michel left grinning.

"Now, how did you know that?" Christine asked the ceiling before her next student got there.

"Simple," Erik said from the doorway (unseen). "A singer's voice is a reflection of his mind. Young *Monsieur* Jean-Michel is a conflicted young man; most are, at that age. If you give him a tangible symbol of the conflict, so that he can fight while he sings, it helps him to clarify things in his mind—and his voice reflects the change."

"If a singer's voice is a reflection of his mind, that certainly explains yours," Christine teased. "Complex, layered, versatile, volatile, occasionally twisted..."

Erik chuckled, the sound coming from the far corner of the room. "Careful, my love, you'll make me blush."

The rest of the day was fairly low-key. A couple of times Erik whispered some suggestions in Christine's ear, unheard by her students, but he did not make another appearance until after her last student had left.

As Christine was packing up her bag again, she turned around to get her music and almost bumped into Erik, standing there tall and graceful in his dark suit and white mask. "Will you stop startling me?" she demanded.

He cocked his head while he considered it, and then shook his head in negation. "No, probably not." He picked up her bag for her, slung it over his arm, and offered her his other one. "Shall we go?"

Christine hesitated, looking at him. "Do you go out masked like that now? In daylight?" she asked. The Erik she remembered was so cautious that he hardly ever went out except at night, either masked or with a false nose.

He shrugged, an elegant lifting of one shoulder. "Since the wars, I am not the only

man on the streets with a facial deformity anymore. People notice, but they do not usually
approach me about it." He picked up his hat
from the piano (when had he put it there?),
pulled it low over his eyes, and offered his arm
again.

On their way out of the opera house, they
passed *Madame* Giry as she was going from
box to box on the grand tier polishing the mir-
rors. She turned and saw the two of them arm
in arm, and clasped her polishing rag rapturously to her breast as her face lit up. She curtseyed deeply to Erik, who bowed in return.

"Oh, sir, it is good to have you back," she
said to him. "Will you be having your regular
box from now on?"

"Thank you, Mme. Jules; that remains to be
seen," Erik told her in a dignified but friendly
voice.

"I was so happy, *monsieur*, when *Madame*
de Chagny told me you had returned. You must
let me know if you need anything, *Monsieur*
Ghost, and I will get it for you."

He bowed again. "Thank you, *madame*. You
are the soul of generosity, as you always have
been."

Christine cast an amused glance his way after they had left the building. "Are you ever planning to tell her that you're a real, live man?"

"Oh, she knows," he said. "*Madame* Jules Giry has always been a lot cleverer than people gave her credit for. I was pleased, when I read in your letters that you had befriended her."

Christine smiled and said nothing. Walking with Erik in the late afternoon sun, she found that he did get some raised eyebrows when people noticed his mask, but no one said anything to him. When they reached her flat, she rang for Anneke. "Hmm, I hadn't thought how I shall introduce you," she murmured to her companion. "I don't even know your surname, Erik; how silly is that?"

"Not silly at all, since I have none," he replied. "And as for introductions, perhaps we should stick as close to the truth as possible. It's far easier to keep track of than lies. I would know."

Anneke came bustling out from the kitchen. "Yes, madam?"

"Anneke, this is my friend *Monsieur* Erik, who used to be my voice teacher. He'll be staying for dinner; would you inform Cook, if you please?"

Anneke curtseyed. "Of course, *madame*." She hesitated a moment, eyeing Erik's mask. The tension in the air thickened.

He straightened and glared straight into her eyes. "Would you like to ask a question, Anneke?" he asked, his voice low.

"Oh! Forgive me, sir—I was just wondering... You see, *madame*'s son is also named Erik, and I was—"

Christine laughed, dismissing the tension. "Yes, I named him after my teacher, because I thought my teacher had died. It turns out he did not, and he has promised to begin teaching me again. Now then: I'd like you go and tell Cook that we want supper at seven, and then bring us some tea in the drawing room. After that, I'd like you to run up to the nursery and ask Nurse to bring Erik-Daaé down to the drawing room in a half-hour or so. And Anneke—don't tell her about *Monsieur* Erik's mask; she might tell Erik-Daaé, and I want to be the one to explain it to my son."

Seeing that Christine treated the subject of the mask in such a matter-of-fact manner eased Anneke's obvious discomfort with it, and she curtseyed and scurried off to do her mistress' bidding.

As Christine led Erik into the drawing room,

he remarked, "That begs the question of what *are* you going to tell your son about my mask? Suppose he should want to see my face? I am unused to small children, Christine, and tend to terrify them even without them having to see me." He put her music bag down on the piano and continued, "I would hate to think of scarring your son's psyche for the remainder of his life." His tone was dry, but there was an undercurrent of apprehension.

"Leave that to me," Christine told him as she faced him and took his hands in hers. "I know he will learn to like you; I am only concerned that you might not like him because he is Raoul's son."

It was the first time either of them had broached the topic of her marriage so boldly, or indeed brought up any of the more serious things Christine had written about. She looked up at him with some degree of trepidation.

Erik had already decided, the night he'd read all her letters, what his response would be when she brought up her marriage. He had already done all the soul-searching necessary, when he had read her letters about her life with Raoul. Now he was at peace. Slowly Erik drew her into his arms, prepared to release her the instant

she balked. She went willingly, which still surprised him.

"Should I berate you for your marriage,
when I sent you away with him in the first
place? Should I blame you for allowing your
husband his marital rights? Your son's paternal
bloodline matters not; he is still yours." His
voice took on a gentle amusement when he
went on, "I doubt that even de Chagny could
ruin a child that was yours. As I told you yesterday, there's nothing about you that I don't
love. I am sure that your son falls into that
category as well."

"Thank you, Erik," Christine said. She
tipped her head back and stood up on her toes,
to lift up his mask and give him a brief but
heartfelt kiss.

That kiss lengthened into others, but the
sound of a step in the hallway made them part
quickly. By the time Anneke had opened the
door and entered with the tea tray, Erik was sitting down at the piano and Christine was innocently unpacking her music bag. Erik began to
play while Anneke poured out the tea.

"Thank you, Anneke; I'll take over," Christine said. After the maid departed, she and Erik
glanced at each other like a pair of guilty chil-

dren. They burst out laughing.

Erik had a nice laugh; Christine had never heard it before. She had heard the occasional cynical chuckle, but Erik being amused enough to laugh freely in her presence was something new. She liked it.

"Perhaps we had better stick to tea and music for now," he suggested smoothly. "Else we may end up starting a scandal among your servants."

Blushing, Christine agreed and brought him his tea.

"Tell me what your son is like," Erik invited, putting his cup down and continuing to play, almost absently, a sprightly little melody that Christine suspected he was improvising right then without even thinking about it.

She pulled up a chair near the piano, and sat down. Sipping her own tea, she thought about it. "He's quite shy," she began. "It takes him a long time to be comfortable around other people. He loves music, even opera, but doesn't show much aptitude for it quite yet. It's still too early to tell, though; he's not yet three, although he sounds older when he speaks."

"What operas does he enjoy?"

Christine grinned. "Carmen. He can't get

enough of the bullfighting."

Erik tilted his head in such a way that made Christine think he was grimacing behind the mask. "Bizet?" he said scornfully. "What about Gounod? What of Mozart? *Don Giovanni, Die Zauberflöte?*"

She shook her head. "No, he mainly loves the Bizet."

Erik sighed. "That would doubtless be the Chagny influence." He finished the song he was playing and stopped to flex his hands and stretch his wrists. "It has been a few weeks," he apologized. "Kaveh maintained that I didn't need a piano in our flat, as we were only going to be in Paris so short a time. I'd like to see him go without air for as long as he's made me do without a piano," he said darkly.

"You're welcome to come and use mine, any time you wish," Christine offered. She finished her tea and set the cup down.

He darted a swift, yellow glance at her. "Be careful with what you offer, Christine; I'm likely to take you up on it."

She rose and went to him, placing a hand on his shoulder. "Erik, you are very welcome, any time you wish."

He took her hand off his shoulder and held it

against his masked cheek for a moment before releasing it and changing the subject. "What would you like to hear, my dear?"

"Something of yours." Christine went and stood in the curve of the piano.

"Very well." Erik closed his eyes and paused for a moment almost as if he were praying, and then launched into a high, soaring melody that was breathtaking in its loveliness until he added a deeper, dissonant harmony. Christine closed her eyes to listen better as the dissonance gradually lifted and the high melody descended until they met in the middle. There was a whole rest before he began the second part, which was a variation of the first melody but with very close, complex harmonies this time. It was a love song, she realized, opening her eyes suddenly. More to the point, it was *his* love song to her. Erik's gaze was fixed upon her face as he told her through music all of his thoughts of the past and hopes for the future.

"That was beautiful, Erik," she said when he'd finished, her voice a little shaky.

Eyes glowing, Erik started to rise and go to her, but just then there was a knock on the door. The nurse, a stout, florid woman in a white apron, pushed it open.

"Here's your little man, *madame*. Anneke said you wanted him sent down." She opened the door wider, and little Erik-Daaé peeked around it with huge, frightened blue eyes.

"Erik-Daaé! Come in, darling," Christine said happily. "Thank you, Nurse; you may go. I'll ring when I'm ready for you to come and get him."

The nurse gave the little boy a gentle nudge to get him into the room, and then closed the door behind her.

"Erik-Daaé, come here," his mother said. "I want to talk to you for a few minutes before you meet my friend."

Not taking his eyes off the masked stranger at the piano, the little boy went into his mother's arms and clung to her. At the piano, Erik began playing again, that same sprightly little tune he had been playing while they talked a few minutes ago.

"You remember when we talked last night, and I told you about my teacher? Well, that is *Monsieur* Erik, the man who taught me how to sing. He can do magic with his voice; maybe after we get finished talking, he might show you a little. Would you like that?"

A cautious nod.

"And do you see his mask?"

Another nod, the uncertainty giving way to a little curiosity.

"That is part of his secret. You remember I told you that *Monsieur* Erik had a secret?"

An eager nod this time. The child was apparently not immune to curiosity.

"His secret is his face. You see, *Monsieur* Erik's face doesn't look like other people's faces. His face is so special that he is the only person in the world who has a face like that."

Erik the younger regarded Erik the elder with a frank, inquisitive gaze.

Erik went on playing, listening hard but to all appearances ignoring the little boy entirely. Christine's son tugged on his heartstrings, though; except for his dark hair, he looked exactly like Christine. He imagined Christine as a small child, with wide, blue, curious eyes, and had to smile at the picture. He realized that when Christine had been Erik-Daaé's age, he himself was already in his twenties, living in Persia and wielding the Punjab lasso for money. His playing faltered a little with his sharp stab of regret; then he resumed.

Christine went on talking. "*Monsieur* Erik

wears the mask because sometimes people don't know how to react to a face as special as his. I remember how surprised I was when I first saw it." Her voice took on a nostalgic quality as she told her son, "I was so curious about his mask that while we were singing together I reached out and took it right off him! And that was extremely rude of me. *Monsieur* Erik was very angry, and I was sorry that I had been so unkind."

She sent Erik an apologetic smile as he played, and he gave her a single nod in return.

"Some people have even been frightened of Erik's face, because it looks so different from theirs," she went on. "But it really isn't anything to be scared of; it's just special, that's all. Would you like to meet him now?"

"Can I see his special face?"

"That is up to him. He knows opera, though, *cheri*; maybe he will play you something if you ask."

Erik-Daaé slid off his mother's lap and went over to the piano. He stared fixedly up at Erik until he finished playing the song.

Erik turned to regard the little boy.

"Erik, this is my son, Erik-Daaé." Christine made a formal, if unnecessary introduction.

"Hello," Erik greeted the toddler seriously.

"Do you know opera?" Erik-Daaé asked.

"I do."

"Do you know the Toreador song?"

Erik met Christine's gaze with amusement, and started to play. He took Escamillo's part and Christine took Carmen's even though it was lower than she liked, and they sang the other parts together. Christine dropped out for Escamillo's solo in the middle of it, which described bullfighting in all its gory detail, and then they finished the song together.

Erik-Daaé was thrilled. His mother had never sung that part before! He joined in during the last line, one beat behind on every word.

"Was that what you wanted, young Erik-Daaé?" Erik asked the boy.

Beaming, the toddler nodded eagerly. He climbed up onto the piano bench next to the man, and then clambered over onto Erik's lap.

Christine's jaw dropped. Erik-Daaé was never this demonstrative with strangers.

Erik was startled. What was he supposed to do with this child on his lap? Hesitantly, he put his arm around the boy to reach the keyboard, and started to play again. "Would you like to play a song with me?" he asked.

Erik-Daaé nodded.

Erik took the little boy's hand in his own, and spread out the fingers. He placed Erik-Daaé's tiny hand on the keyboard, noting with amusement that the boy could only span about three or four keys. Well, that's all he would need for this song, for the most part. Pressing Erik-Daaé's little fingers down in turn, Erik plinked out a recognizable tune.

"There now, do you know that one?"

"Yes! *Sur le Pont d'Avignon!*" the toddler crowed. He looked at his mother. "*Maman*! I can play!"

"I can see that, *cheri*. That was very well done," Christine applauded.

Suddenly with no warning, Erik-Daaé looked at Erik's mask. "May I see your special face, *monsieur*?" he asked.

Erik froze. So far the child liked him, but he knew that as soon as young Erik-Daaé saw his face, he'd run screaming back to his mother. He glanced at Christine in panic.

She just smiled at him.

Erik sighed. Well, it had been nice while it lasted. "Very well, young master," he said, reaching up to untie his mask. "But you must promise me not to tell anyone about my face.

Can you keep it a secret?"

"Yes, *monsieur*."

Erik steeled himself for the wails of terror, untied his mask, and bared his face to the child.

Erik-Daaé's eyes widened and his mouth fell open in shock. He noticed Erik's lack of a nose, and reached up to touch his own.

Erik expected the child to start crying any second. He was quite surprised, though, when Erik-Daaé reached up a curious hand to trace the contours of his cheekbone. The tiny fingers moved over his jutting brow, over his pitiful excuse of a nose, and down over his misshapen lips. One finger came a little too close to his right eye, and Erik recoiled to avoid getting poked.

"What do you think, Erik-Daaé?" Christine asked quietly. "Isn't that a very special face?"

The little boy nodded vigorously. "Yes, *Maman*!" Once again, he felt of his own face: his straight little nose, his smooth brow. With some degree of dissatisfaction, he asked, "How come my face isn't like that?"

"If other people had faces like *Monsieur* Erik's, then it wouldn't be special anymore," was Christine's sage reply. "He is the only person in the world who looks like that."

This answer seemed to satisfy her son, and being so young, he soon lost interest in Erik's face. He slid down off his lap and went over to his mother. "*Maman*, I'm hungry," he announced.

With a chuckle, Christine rang for the nurse to take him away and feed him supper.

"Well, that seemed to go fairly well," she said briskly after her son had departed.

Erik, carefully re-masked, agreed. "I had no idea..." he trailed off, shaking his head. "Why wasn't he afraid of me? People are always afraid of me. Especially children. Children are always afraid of my death's head."

"Well, he's young. He has nothing to compare your face to, in his experience," Christine pointed out. "He has never seen a corpse."

He nodded. "Still, I was expecting hysterics. Not to hear them was a most pleasant surprise." He looked up from the keys, and Christine could see tearstains on his mask. "He is wonderful, Christine. You've done very well with him, my dear."

"You did quite well with him yourself," she said. "I could see the light of hero-worship in his eyes when he looked at you," she teased, trying to lighten the mood.

It worked. Erik scoffed. "Sing a little Bizet for him and I become his hero? That must be more of the Chagny influence, if he is so easily impressed." His yellow eyes twinkled.

"Oh, I don't know about that. He might get some of it from me. I have been known to impress too easily in my time," Christine retorted mischievously. "I once mistook a man for an angel, just because he sang through the walls of my dressing room!"

Erik laughed. "Touché," he said.

Supper was an awkward affair. With Anneke in the room serving, Erik could not remove his mask. He lifted it gingerly for each mouthful, careful not to show too much of his face as he ate.

Anneke, though, seemed to want to make up for her behavior earlier, and was very attentive to him. "More wine, *monsieur*?" and "Will you have more potatoes, *monsieur*?" Christine was pleased with her servant, and had to hide her smile.

After supper, they went back into the drawing room, where Christine asked, "You know so much about me, because of my letters, but I know very little about you—little of your life before we met, and nothing at all after we parted. Won't you tell me about it?"

So Erik told her of his childhood, spent alone in the company of a paid servant, cloistered in a far wing of his parents' house outside Rouen. His mother would visit once a week or so, and his father never visited at all.

When he was nine, he said, his mother died, and then no one visited. The only person he saw was the servant, who had been terrified of his demonic visage; Erik lasted almost a year alone with her. Then one day she made the mistake of using a whip to try to cast out the demon in his flesh, and he had shoved her away from him. Unfortunately, it had been at the top of the staircase, and the old servant tumbled down and died.

Frightened, Erik ran away. The gypsies had come to town, and charmed by their music and easy manners, he had run away with them. Unmasking himself for money, he continued with them for four years, learning their tricks, language, and music.

Then the gypsies had traveled back to the Rouen area, and, afraid to show his face so near his birthplace (for he knew there had been many rumors), Erik had run away again and headed east.

The next year had been spent as a drifter. He

went from fair to fair at first, showing his face for coins, and picking up whatever skills he possibly could. He would hear of someone who had great skill as an architect, or as a mason, or as a musician, and travel to their town. He found particular pleasure in learning stonemasonry, as he had been told that was his father's profession. He would learn a new skill and then travel on. He stopped unmasking himself for pay and started earning it through his talents instead.

His mid-teens found him in Russia, where he was captured by some runaway English soldiers and tortured like a beast. He glossed over this time when relating it to Christine; he only said it had left scars, both on his body and his mind. It was the gypsies who had rescued him when they heard him humming a Romani song, and they realized who it was.

The Romani leader, being descended from chieftains of the Punjab area of India, was an expert at the Punjab lasso. He taught Erik how to wield it. Erik stayed with the Romani long enough to master the lasso, and then he tracked down every single one of the eight soldiers and strangled them.

The lasso became his weapon of choice, and

he soon outstripped his teacher in skill with it.

He did not meet Christine's gaze, and his low, steady voice did not falter. He found it strangely cleansing, to tell her about the horrors of his past after keeping it locked up inside for so many years. He began to see why religious people went to confession.

Christine held his hand firmly, even when he talked of the strangling.

He traveled with the gypsies through India, and then continued to Persia in his late teens. In Persia, he just went downhill. Having killed already—not just once, but eight times over—he found it easier to go on and kill the ninth… and the tenth, and so on. He was in a high position of power there, as the court architect among other things. That was when he had met Kaveh. He made friends, as much as a man was allowed to, with the sultan's favorite daughter. She was betrothed but not married yet and still lived in the palace. She was bored. Erik entertained her and talked with her (always with both of their faces covered up, and with a gigantic eunuch bodyguard close at hand) and when she got bored with that, he revealed his assassination skills. When the shah discovered his talents, Erik began killing for pay. Then for the first time, at the urging of the bloodthirsty little sultana, he began killing for entertainment. By this point the last twinges of conscience had long since ceased to plague him.

He told of Kaveh's saving his life when the palace was finished and the shah ordered his execution, and of his subsequent escape to Constantinople. When he had to flee Constantinople he got homesick for France, and eventually made his way back to his home country. There he had worked as an ordinary contractor for nearly a year until one of his designs caught the eye of the young architect who had won the bid to build the new opera house.

He had helped design and build the Paris Opera, working as Garnier's assistant. When the Paris Commune took over, he insinuated himself among their leadership so that he would have the opportunity to continue working on his beloved opera house. He built himself a house in the fifth cellar, and when the commune collapsed and the Communards started being captured, he retreated to it. He had stayed there quietly for a few years, knowing that his association with the Communards would get him captured if he were found. The gendarmes would not care that he did not believe in the Communards' cause and had only used them for his own advantage; if found, he would still be executed alongside them.

He planned to spend the rest of his life down there, in the cellars of the Paris Opera. He never wanted to be seen again. He wanted to have nothing more to do with other people. One thing, though, that he wanted to experience out of his lifetime of pain, was once—just once—he wanted to be with a woman.

He had traveled all over Europe, but had never gotten any closer to a woman than doing ventriloquism tricks for the little sultana with the massive eunuch between them. He had no delusions about his ability to attract feminine attention; he had tried, several times, but with no success. His constant aura of threatening menace tended to alarm any women who came within two meters of him. They would usually shy away with frightened looks.

He did, however, have money in his purse—and this was Paris, after all. He thought he would have no difficulty purchasing the favors he wanted, but it hadn't gone the way he'd planned.

His voice cracked in an agony of shame, as he confessed to Christine the part of his past that he was most ashamed of, that had tipped his already unbalanced mind into total madness. He had burned out his conscience with all the killing, but aside from that he had remained relatively sane. It was only after his one and only experience with a woman that his last tenuous links with reality had snapped for a few years.

The first woman he approached had initially accepted him and then demanded to see his face before delivering her services. He refused, and found a different woman.

The second one had accepted. She had gotten him into a vulnerable position and then ripped the mask from his face. He had thrown her against the wall in a rage. She'd shrunk back in fear, calling him a devil, and thrown her rosary at him. He'd darted out his hand and caught it neatly, and then started to approach her, still roaring with rage. She'd attacked him then; his face still bore the scars from her nails on his face. Finally, in a frenzy of humiliation and bloodthirsty rage, he had strangled her with her own rosary.

Hers was the death that haunted him worse than any other, the one who had incited him to murder her by using her own symbol of faith instead of his lasso. He had disposed of her body and come quite close to joining her in the Seine. At the last moment, he had decided that continuing to live would be a much worse and more deserved punishment. So he had quickly finished up the last of the business that kept him aboveground.

Then he had gone to ground like an animal.

He had never dared to approach a woman again. He cried out his anguish to the Almighty, but in the black pit of his depression his contrition did no good. He feared that even if God existed, He wouldn't pay any attention to the remorse of a man who murdered women with rosaries. Over time, Erik's shame over his actions was slowly worn away by bitterness.

He poured his feelings into his beloved opera "Don Juan Triumphant," a lifetime of pain inflicted by those who hated him for things he couldn't help, and a decade of bitterness, sin, and despair.

He had few clear memories of that time, he told Christine quietly. He did not like to remember the monster that even his best friend Kaveh had called him. It was all a blur to him now, every killing, every threat, every bit of blackmail. He hated to recall how he had treated Christine, with all the lies, threats, kidnapping, and manipulation. If he could change anything about the last twelve years of his life, it would be to have left Christine alone and never paid any attention to her. He had brought her nothing but misery, and had infected her with a bit of the darkness that filled his own soul.

"In all of that darkness, you were the one ray of light for me. I've forgotten much of those years, but I remember every interaction we ever had. Even the ones I'm most ashamed of. I honestly never meant to hurt you in any way, but with my background it was probably inevitable." Christine sat there gravely and silently holding his hand while he recited his tale.

Expecting rejection and betrayal, his voice hardened as he asked, "So what do you think of me now, my dear?"

Christine had known that Erik had a violent past, but she hadn't known the extent of it. She realized suddenly just how very, very lucky she was that he hadn't killed her the instant she had unmasked him all those years ago. All of his cryptic remarks and bitter warnings about "curious women" made sense to her now in light of what he told her of the prostitute. Even his rak-

ing his own face with her nails—her most horrifying memory of her time with him—now had
some basis in his experiences because it was
what the prostitute had done to him. His story
was the darkest and most appalling thing she
had ever heard, but at the same time she could
plainly see his anguish, shame and very real
sorrow over the things she had done…and his
despair at ever being forgiven. If she could forgive him his crimes against herself, then she
could forgive him his crimes against that
woman and the other people he had killed.

Her eyes filled with tears and she didn't try
to hide them. She told him, "Erik, as I told you
years ago: I think you are the most wounded
and sublime of men."

"But you don't still claim to love me," he
said bitterly.

"I do love you, Erik; now more than ever, I
think, because you have let me know you
more."

"How?" he demanded. "How can you love a
thief? A monster? A *murderer of women?*"

She shrugged helplessly. "My love, it's not
for me to judge you for your past, and you've
never been a monster to me. Well," she added,
forcing herself to honesty, "not for long, any-

way." She had been terrified of him after tearing his mask off, but her terror had lasted only until he had started playing his "Don Juan Triumphant." His agonized music had brought her some understanding. So did hearing his rational explanation of the dark river of madness that had swept him up in its wake after all his crimes.

Erik started to weep. He slid off the divan and knelt on the floor in front of Christine, burying his face in her skirts. Christine untied his mask so she could stroke his thinning hair as he sobbed his long years of misery into her lap. She rubbed his shoulders a little, noting absently how much more muscular they were than the way she remembered them: thin and bony like birds' wings.

When he finally calmed, he used the mask as a handkerchief to wipe his streaming eyes. "How can you ever forgive me for the things I've done?"

"They're not for me to forgive, Erik. You should perhaps go to a priest and make your confession at some point, but I have nothing to forgive you for."

"Priests are all grasping crows. I need to know if *you* can forgive me!" Still kneeling, he looked up at her with his face bare. "Can you look at Erik's face and tell him you forgive him for his past?" he asked, his voice still a little choked. He used his old habit of referring to himself as someone else, whenever he felt unworthy of being a real person.

"Yes, my dearest. I forgive you." She held his gaze steadily.

"Can you tell him you love him?" he asked, clutching both her hands desperately.

She smiled sadly at his use of the third person, knowing he used it to distance himself from his humanity. She reached out and caressed his sunken cheek. "I love you, Erik."

He closed his eyes and, hardly daring to breathe, started to ask, "Can you tell him..." but he shook his head and trailed off. "No, not that."

"What is it, my love?"

He shook his head again. "No... no, not that. It's too much to ask." He put his head down again, as if ashamed.

"Erik, please don't shut yourself away from me. What is it?" Christine pressed.

He straightened his slender shoulders as if he was bracing himself, cleared his throat and looked up at her again. "Tell me you'll marry me," he said. He did not speak of himself as someone else this time.

It wasn't so much a question as it was a dare, a challenge. There was no third person and no distancing this time—just a man proposing to a woman that he loved—

Christine's face lit up with joy as she met the challenge. "I will marry you, Erik."

—And receiving her answer.

Not even taking the time to stand, Erik pulled Christine right off the divan into his arms. Kneeling on the floor, they clung to each other and wept together, mingling their tears and kisses just as they had once before. This time, though, there was no pledge of death and no heart-wrenching separation; instead, there was only the assurance of a life spent together.

Chapter 11
"Hope and a Future"

Erik left Christine's flat that night with a heart so light he felt as if he were flying. He knew he wouldn't be able to sleep; he couldn't go home, because he just had to sing. He would burst if he didn't sing. There was only one place to go.

He was nearly running by the time he reached the Rue Scribe. He no longer carried the great iron key that unlocked the secret side door to the opera, but it didn't take him long to pick the lock and begin making his way down to his former home.

It was dusty and musty. He turned on the

gaslights and set to work cleaning and tuning the organ. He saw no evidence of mice, but with all the dust and dampness, it was filthy and badly out of tune. It took him much of the night, but finally it was ready, and with a thrill of anticipation he sat down to play.

Ah, he had forgotten the bliss, the freedom, of playing the organ—multiple manuals, all those stops and pedals—he was in heaven. Without even realizing it, he started playing from his old "Don Juan Triumphant"—except that its aching pain and despair no longer fit him. For the first time in years, his heart held hope and joy. He had to modify the music to reflect that, and ended up playing and singing there in the cellar for the remainder of the night.

Shortly before dawn, he rubbed his gritty eyes and looked around as if he had just awakened from a daze. "Don Juan Triumphant" isn't finished after all, he thought to himself. Now I need to compose the second half of it: "Don Juan Redeemed"!

But his old house was disordered, and it distracted him. No one had been in it for five years, and it was cluttered and dusty. Erik began going around and picking up a little: shelving a book, hanging up a cloak that had fallen to the floor, sorting through some papers that were scattered around.

In a closet he found something that he had almost forgotten he had made. He picked up the small piece of rubber and started to laugh.

He remembered bragging to Christine, years ago, that he had made a mask that made him look like any other man. So much had happened since then that he had dismissed the memory from his mind—especially since he had been able to successfully re-enter society while wearing his usual mask of white silk. The people in his small village in Provence just accepted him as a rich eccentric, and the people of Paris were too polite to mention it. He had discovered long ago that if he was matter-of-fact about the mask, other people were more likely to be as well.

Smiling, he took the rubber mask into his bathroom and washed the dust off it. Shaking it dry, he removed his white silk mask and fixed the rubber one to his face. He tied the cord around the back of his head and fluffed out his hair over it.

For once, he wished he had a mirror.

He turned and looked around the room. He

saw the coffin and winced. Had he really been that morbid? The memory of his mental imbalance—the paralyzing fear, the murderous rage he used to feel, shut up like a rat in a cage down here in the cellars—embarrassed him.

No matter. Moving to Provence with Kaveh had turned out to be a good change, and now it was time to make another. He went over and picked up one end of the coffin. It was heavy, but Erik had always been strong—and since regaining his health was much stronger than he used to be. He had no trouble dragging it out of his house. What to do with it, though?

Ah. He had it. Grinning a little to himself, he loaded it into the boat and rowed it along the shoreline until he reached the little cavern where he and Kaveh had put his gravestone. He dragged the coffin up out of the boat and into the cavern, leaving it beside the grave marker. Leaving his empty coffin sitting next to the marker with his name on it amused him; the symbolism of it gave him a sense of satisfaction as he made his way back down to his house. The Erik who had lived below the opera and slept in a coffin was dead; now he was a new Erik, about to embark on a new life.

Suddenly tired, he tucked his white silk

mask into his pocket. He left his cleaning and returned to the boat; he rowed across the lake and then began the long trek back up to the surface.

There were not many people on the streets just yet, but the ones there were did not give Erik a second glance. He smiled with satisfaction, and was extremely pleased when one gentleman smiled back and nodded to him.

Once again, Kaveh was just sitting down to breakfast when Erik came in. He leaped to his feet when he saw the tall stranger sauntering into his dining room with no warning. He started sputtering. "*M-monsieur*! What—who—what are you…"

"Calm yourself, Kaveh; it is I," Erik told him. "Like my new mask?"

Kaveh sat down weakly, gaping at him. The new mask covered only the center portion of Erik's face, leaving his chin and brow uncovered. It had a fine, aristocratic nose, and covered Erik's sunken cheeks with well-formed, slightly rounded ones. It came to just below his nose, and it was shaped in such a way as to minimize the misshapen look of his upper lip. His lower one was only slightly twisted, so the mask didn't come down that far. One of Erik's

good features had always been his teeth—
straight and white behind his malformed lips—
and he showed them now in a mischievous
grin.

Erik was still ugly; there was no escaping
that. His brow still stuck out too far, his chin
was still bony, and his eyes were still unnerv-
ingly yellow. But the mask made him look like
any ordinarily ugly man instead of like a grotesque and hideous living corpse, and Kaveh
couldn't believe the difference it made.

"Erik, I—this is amazing! I cannot believe
it! Where did you get that mask?"

Erik sat down and helped himself to some
breakfast. "I had made it a long time ago, when
I hoped that Christine would marry me. Since
she has finally agreed to, I went to the opera
last night and found it again."

"Well, it looks very lifelike..." Kaveh
dropped his fork. "What did you say?"

Erik smiled, looking down demurely at his
breakfast. "Christine has accepted my proposal
of marriage." He looked up again, eyes shining.
"She actually said those words, *daroga*: 'I will
marry you, Erik.' Oh, she is such a good, sweet
girl!"

Kaveh grinned and stood up. He offered his

hand to Erik. "Congratulations, Erik! I am very happy for you."

Erik rose and shook hands, beaming. "Will you stand up with me at my wedding, Kaveh?"

"I'd be honored to, my friend. One question, though: what name do you plan to bestow on your new bride?"

The light died in Erik's eyes and he scowled as he sank back down into the chair. "You know, Kaveh, sometimes I really don't like you."

"I know, I know," Kaveh told him with sympathy. "Better to think of it now than later, though, eh?"

"No; better to think of it after I sleep. I'm a bit tired—I was too busy laying to rest a ghost last night to get any sleep." He rubbed his eyes. "Forgive me for snapping, old friend; I'm not fit company at the moment."

Erik slept like the proverbial dead, and did not stir until mid-afternoon. Kaveh and Darius were out; the only one who answered the bell when Erik rang for hot water was the timid young housemaid.

As he washed and shaved, Erik pondered the problem of his name. He might be able to find the priest who had baptized him; such a man would definitely have seen his face. Assuming he had even been baptized, he thought cynically; his parents may very well have just assumed he was hell-bound anyway, and not wanted to bother giving him a name. Perhaps the local church would have other records as well?

He thought he might be able to remember his mother's name, but he couldn't remember his father's; he thought he might be able to find his parents' house again, but after the accidental death of the old servant woman, he feared being arrested.

Unless... his eyes fell on the rubber mask, sitting innocently beside the basin. The rudiments of a plan started to glimmer through his mind, and he nodded to himself. It was a little unorthodox, but he knew what he would do. It would help him learn what he needed to know in order to marry Christine, and it would deeply annoy his best friend at the same time. There was no down side. He grinned to himself as he put on his white silk mask.

He would leave tonight. Right now, he had to get back to Christine and tell her he'd be out of town for a while. He rang for the maid again. "When Darius returns, tell him I'd like him to pack my valise for a week," he told her. He didn't expect it to take that long; Rouen wasn't that far, but it was best to be certain.

"Yes, sir, and there's been a message for you," she replied. She held out a tray with a note on it.

"Thank you," Erik said, taking the note and waving a dismissal.

My dear Erik,

At the risk of seeming too forward, would you like to come to supper again this evening? My son has been asking about you ever since I informed him of our engagement.

Our engagement. What a lovely thought that is!

Much love,

Christine

Erik's eyes softened as he read the note. He tucked it into his pocket and went to get his cloak.

When he got to Christine's flat and rang the bell, Anneke opened the door. "Oh, come in, *monsieur*!" she greeted brightly. "I'll just go and tell *madame* that you're here. And, *monsieur*—if I may be so bold—may I offer congratulations?"

"Thank you, Anneke." Erik was pleased that Christine had already told her staff. He had somewhat feared that she would want to make this a secret engagement. The maid took his cloak and showed him into the drawing room, where he immediately sat down at the piano and began to play one of the melodies from "Don Juan Triumphant," that he had been working on last night.

"Erik!" Christine appeared at the door looking radiant, and approached the piano. Erik rose and met her halfway across the room; she came into his arms and embraced him for a few moments.

"I am glad you got my note," she said, stepping away. "Shall you stay to supper then?"

"Unfortunately, no," he replied, regret coloring his voice. "I must make preparations for a short trip. I shall have to leave Paris for a few days, I'm afraid."

"Oh." Christine's face fell. "Where will you go?"

"I have some business to take care of, up in Rouen, before we shall be able to marry. I hope to only be gone a few days."

"What business is that?"

Erik shifted uncomfortably. He didn't really want to tell her, but on the other hand he'd already told her everything else about him—why not this as well?

"I must go to the place I was born, and try to find out what my name is," he finally said. He was glad of the white mask; he was sure that he was blushing horribly beneath it. "I know where my parents lived, but I have no idea of what their surname was; my mother never told me. It will be hard to find a priest to marry us if I have no name to give you."

"Oh, I see." Evidently she hadn't thought of that. She sank down on the divan.

Erik sat down beside her, holding her hand in both of his. "I also wanted to give you some time to reconsider, if you wish." He shushed her immediate protest and went on. "Right now, your son will be the Comte de Chagny, and as such, he will have power, money, and prestige. If his mother marries a no-name, face-less vagabond—especially if she then goes back onto the stage," he added with a twinkle in his eye, "—then Erik-Daaé's situation may change. The other Chagnys could easily try to claim his title or even disinherit him. These are things you must consider."

Christine nodded, giving Erik's hand a squeeze. "I did consider them, Erik, before I even told my staff of our engagement. I could hardly sleep last night for thinking! My son might be the *Comte de* Chagny when he turns twenty-one—and I would certainly not wish to deny him the prestige that comes with the title—but Bonaparte's titles are fairly meaningless nowadays anyway. He's also the son of an opera singer and the grandson of a Swedish peasant. He will never be accorded the respect of someone whose parents were both noble. He shall have to learn to earn a living anyway. Having a stepfather who is a world-class musician, architect, and any number of other things as well, will not do his status any harm."

Erik stiffened. He hadn't actually thought ahead enough to realize that he would be young Erik-Daaé's stepfather. It would be almost like having a child himself! What a terrifying thought.

He liked the boy, though, and he would have a special place in Erik's heart as Christine's son anyway. The fact that young Erik-Daaé wasn't frightened of his face was such an unexpected blessing that it made his heart swell with relief.

He kissed Christine gratefully and settled down to enjoy the rest of his brief visit.

Chapter 12
Discovering the Past

E rik got on the night train from Paris, and by dawn he was in Rouen. He thought he remembered how to get to the house he'd known as a child—it had been more than thirty years, but his memory for detail had always been sharp.

First thing he did was check in at a local inn. He gave them a false name, trying not to smile at the thought of Kaveh's reaction. He made arrangements to hire a horse, and then went up and unpacked his bags. He pulled out an old Persian-style uniform and looked at it wistfully, but ended up setting it aside. Better not to stick out too much here, especially at first. He changed into a clean suit, and brushed his hair. Hmm. Should he wear the wig or not?

Not, he decided. His head would be covered anyway. He reached into his bag and pulled out one last item: one of Kaveh's favorite astrakhan caps. He placed it on his head at a jaunty angle and inspected himself in the mirror. He wasn't swarthy as Kaveh was, but at least with his yellow eyes and astrakhan cap, he certainly didn't look French. If he spoke with Kaveh's accent and sprinkled a bit of Farsi into his conversation, he might be able to pass himself off quite nicely.

The servant knocked on the door. "Sir, your horse is ready," she announced.

"Thank you," Erik called. He opened the door, pleased when the maid's eyes fixed on his hat instead of on his face. This trip would be the trial run of his new mask.

It was a nice day for a ride. Erik made his way back along the route he remembered running away from, as a child. Little had changed in thirty years. He found the house of his youth with little trouble, but reined in and stared at the emblem on the front gates, dumfounded.

He knew that crest. He'd seen it before.

Not on these gates, though; the only time he had ever been outside as a child had been the night he'd run away when, fearful of discovery, he had stolen across the back of the property and had never seen the gate at all.

What was the meaning of the emblem on the gates?

He walked his horse right up to the gates and stood up in his stirrups to see the estate. All the rest of it looked the way he remembered it from looking through the windows as a child; there was no doubt that this was the house of his childhood.

Scowling, he wheeled his horse around and headed back into town. A brief visit to the town records office would be able to clear this up for him.

He was eager to find out why the home of his youth now sported the Chagny crest on its gates.

The town records clerk was small and grey: grey hair, grey eyes, grey suit. He wore small, wire-framed glasses (grey) and peered up over them at Erik. "Yes, *monsieur*?"

Perfectly imitating Kaveh's musical Farsi accent, Erik introduced himself. "I am Kaveh Tallis, the *Daroga*—the chief of police—of

Mazenderan, Persia. I am hoping you can help me track down a certain Frenchman in whom the Shah of Persia has an interest."

The clerk's dull face lit with interest; Erik's foreign accent, not to mention the story, struck the little man as exotic and exciting in this sleepy little town. "Of course, of course, *monsieur*! In what way may I be of assistance?"

"I only know the Frenchman's given name, not his surname. I know he originally came from this town, though, and I have located the estate where he was born and spent his youth; perhaps you can help me discover his surname?"

"Of course, sir; I know every major family within a day's ride. What is your Frenchman's given name?"

"Erik. Spelled with a 'k.'"

"Erik, hmm." The clerk rolled his eyes up into his head as if trying to find the information in his brain by sight alone. "Erik, Erik, Erik. Where was he born, *monsieur*, and when?"

"I believe him to be in his mid-forties or so. He was born on a large estate about three miles east of here; the one with the crested wrought-iron gates."

"Ah, yes, the Chagny estate! I know that one."

"Yes," Erik said cautiously. "I believe that to be the name. It is owned, I take it, by a family named Chagny?"

"Oh, yes, a noble family, sir. The original owner of that house was quite a rich man, and titled, as a gift from Napoleon. Why, he was the first Count de Chagny, he was."

"What about the Count de Chagny named Philippe?" Erik asked. "I met him in Paris once, you see," he hastened to explain why a Persian police chief would be acquainted with a Parisian count.

"Oh, Philippe was the nephew of the original count," the clerk explained. "The title was originally given to Count Erik."

"Count Erik?" Erik demanded, frowning. This was an odd coincidence.

"Yes; apparently he was a master mason before his service to the Emperor."

"Did he have any children?"

"Yes, but only daughters, which is why the title reverted to his brother upon the old count's death."

"When did the Chagny family buy the estate?" Erik wanted to know. This was getting confusing.

"Buy it, sir? But no. That estate was given to

old Count Erik along with the title. It has been owned by Chagnys for fifty years, at least."

An uncomfortable idea began to make itself known in Erik's brain. If old Count Erik had owned the house while he himself was living in it... was it possible that he might have been the son of the old count? A bastard son, perhaps, which—combined with his face—would have led to his being hidden away all his life?

There was only one way to find out.

"Who would have been the family priest?" he asked. "And where may I find him?"

Chapter 13
A Major Confession, with Penance

Father Arnaud had had a long and eventful life. He had come to the priesthood after a wild and debauched youth; now in his twilight years, he liked the quiet church life with its little secrets and dramas—he would never divulge them, but he did vicariously enjoy the private details afforded by confession.

Now he was getting on in years, and little surprised him. He was therefore not taken aback in the least by the tall and very ugly foreigner standing before him scowling. What did take him aback was the pair of intense yellow eyes glaring at him from below the overhanging brow. Where had he seen those eyes before?

"Are you Father Arnaud?" the stranger demanded.

"At your service, sir."

The tall stranger bowed. "*Daroga* Tallis of Persia. The town records clerk tells me you might be able to help me track down a certain Frenchman who appears to have some connection with the Chagny family."

"As much as is in my power, sir, I will help you."

"Did you perform baptisms for *all* the children of the late Count Erik de Chagny?"

Arnaud noticed the odd emphasis the man put on "all," and wondered about it. He nodded slowly. "I did, yes."

"Did the count have any sons?"

The priest tried to deflect the question with another. "If he'd had a son, wouldn't the title have gone to him, instead of his brother when he died?"

The foreigner shrugged. "Not if the son were illegitimate, no. The Frenchman I seek is also named Erik, and he was born and spent his childhood in the old count's house. I do not know his surname; I now have reason to believe that he may have been a bastard son of the old count."

At last the priest could answer honestly. "The old count had no bastard children, sir. I can promise you that." He thought he knew now who the Persian was looking for. The trouble was that most of his information had been given in confidence, and he wasn't at liberty to share any of it—and certainly not with foreigners.

"Then what of the Frenchman's story? He was born in the old count's house, given the same Christian name as the count, but then kept away from the rest of the family until he ran away."

"Are you sure it was Count Erik's house? There are other large estates around here."

"I am sure."

"I'm afraid I cannot help you, *monsieur*. I am sorry." This foreigner was asking altogether too many questions that Arnaud wouldn't be able to answer. Best to have him gone altogether.

The tall stranger frowned. "You know, don't you?" he demanded.

"I know many things, *monsieur*, that I am not free to discuss with strangers. I cannot help you in your search."

The priest started to turn away, but the stranger grabbed his shoulders in a viselike grip. "You'd better tell me what you know, old man, or you may regret it!" His voice hardened as his fingers tightened on the old man's thin and bony shoulders. His furious yellow eyes promised dire consequences.

Father Arnaud stood firm and dignified in the face of the man's threats. "I'm sorry, sir; I'm not at liberty to divulge any private details of any of the families I serve. Please unhand me, *monsieur*; you're hurting my shoulders." He spoke without any hint of fear, and the foreigner dropped his hands from the priest's shoulders as if he'd been burned.

Erik changed his tactics. He stepped back with an apologetic gesture. "I am sorry, Father; my search is frustrating, though, and much hinges on the outcome. I wonder, though..." he paused, thinking rapidly.

"Yes, *monsieur*?"

Erik made his decision. Not only would it please Christine, but priestly confidentiality would also seal the priest's lips about what he was about to convey. "I would like to make my confession, Father. Will you hear it?"

Father Arnaud frowned, puzzled. "I thought, as a Persian, you would be a Musselman."

"I am not." Erik wisely left his denial open, as he was neither Persian nor Muslim.

"Then I'd be happy to hear it, *monsieur*."

In the confessional, Erik rested his arms on the dividing shelf and began—a little self-consciously, as he switched back from Kaveh's accents to his own. "Father, forgive me, for I have sinned. I have never made confession before."

It was clear from Erik's demeanor that what he had to say transcended catechism and confirmation and the proper order of things. Arnaud saw this and merely folded his hands. "Go on, my son."

"I am not Persian. My name is not Tallis, nor am I a *daroga*; in fact, my past is such as would lead me to avoid any contact with police. I borrowed the name of my friend Kaveh Tallis in order to conduct my own private inquiries here in Rouen without being arrested.

"You see, I am the Erik who was born in the Chagny estate. Due to a certain peculiarity in my appearance, I was kept away from other people so as not to frighten them." Erik paused, not knowing how to continue.

"Go on," the priest urged. He drew his brows together in a frown. Some of this man's story seemed valid, and matched what Father Arnaud knew to be true, but other parts did not. He asked a testing question. "What peculiarity is this, son? You're not overly good-looking, but I've seen less handsome men than you."

"I really doubt that," Erik replied dryly. He shrugged and went on, not wanting to unmask himself at this point. "When I was young, I accidentally caused the death of the old woman who looked after me. I ran away. I have never been back to Rouen since then. I have never known my surname, and now it is of the utmost importance that I find out my true identity."

Erik hesitated, not really knowing what the priest expected him to say.

Arnaud prodded him gently. "Was this what you wished to confess? The death of the servant woman?"

Erik let out a bark of cynical laughter. "Oh, if only that were all! No, Father, there have been others. Countless others. You see, when I left Rouen I fell in with a troupe of gypsies…"

The priest said nothing, merely listened, as Erik recounted for him all the atrocities he had committed during his lifetime, and all the ones that had been committed against him: the beatings, the torture, the terror, derision and scorn. He told what he could remember, anyway; he knew there had been others, but since his mind had been unhinged for some years, those memories were hazy. He explained that he wore a mask in public because of people's reactions to his face.

He told of those "rosy hours in Mazenderan," when he had been at the height of his power, and of Kaveh's saving his life when the shah wanted him executed. He told quite frankly about killing the prostitute with her own rosary; he clenched his eyes shut tight, not wanting to see the priest's probable expression of horror-stricken condemnation.

If he had looked, he would have seen only pained compassion in the priest's eyes.

He spoke of his experiences in the opera house—yes, even about what he did to Christine. He described their reunion a few days ago, and explained that he could not marry her without a name to give her. That was why he was here, although he admitted that it was partly due to Christine's suggestion that he had even thought of making his confession in the first place.

When Erik finished talking, there was nothing but silence for a few minutes. Finally, Father Arnaud took a deep breath and wiped his eyes. "Erik, my son, the story you've just told me is one of the most tragic and incredible tales I've ever heard—and yet, as it was told me within the bonds of a confession, I am bound to credit it. Just let me ask you a few questions, if you please?"

"Very well, Father," Erik replied. He felt drained, remembering and speaking of his past crimes.

"Have you repented of your sins, and turned away from them?" Somehow the priest knew that this was as close as Erik was going to get to saying the Act of Contrition.

Erik remembered his heart-wrenching guilt and pain as he had sobbed in Christine's lap, and nodded slowly. "Yes, Father." His voice conveyed his emotions as his masked face never could, and the priest nodded thoughtfully to himself. Erik was probably as close to feeling "perfect contrition" as anyone that he had ever seen before.

The priest asked, "And this young woman who means so much to you—you say she returns your love and wishes to marry you?"

Erik's head came up, and he blinked. "Yes." He glanced away, momentarily overcome by his own unworthiness of such a fortune.

"And she has seen your unmasked face?"

"She has. She has seen it, shed tears over it, and kissed it. And yet she says she loves me." A note of wonder crept into Erik's proud tone of voice, and the priest smiled inwardly. He was becoming more convinced that this was, in fact, the same Erik.

"Then I would say we must do whatever is necessary to make sure your soul is unstained before you marry her," the priest said, still smiling. "We must discuss the matter of your penance."

Erik raised an eyebrow and sarcastically asked, "And how would you suggest I atone for all those murders and tortures, Father? The Church frowns on suicide, I'm told."

Arnaud nodded. "Erik, I will not sugar-coat this: you have sinned greatly in the sight of the Lord. However, you have repented of your sins, and seem perfectly contrite about them. You have also suffered terribly during your life at the hands of other men. I would say that any penance I could assign you, to atone for your sins, would pale in comparison to what you have already endured and what you have in-flicted upon yourself.

"Therefore, for your murders and other acts of violence, I assign you nothing. You have already suffered; you have repented; you have changed your ways. For one other sin, though, I shall have to assign a penance."

"Which one is that?" Erik asked, bewildered.

"You lied to a priest about your identity. That's the only sin that you seem unrepentant about, so I'm assigning you either five 'Hail Marys' or a donation of seven francs, to help you realize the error of your ways."

Erik stared through the grille in shock at the smirking old priest. "Father, I don't know what to say."

Arnaud's smirk broadened into a grin. "You start with *'Ave María, grátia plena, Dóminus tecum'*[7]..."

"Seven francs, you said?" Erik asked drily.

"Then you accept the penance?"

Erik nodded, beginning to see the humor of the situation. Seven francs was pocket change, and both men knew it. "I accept." He fished the

---

[7] Hail Mary, full of grace, the Lord is with you...

seven francs out of his pocket and slid them across the shelf toward the priest.

Father Arnaud, trying not to smile, held out his hand towards Erik and spoke the words of the Prayer of Absolution.

As he finished with, *"... ego te absolvo a peccatis tuis in nomine Patris et Filii et Spiritus Sancti,*[8]" Erik felt a curious freedom. He had begun his confession for the sole purpose of binding the old man to secrecy about his real identity and looks; he never expected or even hoped to gain absolution for his sins. Now that it was offered, though, he felt as though a vast weight had been lifted from him.

He sighed, sitting up and rolling his shoulders; the relief was so great it was almost palpable. "Thank you, Father."

"Now then, Erik. The confession is officially over but I wish to assure you that anything else we say while we're in here will be treated with the same discretion. I will tell you what I can of the family you're asking about."

"You do know, then," Erik surmised.

The priest shrugged, lifting one shoulder the

---

[8] I absolve you from your sins in the name of the Father, and of the Son, and of the Holy Spirit.

way Erik always did. "I know a few things. I hesitate to speak of them, though. How do I know you are who you say you are? You look... different from the child I baptized." He paused, embarrassed, and then clarified. "Better."

Erik raised his eyebrows. "You swear not to speak of this to anyone?"

"You have my word before God not to speak of it to anyone without your permission."

"And don't faint, either," Erik muttered as he reached for the ties of his rubber mask. He loosened it and brought it away from his face, showing his full visage to the priest.

Arnaud's jaw dropped.

"Is this more the face that you remember?" Erik asked.

The priest nodded. "Erik!" he said in awe. "It really is you!"

Erik nodded. "So tell me what you can, Father. Starting with..." he hesitated, and when he finished the sentence his voice came out sounding almost plaintive. "What is my name?"

"Carpentier," the priest said quietly. "I baptized you Erik de Carpentier. I can speak more freely of your baptism and christening, now that I know it is you. You are not illegitimate;

you are the lawful eldest child of Count Erik de Chagny and his wife, Countess Marie-Therese. Count Erik always chose to be known by his title—as I believe the rest of the family has done as well—but the actual surname is Carpentier.

"Your mother sent for me when you were born, to protect you; she was afraid your father would kill you because of your face. She wanted someone besides herself and the midwife to know of your existence and appearance, because your father told everyone that you died at birth."

"And what did you do when you saw me?" Erik wanted to know. The story was painful, but his thirst to finally discover who he really was soon overcame the hurt and drove his questions.

"I named you and baptized you, and made arrangements with your mother and the old count for your secret upbringing. I sent the servant to them who watched over you."

"The one I killed," Erik said dully.

"In self-defense, yes; and while we're on the topic, my boy, I really must apologize for her superstitious nature. Had I known she would end up abusing you because of your face, I would have sent someone else."

"Uh… that's… no matter, Father; it's in the past," Erik said. He was uncomfortable being apologized to. It hadn't happened that often.

"True, true. Now, the question remains, what are you planning to do with this information?"

"Do? I shall marry Christine as soon as I possibly can; that is, assuming she'll still have me after she learns the truth about my birth." Erik sobered as he put his rubber mask back on.

"Why would she refuse? Marrying the son of the original Count de Chagny will probably be a step up from marrying a retired Opera Ghost," the priest said.

Erik smiled sardonically. "Oh, did I forget to tell you? Christine is the widow of the late Count de Chagny, Raoul. Their son is the present count; or will be, when he grows up."

Father Arnaud blinked several times. "You mean… your fiancée is Count Raoul's widow?"

Erik nodded. "Yes; you know her?"

"Of course I know her, son; I've been their family priest for almost fifty years," Arnaud replied crisply. He shook his head in amazement. "You're *that* Erik? Count Raoul's rival, and the one she named her son after?"

"...Yes..." Erik suspected where this line of questioning was going, and sought to forestall any false assumptions. "The boy is definitely her husband's child, though; until just a few days ago, Christine thought I was dead and I thought she was still happily married. I don't want you to think that she and I—"

"Oh, I know that, son, I know that. It's quite the coincidence, though, isn't it?" Arnaud distinctly remembered hearing Raoul's confession, years ago, of waking from his bed and shooting at what he suspected was his rival in the dark. The young man claimed that he'd shot at Erik, a cat, or two stars; he couldn't be sure which. Arnaud had thought the young man raving at the time, but in retrospect, the situation looked much different.

"It is, yes," Erik agreed, starting to smile at the humor of the situation in spite of his discomfort at finding out that his former rival was in fact his own cousin!

"So I assume you'll want to visit the Chagny solicitor, then?"

"What for?"

"Why, for arranging the transfer of the title, of course. Erik, you are the rightful Count de Chagny, and would have inherited the title if your father had acknowledged you. With my statement of witness and the records of your baptism, you could easily reclaim the title if you wish."

Erik shook his head slowly. It was too much to take in, all at once. "I shall have to discuss that with Christine. The title means nothing to me; I just wanted to find out my name so I can marry her. I shall leave the matter of the title in her hands; after all, if I reclaimed it, I'd be taking it away from her son. She should be the one to decide."

"Fair enough, but remember I am completely at your service if you should choose to pursue it. Your father did you a heinous wrong, Erik. As the family priest, I'd like to try and make it up to you, as far as is within my power."

Erik thanked the priest and shook his hand when they left the confessional together. He went straight back to his room at the inn; he had a letter to write.

# # #

My dear Christine,

I've had a large measure of success finding out about my name and family. The town records clerk answered some of my questions, and he directed me to an old priest in town who answered the rest of them. You may know him, a Father Arnaud. By the way, you'll be pleased to know that I did, in fact, end up making my confession to him; not only that, but I must re-assess my previous opinion of all priests as grasping crows. There is at least one who is not, even though he fined me quite heavily as penance. I can afford my train ticket back to Paris, but only just.

You will be astonished when you hear my story, though; I can hardly believe it myself. Such coincidences usually happen only in stories and not in real life! But I will tell you what I know, and let you decide for yourself what is to be done.

My father's name was Erik de Carpentier, and my mother's name was Marie-Therese. While I am pleased to discover my own surname, it comes with an additional—and slightly uncomfortable, for me anyway—bit of baggage.

Erik de Carpentier was the first Count de Chagny.

I am his legitimate, first-born son.

Father Arnaud showed me my baptismal records. Apparently, my mother sent for him and the christening was accomplished without my father's knowledge or consent. He had been planning to simply kill me and hope for another living son who actually looked like a living son (instead of having a living son who looked like a dead son). Unfortunately for him, all he got were daughters. He still refused to acknowledge me, and when he died the title passed to his brother, and then to his brother's son Philippe. They chose to be known by the title, rather than their surname.

It seems, my love, that your deceased husband and his brother were my own cousins.

Christine's hand flew to cover her mouth as she read Erik's clumsy left-handed printing, and when she finished reading she let out an amazed laugh before going back to the beginning and reading the whole thing again.

It was too preposterously coincidental for words. Erik, a Chagny? *Erik?*

Erik was Raoul's first cousin, she realized. And more to the point, he was the rightful heir to the title of Count de Chagny, and had only been denied it because of his deformities. She went on reading.

How humbling; after all my years of railing against that family, only to find out that I am part of it—I may never recover from the shame.

I had always thought my father was a working man. My old nurse had told me that he was a "master mason" – but the priest explained that the old count had done some favor for Bonaparte and had been awarded the title of count; he had not picked up a chisel since he was a young man in Napoleon's army!

Father Arnaud seems to think that I could reclaim the title with little effort if I wished, since he can provide proper church records of my legitimate birth. Since the title now belongs to your son, I shall leave the decision up to you. Would you rather marry the true count (for if my father had acknowledged me, the title would never have gone to Philippe and thus to your husband), and have your son revert to being viscount? Or would you rather he keep the title, and you simply marry Erik de Carpentier? For myself, I do not care about it one way or the other; my sole ambition in this life is to marry you and spend the remainder of my life in your delightful company, wholly devoted to your happiness. The dubious "honor" of being a Chagny pales in comparison with that thought (as does everything else under the sun). For after all,

"O toi, doux objet de ma flamme,
Toi seule y peux calmer le trouble de mon âme!

Tes accents
Tendres et touchants,
Tes regards séduisants,
Ton doux sourire
Sont les seuls biens que je désire."[9]

I shall return to Paris early the day after tomorrow. I wish to speak further with Father Arnaud tomorrow, but after that I shall be on the night train. I shall write you when I return.

My heart is full of you, my beloved; I need you more than my next breath, and I miss you terribly. I can hardly wait to see your lovely face and hear your beautiful, scolding voice again—for you will scold, and quite dreadfully, when I tell you how I learned all of this; I know you will, and so will Kaveh. That man was born to scold.

Until then I remain,

Forever your devoted
Erik

---

[9] O, you sweet object of my passion,
Only you can calm the turmoil in my soul!
Your accents
Tender and poignant,
Your tempting glances,
Your sweet smile
Are the only blessings I crave

Christine smiled at the lines from *"Orphée et Euridyce"* that he had included, and her eyes filled with tears. Sometimes she felt she didn't deserve a love as powerful and compelling as the love that Erik offered her... and yet, she would never be able to turn him down. She would simply have to make herself strong enough to bear the passion of a man like him—for she knew that, now she had found him, she would never, ever be able to let him go.

Then there was the matter of his title, which he had been denied because of his deformity. Her decision was the work of an instant: Erik would never again be denied his birthright because of his face. The title of viscount was still nothing for her son to scoff at, and in the meantime she was determined that Erik would finally begin to get some of the respect and power that was due him.

She nodded once, and went over to her writing desk. She sat down and immediately drafted a letter to the Chagny solicitor.

Dear M. Coté:

Thank you for your kind congratulations on my engagement. I have just learned some star-

tling news, however, of my fiancé's family background, which will necessitate your making some changes in your records.

It seems that my fiancé is the rightful Count de Chagny, the legitimate son of Count Erik de Chagny. He will contact you soon with the legal documentation of this; meanwhile, be aware that I fully support his claim, and am perfectly satisfied for my son Erik-Daaé to be viscount when he reaches adulthood.

We will inform you of our wedding-date as soon as we have decided on one. For obvious reasons, we wish for his reinstatement as Count de Chagny to take place before we are married. Thank you for your kind attention to these details, and I look forward to seeing you again soon.

Sincerely,

Christine Daaé de Chagny

Christine rang for Anneke to come and get the letter delivered to her solicitor right away. After the maid had left with it, Christine sat there at her writing desk musing quietly. She remembered Raoul's talking about visits to his family's country home, just outside Rouen, when he was a child. Raoul was close to her own age, and by the time he was visiting, Erik would have been long gone. Philippe, though— Philippe was close to Erik in age. A lump rose in her throat when she realized that Philippe probably went there as a child to play with his girl cousins, little knowing that he had another cousin, masked and lonely, imprisoned in a far-off wing of the house.

No, she had made the right decision. Erik would regain his rightful title, and Christine would fully support him in it. She was tired of his being denied all the good things in life, just because of his face. Enough was enough.

Erik would be the Count de Chagny.

Chapter 14
A Secondary Confession

E rik arrived back at the Paris flat he shared with Kaveh and immediately dispatched a note to Christine, inviting her for supper. He had a lot to tell her and Kaveh both, and he didn't want to go through everything twice. He decided to continue wearing his white silk mask while he was in Paris; he thought it would make a pleasant surprise for Christine if he were to wear his new one for her for the first time at their wedding.

Having nothing else to do, and itching to get his fingers on a keyboard again, he returned to the opera and spent the remainder of the day in his old house in the cellars working on his new piece, "Don Juan Redeemed."

He lost track of time as he played and wrote feverishly, until suddenly it was mid-afternoon and Christine stood next to him, smiling.

He gasped and dropped his pen, making a red scrawl across a couple of the keys. "You— you startled me," he stammered.

Christine gave a delighted laugh. "Serves you right, after all the times you've crept around and startled me," she shot back. She came up behind him and put her hands on his shoulders. "I'm so glad you're back, Erik!"

"Are you? Welcome me, then," he requested, sliding off the bench and slipping his arms around her waist to draw her close for a kiss. One kiss led to several others, until Erik felt properly welcomed.

After a few minutes they had to pause for breath. He leaned his forehead down against hers and said, "I'm happy to see you, my dear, but what are you doing here?"

She shrugged, stroking her hands over the back of his neck. "I was curious to see your old house again after so long. Then when I reached the bottom of the Communards' Road, I heard you playing and just had to come and see you.

You've been gone far too long!"

He chuckled. "I agree, and it was only a few days! But now…" He bent to brush her mouth with his own again, briefly, before he straightened up and slid back onto the organ bench. He flashed her an enigmatic yellow glance and flung out his challenge from many years ago. "Let us sing from the opera, Christine Daaé!"

He launched into the duet from Othello, just as he had done long ago when she had torn his mask from his face. Christine smiled and played along, singing, *"Chi è là? Otello?"*

"Si!" Erik replied, asking, *"Diceste questa sera le vostre preci?"*

They continued into the duet, but all the hatred, jealousy, and fear that had been present during their first duet had melted way, leaving behind only passion and intensity. They were both waiting for the denunciation…and the inevitable unmasking that followed it. Christine sang hopefully, *"Ch'io viva ancor; ch'io viva ancor; ch'io viva ancor…"*

This was it. *"Giù!"* Erik thundered. *"Cadi, giù, cadi, prostituta…"*

"Pietà!" Christine cried, reaching for his mask. She ripped it off his face and stepped back as he rose from the organ bench.

Erik, as Othello, finished his line. *"Muori!"*[10] His yellow eyes flashed and he grabbed Christine by the shoulders, holding her still so she could look up at his naked face.

The intensity broke as Christine gazed upon him with a soft smile. "No, Erik. Not death this time, but life." And she pulled his face down to kiss it.

Her lips traveled from his forehead, down his gaunt cheek to his bony chin; they touched his own malformed lips, lightly as a butterfly; they lit briefly on his tiny, pitiful excuse for a nose. She kissed the lids of his deep-set golden eyes and went back to his prominent forehead before she returned to his lips again. A single tear escaped his tightly-shut eyes and she

---

[10] The duet spoken of here and in the original novel is one of the final scenes from "Otello," where Othello comes in and denounces Desdemona, his beloved wife, as a whore. He's been led to believe, by his unscrupulous advisor, that his wife is having an affair with Cassio, his captain. The scene ends with his stabbing his innocent wife to death.

Desdemona: Who is there? Othello?
Othello: Yes. Have you said your prayers this evening?
(They sing about Cassio's death and Desdemona continues to defend the captain while protesting her own innocence. Otello threatens his wife with death, but she sings...)
Desdemona: I still live, I still live, I still live...
Othello: Down you fall, down you fall, prostitute!
Desdemona: Mercy!
Othello: Death!

caught it on her tongue.

He slid his arms around her and tightened them, pulling her flush against him. He bent to kiss her again, one hand sliding up to tangle in her hair, holding her close so she couldn't withdraw. She didn't withdraw; instead she moved even closer, holding him tightly as her mouth clung to his. His heart swelled at Christine's trust and acceptance, and only when his desire threatened to overcome his control did he finally end the kiss. He kept his arms around her and gently rested his cheek against her hair.

The irony of the situation struck him then, and he huffed out a little laugh. "Now, if you'd only done that the first time we sang that piece, think how much better things would have gone!"

Christine's shoulders started shaking. Was she crying?

He released his grip and stepped back, relieved to see that she was laughing along with him. She shook her head. "Erik, what in heaven's name am I going to do with you?"

"More of the same?" was his helpful suggestion.

"I'm serious!" she protested, but her laughter belied her claim.

"So am I," he maintained. "Sing with me, Christine, and kiss me every now and then, and I shall be gentle as a lamb."

Christine arched a skeptical eyebrow. "Gentle as a lamb, is it? If that was an example of your gentleness, *monsieur*, then your passion must be a fearsome thing indeed!"

Erik didn't know what to say; he opened his mouth and then closed it, flushing a little.

Christine gave him an impish smile and a light kiss on his gaunt cheek before handing him his white mask and changing the subject. "Shall we go, then? Are you all finished here?"

Erik looked around at the house that had been his cell for longer than he cared to remember, and nodded. "Yes, I think so. Why?" he teased. "Are you worried that I'll start haunting the place again?" He tied the mask back on.

"I hadn't been, until I happened to come down after my lessons and heard you thundering away down here just like you used to!" Christine retorted. "And then... Othello, Erik? Why Othello?" She shook her head.

He just smiled under his mask and offered her his arm. "It's a painful memory I wanted you to help me heal," he explained. "And you did so admirably. Thank you."

"The pleasure was all mine," was her amused reply as she took his arm and they left the cellars together.

"No," Erik muttered under his breath as he rowed them across the lake toward the passage that led to the Rue Scribe exit, never taking his eyes off Christine's luminous beauty. "It wasn't all yours, my dear."

Later that evening before supper, Erik, Christine, and Kaveh sat together in the drawing room of the Persian's rented flat. Erik started to tell them both about his inquiries. He did not get very far into the story before the expected interruption.

"You did WHAT?" Kaveh cried in outrage.

"I borrowed your identity in order to conduct my investigation."

"You told them you were Persian, you mean." Kaveh hoped this was the case.

It was not. "I told them I was Kaveh Tallis, *Daroga* of Mazenderan."

"What? Why? *Why?*" Kaveh demanded. "Why on earth would you do such a thing?"

Erik bit back a smile. He'd known that this was how Kaveh was going to react; he'd been looking forward to it for days. A quick glance over at Christine told him she was shocked, but slightly amused. She had no idea of the amount of history he shared with Kaveh; no doubt she thought the Persian was over-reacting.

"The last time I was in that area, I killed someone by accident. I did not want to be arrested for it at this late date. Oh, I also borrowed your voice and your accents," he added, employing both at once for Christine's benefit.

Darius was just pouring out the tea when he heard Erik speak in his master's very voice and tone, and swiftly turned his chuckle into a cough when Kaveh turned glaring jade eyes on him.

Christine giggled.

Kaveh fumed. "Anything else?" he asked finally.

"Yes, actually," Erik told him, producing Kaveh's astrakhan cap from his valise on the floor. "Hope you haven't been missing this."

"It's my favorite one, Erik!" Kaveh sputtered.

"And I can see why!" Erik teased, turning it over in his hands, admiring it before he tossed it to his friend. "It's quite handsome; I appreciate the loan of it. The loan of everything, really, since posing as you enabled me to complete my inquiries without any police interference."

Kaveh subsided, shaking his head. "So glad I could help," he said, his voice dripping with sarcasm.

"So am I, *daroga*, so am I," Erik replied cheerfully.

"So what happened? What did you find out?" Kaveh asked, his interest finally overcoming his outrage.

Erik glanced at Christine. "You got my letter?"

"I did," she told him, eyes dancing. "Your news was… surprising, to say the least."

"What news? What did you learn, Erik?" Kaveh was nearly on the edge of his chair.

Erik took pity on him. "It seems, old friend, that all this time you have been abusing me, scolding me, lecturing me, and ordering me around… you have been doing so to a member of the nobility."

"What?"

Erik leaned back, stretching out his long legs in front of him. "You're looking at the son of a count."

"No!" Kaveh blinked, disbelieving.

"Yes. And that's not all," Erik went on. "Tell him, Christine."

"It seems, M. Tallis, that Erik is actually—and rightfully—the Count de Chagny."

Kaveh's eyes got even wider. He sat there in shock for just a split second before throwing his head back and bellowing in laughter. "You are serious?"

"As the grave," Erik replied, deadpan.

Kaveh laughed harder. He pointed at Erik helplessly, and leaned back in his chair, laughing so the tears came. "You! A Chagny!" he chortled.

Erik started to frown. "It isn't *that* funny," he snapped.

Kaveh nodded, still chuckling. "Oh, yes it is! After all your curses and imprecations against that family… and now you're one of them! Erik, this is the funniest thing I've ever heard in my life."

"So glad you're enjoying it," Erik told him acidly.

"Oh, I am, I am!" Kaveh replied, wiping tears of merriment from his eyes. "This is the best thing I've ever heard. So ironic!"

"When you're quite finished," Erik snapped, "perhaps we can begin discussing what we are to do?"

With a broad smile, Christine handed Erik a folded sheet of paper. "Here; while M. Tallis is regaining his composure, I want to show you this."

It was a letter from her solicitor, received that morning.

Dear Mme. de Chagny:

I read your letter with great surprise and considerable interest. When I began researching the family's files I discovered a rather old letter that actually may confirm your fiancé's claim. I have already begun the paperwork required to make the change you requested; however, nothing can be made official until I have seen your fiancé's documentation and confirmed the validity of the letter.

If he would be willing to come here with it tomorrow, I shall examine the documents. If they are in order, then the family can make no objection and I shall update the records to reflect his reinstatement as Comte de Chagny.

Again, congratulations, and best wishes on your continued health and happiness.

Sincerely,

Fontaine Coté

"You wrote to your solicitor about this already?" Erik asked. "Before we even talked about it?"

Christine shrugged. "You said in your letter that you were leaving it up to me. I've decided you shouldn't be denied your rightful title anymore. Being a *vicomte* will be quite an honor for my son, and nothing to be dismissed lightly. It's far more important that you finally get what you deserve, Erik."

He shrugged. "As long as you and I can be together, it doesn't matter to me one way or the other. I imagine, though, it will also improve your status if you were to marry another count, rather than some nameless, faceless nobody. And as to that, any thoughts as to how soon we may marry? And where?"

"I asked M. Coté to transfer your title before our wedding, so that people will think I'm the social climber instead of you," Christine told him, blue eyes dancing.

"Hmph," Erik snorted. "If that were the case, you wouldn't be thinking of going back on the stage, my dear."

"I wonder what people will say, for me to marry another Count de Chagny, and yet return to singing on the stage?" Christine asked.

"They shall be delighted that you're not wasting such an amazing gift," Kaveh suggested.

"At least, they will be if they know what's

good for them," Erik returned darkly.

Christine and Kaveh exchanged an amused glance. "I hear echoes of the opera ghost there, Erik," Kaveh told him. "Should I start following you around again?"

Erik barked out a laugh. "Good luck with that endeavor, my friend." He turned to Christine. "Have you any preference as to where? I used to dream of marrying you at the Madeleine, but now I think I'd prefer to have Father Arnaud marry us. What do you think?"

"I would love to have him marry us; he's been so helpful to you." Suddenly Christine laughed, a pleasant tinkle of sound in the rather somber drawing room of the flat. Erik looked at her, a question in the tilt of his head, and she explained. "I just realized that you and I are cousins, Erik; cousins through marriage."

Kaveh grinned. "And here you always said you had no family," he teased.

"I suppose I should just be glad that I turned out to be your husband's cousin, rather than his brother," Erik mused. "For cousins can marry, but brothers and sisters-in-law cannot."

The next morning when Christine introduced the tall masked man as her fiancé, M. Coté was slightly taken aback by the mask but too well-mannered to remark upon it. He had a government official with him for their meeting, and they both examined Erik's baptismal records and Fr. Arnaud's letter in minute detail before the official nodded once, curtly, and left the room.

"Well, this is certainly unusual, M. de Carpentier, but everything does seem to be in order. The priest's letter and baptismal records do confirm the information that Madame la Comtesse de Chagny apparently sent to my father, who was *their* solicitor, more than forty years ago."

The young man, who had apparently inherited the business from his father, shuffled through a stack of papers. He found what he was looking for, and held it up to show them. "Here it is. With Count Philippe's sisters having signed away their fortunes to their brothers, they can make no legal objection to the change," he said. "Mme. de Chagny tells me that you wish me to go ahead with this right away, so that the title will be fully yours before you marry. I shall update the family records immediately, and inform the other members of the family."

"Thank you, *monsieur*," Erik replied.

"One question, M. de Carpentier, and… it is a rather personal one," the solicitor asked.

Erik cocked his head to one side. "You wish to know about the mask."

M. Coté nodded. "Forgive me, *monsieur*. I was merely wondering if the mask had anything to do with the reason your father did not acknowledge you as his heir in the first place."

Erik hesitated an instant, seeking out Christine's gaze. She looked concerned, a frown wrinkling her brow. He searched her eyes as if looking for direction, and finally he nodded and turned back to the little solicitor. "My face has been disfigured from birth. I wear a mask because others tend to find my countenance somewhat disconcerting." To put it mildly, Erik thought. He leaned forward in his chair to make sure he had the man's full attention.

"M. Coté, I am planning to increase your salary significantly to reflect the extra work my fiancée and I are putting you to. I trust that will help to make up for the inconvenience of keeping my confidence on the matter of my mask, sir, as only five other people in the world know the true reason for it." He stood up, towering over the rather dumpy little businessman, and took one threatening step closer to him. He lowered his head, fixing the solicitor with a pointed look. "I would trust any of them with my life, sir. If word of my deformity gets around, M. Coté, rest assured I shall know where to find you."

The hard edge of menace in his voice made the businessman go a shade paler as he rose and stammered his assurance to Erik of his discretion and long-time loyalty to the Chagny family.

As they left the office and started down the street, Christine took Erik's arm. "Five others?" she questioned. "You're much more trusting than you used to be."

He shrugged and started naming them, counting them off on his pale, slender fingers. "You, because of your insatiable curiosity six years ago..." he flashed her a challenging look, but she said nothing—it was true, after all. "Kaveh and Darius, because they were the ones who dragged me bodily out of the opera when I was dying and nursed me back to health. That's three. Father Arnaud makes four, because he baptized me as an infant, and your son is the fifth."

"And you'd trust my son with your life, would you?" Christine laughed.

"He doesn't speak to anyone. As long as the person asking him questions about me didn't sing any Bizet to him, I'd be perfectly safe."

Erik spent the afternoon at Christine's house alternately playing with her son and her piano. He visited Erik-Daaé in the nursery and had some fun making the little boy's toys and animals speak to him in various voices. Erik-Daaé's dark blue eyes got even bigger, filled with wonder as his toys came alive and began acting out tiny bits of operas that he'd heard his mother singing from.

"Are you two gentlemen having fun in here?" Christine asked, watching Erik manipulate a small wooden giraffe to sing Aïda's part in her final duet with Radames in a heartbreakingly beautiful falsetto. He sang soprano far better than La Carlotta ever had, she thought with a secret smile.

"Yes, *Maman!*" Erik-Daaé said. "*Monsieur* Erik did some magic and made my animals speak to me!"

"He's good at doing magic like that," was Christine's placid observation. "You'll certainly be happy when M. Erik comes to live with us, won't you?"

Erik-Daaé nodded several times. "Yes,

Maman! And he can sleep in my room!"

Christine pursed her lips and darted a quick glance at Erik, who coughed to hide his chuckle. "Well, I doubt M. Erik would want to do that, son, as I'm sure he would prefer a grown-up room... but perhaps we should talk about that before he moves in."

"Definitely," Erik said hoarsely. He cleared his throat and spoke louder. "Another thing we should discuss is that I had assumed you and your household would be moving in with me, rather than the reverse."

Christine raised her eyebrows. "Ah." She nodded. "You're right, we do need to talk." She knelt down to talk to her son. "*Cheri*, M. Erik and I are going to go downstairs to talk about some things; we'll send for you a little later, and maybe he'll play for you again."

The little boy brightened. "More bullfights?"

Erik sighed. "Perhaps. Or possibly something with some fighting in it?"

"*Oui!*" was Erik-Daaé's enthusiastic reply.

"Thank God," Erik groaned under his breath as he and Christine started down the stairs toward the drawing room. "Maybe we can get him into some Gounod, at least."

Christine chuckled.

They reached the drawing room and Erik sat down at the piano and started to absently pick out a simple melody.

"Erik?" Christine said. "I thought we were going to talk."

"Hmm? Ah, my apologies. It's an old habit; if there's a piano in the room, I have to be sitting at it." He stood up and joined her on the divan. She took his hand and held it, and neither one spoke for a moment.

Erik began. "If you go back onto the stage in a few months, then we shall have to plan to spend at least the opera seasons here in Paris. This leaves us autumns and winters to spend in Provence, perhaps, or... I also know of a lovely estate up near Rouen, that I'm told I now own..."

"You actually own this flat, too," Christine reminded him.

"So I do." Erik leaned back and stretched out his long legs in mock complacence. "Another thing to consider, my dear, is Kaveh."

"M. Tallis? What of him?"

Erik's gaze became distant. "I have certain responsibilities toward him, and I cannot simply abandon him in my happiness. I would not. If you only knew how much I owe him..." his voice trailed off, lost in memories.

"Erik?"

He started. "Oh. Yes. I was merely saying that if you moved in with us, I wouldn't have to worry about Kaveh's finding a new place to live. He is not a rich man; without my contributions to the household expenses, his standard of living would be lower. Considerably lower. He would have to move, with only a single servant, into a much smaller flat." He glanced back at her, a bit of self-consciousness in his bearing. "Not to mention that... well, I would miss him."

"Would you," Christine remarked, amused. It was obvious to her that the two men were the closest of friends, for all their provoking remarks and taunting each other. "That must hurt to admit."

"Well," Erik dissembled. "I've gotten used to the old fussbudget."

"He seems fond of you, too... against his better judgement, I think."

Erik cocked his head. "Well, I'm sure he finds me useful on some basic level. I pay the servants, for one thing. I doubt there is any deep attachment to me, though."

"Oh, I think there is. A friend will lie about

your death to the girl who jilted you," Christine said. "But a *true* friend will help you carry your gravestone."

Erik's suspicious look made her giggle. "How did you know?"

"Did I neglect to mention that I enjoyed a most informative visit with M. Tallis while you were in Rouen?" she asked innocently.

Erik groaned, leaning his head back against the divan and covering his eyes with one hand. "I am doomed."

She lifted his hand from his eyes and kissed it. "You're not doomed, my love. How about this: why not invite M. Tallis and his man to move in here with us after we're married? This flat is certainly large enough to accommodate a few extra people. And from what you say, the Rouen estate is enormous."

Erik thought for a moment. "We would have to sell the cottage in Provence if we did that, as it would be too small for all of us together. Pity; I do rather enjoy living in Provence."

Christine shook her head. "Why not simply add on to it? We could winter there if you wish. And I know you could design a beautiful addition even in your sleep."

"I could, at that," Erik remarked thoughtfully. "It has been a long time; I would enjoy doing that."

"So it's settled then, assuming M. Tallis agrees. I hope he likes children."

"I think that will be the best solution, for Kaveh to move in with us. Assuming he accepts the offer, that is; he may wish to be free of me after so long." Erik gave a self-deprecating shrug. "It will be nice to offer him my hospitality for a change, after having accepted his for so many years. As for children—I assume he has nothing against them. He once had a family of his own, in Persia." Erik's golden eyes twinkled. "We could always put him in the nursery with Erik-Daaé."

Christine laughed. "Erik-Daaé would be petrified of him for at least a month. It's probably better that he gets his own 'grown-up room' as well."

"Speaking of which…"

"Yes?"

Erik hesitated, not knowing quite how to bring it up. He remembered her distressed letter, from early in her marriage, when she discovered that noblemen did not share a bed with their wives. He would be a nobleman himself by the time they married; what were her expectations of him on that front? He hoped desperately that she would welcome him as a husband in every sense, but looking as he did, he dared not presume.

"Erik?"

He cleared his throat again. "How many... uh, how many rooms shall you have to prepare here?" he asked. Her answer would tell him whether she expected him to share her room or have one of his own.

"Two, I would imagine," Christine said, as M. Tallis would no doubt be bringing his manservant with him.

Erik's heart sank. Two rooms: one for Kaveh and one for him. She didn't want him in her room with her, then. "I see," he replied, sounding hollow. He looked away, preferring not to let her see the pain in his eyes. His voice hardened. "No doubt I shall require privacy!"

Christine saw his reaction and her shoulders slumped. "Forgive me, Erik," she whispered. "I should not have presumed..." that you would share my room, she thought but did not say. She sighed. Three rooms, then, instead of two: one each for M. Tallis and his servant, and one for Erik. He was going to be the Count de Chagny; why should he not wish for all the trappings that accompanied the title—including his own private bedroom?

She gestured helplessly, not knowing what to say. "Sometimes I forget my station." Her parents had shared a room and a bed quite happily until her mother had died; it was hard to remember that she was a countess now, and had to behave according to the customs of noble families—including the master and mistress keeping separate bedrooms.

"No, no," he snapped, holding up one hand in a protective gesture. "The presumption was on my part." Voice heavy with sarcasm, he stood up and said, "I would certainly never wish to intrude on you without being invited." He left her there on the divan and headed back to the piano. He started to play something Christine recognized from long, long ago. Instead of a long wail of agony, though, this sounded more like bitter and furious mutterings—perhaps a different portion of his Don Juan Triumphant than she had heard before, but she knew with a flash of insight that it was from that opera.

Christine was left sitting alone on the divan, feeling bereft. Why was he so angry? Even if she had made the unwarranted assumption that he would share her room with her, there was no need for him to be angry. It was quite plain that he was, though, when she darted a quick look at him at the piano. His posture looked forbidding; he was extremely annoyed with her.

With a pang, she envisioned another marriage like her first with Raoul—would Erik, too, visit her in her room only when he wanted to have relations, and then abandon her directly afterwards? Would she see him only at dinnertime and when he was feeling amorous? Her heart sank at the thought. She had been so lonely! If the very thought of sharing her room was enough to make Erik lose his temper, though, how could she expect anything else?

A single tear slid down her face and she turned away from where Erik was playing the piano. It wouldn't do for him to see her crying over her shattered illusions, a silly girl's fantasies. Even though she'd been married, widowed, and had a child, she suddenly realized that she was still very young. She was half Erik's age; why would a man as capable, intelligent, and powerful as Erik even want to be married to such a child as she?

The tears kept coming, but she ruthlessly stifled the sob that sat there at the back of her throat, threatening to escape. Erik deserved better than having to always pick up the wrecked pieces of her dreams. Maybe she could get herself back under control while he was distracted with the music.

She wiped the tears away with her palm and stood up to ring for Anneke.

"Tea, please, Anneke," she requested when the maid made her appearance. Erik went on playing, refusing to even look in her direction.

When Anneke returned with the tea, Christine poured out for them, and then straightened up and took a deep, calming breath before bringing Erik's tea to him at the piano. She hoped he wouldn't notice her slightly reddened eyes.

He fixed her with a golden glare. "Tea?" he snarled. "You condemn me to a farce of a marriage and then think to comfort me with tea?" He slid off the piano bench and stood with his back to her, tall and still. His hands were clenched in fists; she could see them quivering.

"I'm sorry; I just thought…"

"You thought you could just kick your poor faithful dog of an Erik, and then just offer him a cup of tea and he'd come crawling back." He let out a bitter laugh. "You know me too well, *madame*, for you are right."

He half-turned, enough to pick up the teacup and bring it to his lips. "You know that Erik would put up with anything, in order to call you his wife! But it was ill-done, *madame*—it was ill-done indeed!—for you to have raised Erik's hopes as you have!"

"What? What have I done?" Christine was at the barest edge of her control; that sob would not be contained for much longer. His reverting to speaking in the third person didn't help.

He turned suddenly to face her, so sharply that his tea spilled on his hand. He hissed at the pain and set the cup down. "When Erik dared to dream of having a wife and a home just like any other man, you went along with it... just as long as he didn't get too close! But any talk of sharing normal marital relations, the same as any other married couple enjoys, and suddenly it's time to give Erik his own room! Heaven forbid you must endure a corpse in your bed!"

The sob came welling up and burst forth before she could contain it. Burying her face in her hands, she turned away so he wouldn't see her. Her body shook with the force of her weeping.

Behind her, Erik folded his arms and

frowned behind his mask. What did her crying mean? As it continued, he began to get uneasy. "Christine?"

She made no reply, and the sight of her slender, shaking shoulders smote him to the heart. His wrath dissipated completely and he came up close behind her, without touching. "Christine? I—oh, forgive me! I am a beast, I know I am, but forgive me, please! I'll take my own room if you wish, and be grateful you allow me into your house at all!"

"Oh, Erik!" Christine sobbed, turning to throw herself into his arms. She buried her face in his shoulder and put her arms around him tightly.

He embraced her and rested his face against her hair. "Forgive me, please, my love," he pleaded in a broken whisper. "You know what a damnable temper I have."

Christine let out a half-laugh, half-sob, and nodded against his shoulder.

"I should have killed myself before taking it out on you," he muttered, filled with self-loathing. When he had been reunited with Christine, he had sworn to himself never to make her cry again, and here she was sobbing in his arms once more.

He held her tightly against him, stroking her hair, until she had calmed. She took a few deep, shuddering breaths and stilled.

Carefully, he tipped her face up to his, so he could read her expression. Grief and confusion showed plainly, and he sighed, taking out his handkerchief. "Here, let me help you," he murmured, drying her face off with gentle fingers. "I am sorry, Christine," he repeated.

She took the handkerchief and finished drying her eyes. She shook her head. "There's no need," she said quietly. "It was my fault—but Erik, we seem to have quite a misunderstanding going on here."

"Have we? Tell me," he requested, his voice still quiet.

Christine shook her head. "It's—it's only something I had expected that I had no right to expect. That's all."

Erik's chest lifted quickly, once, with his sharp intake of breath. "I'm familiar with the concept, *madame*, believe me," he replied dryly. "What were you expecting? Tell me."

"I was expecting—that is, I was hoping— that you wouldn't be so enamoured of your new station in life that you wouldn't want to share my room."

"Wha…" he was so startled by her question that he jerked back. "What?"

"I had hoped that we would share a room, but then you mentioned needing privacy… and then you got so angry at the thought of having your own room, that you left me sadly confused."

Erik blinked several times. "Do you mean to tell me that you want me to share your room?"

"Of course, my dear! If you read all my letters, you'd remember how upset I was that… well, that my husband didn't. I was so lonely, Erik, all the time but especially at night. I was so looking forward to not being alone anymore that it was quite a rude awakening when you said you'd want your own room."

Erik could have smiled in relief. "No, love. You said you'd have to prepare two rooms, for when we moved in here. One for me and one for Kaveh."

"And what about his servant? We're not going to turn Darius out of doors, I hope."

Erik's mouth opened and closed. "Darius is a servant. I… I had assumed that the housekeeper would be the one preparing his room. Not you."

"But I don't have a housekeeper, *mon coeur*.

Just a nurse, maid, and evening cook. I may be a countess, but I grew up poor. I'm not too proud to make a bed from time to time."

He tightened his arms around her, burying his masked face in her hair. "You mean you weren't telling me you didn't plan to... that you wouldn't allow me..."

"Wouldn't allow you what?" Christine tipped her head back to meet his eyes.

"Wouldn't allow me conjugal rights?" Erik finished with difficulty. "Not that I would blame you," he added hastily, "for indeed, what woman could possibly be willing to take someone who looked like me into her bed?"

For answer, Christine reached up behind him and untied his mask, letting it flutter to the floor. "I would, my love. I'll never call you handsome, but your face is dear to me because it's yours. I love you, Erik, and someday you'll understand that means I love all of you, face and all."

Erik's deathlike visage took on a look of faint hope. "So you're telling me that you'd like me to share your room? That you'll even allow me..."

Christine smiled, standing on her toes to brush her lips to his prominent cheekbone. "I'll allow you any conjugal rights you care to name," she promised. "Just, please, promise me you won't leave me alone in my room afterwards."

Erik exhaled, a long, relieved breath. He hadn't even been aware that he was holding it. "Never," he promised. "You couldn't possibly be rid of me that easily, then or ever." He leaned down to kiss her. And kiss her. And…

"Gentle as a lamb, was it?" Christine teased after a few minutes, resting her head on his shoulder to catch her breath.

"Forgive me, love," he said. "I admit, all those thoughts of conjugal rights are rather in the forefront of my mind at the moment." He smiled ruefully and turned away to take a sip of tea and calm down his racing heartbeat.

"I know exactly what you mean," Christine admitted. "You make me feel things when we kiss, Erik, that I've never felt before. And I was even married!"

He snorted. "That's hardly the way to take my mind off the subject, *madame*." He sat down at the piano and started playing. The melody this time was a variation of the previous one, only with an undertone of longing rather than melancholy.

Christine noticed the difference and smiled impishly. "Then we should probably set a wedding-date for sooner, rather than later. M. Coté says he should have your new title made official in a matter of days; shall we arrange to be married as soon as we hear from him?"

Erik raised his eyes to hers in elation. "I shall write to Father Arnaud immediately; we can be married in a week! Is there anyone you'd wish to invite?"

Christine thought a moment as Erik went on playing. "I'd love to have the Girys there, and perhaps Sorelli and her family. How about you?"

He played for a moment without answering, and then said, "Kaveh has agreed to stand up with me, and I should like Darius to be there as well. Other than that, no one."

"A small wedding, then," Christine summed up. "Good. Large ones take longer to plan."

"Ah, I knew I loved you for a reason."

Chapter 15
A Bit of Mischief

The next day Erik received a letter from M. Coté, stating that the title had been officially granted to him. The solicitor's fawning congratulations to the new Comte de Chagny made Erik smirk even as he hurried over to his desk to write a couple of letters.

The first was a brief note to Christine, telling her the news, and the second was a letter to Father Arnaud.

Dear Father Arnaud,
First of all, I wished to thank you again for your assistance in the matters of both my inheri-

tance and my soul. You have my sincere gratitude.

Your letter, and the documentation of my birth that you were good enough to provide before I left Rouen were enough to ensure that the title is officially mine, and my solicitor confirms it. Madame de Chagny insisted on it before we are wed, so that she "would be seen as the fortune hunter," rather than I. What man could possibly resist loving such a delightful woman? As to that, Father, we would like to have you marry us on Friday morning, if you are willing.

When I visited your church, I noticed that it lacks an organ. I happen to own a very fine one, and pending your approval, would like to donate it to your church. I ask only that I be allowed to play it once in a while; I think you will find my abilities acceptable for the task. Ideally, I would like to get it installed prior to my wedding, as I have composed a nuptial mass that I would like to play for my bride.

I am planning to visit the Chagny estate early this week to make preparations; may I call on you when I arrive in Rouen? I look forward to hearing from you at your earliest possible convenience.

Yours respectfully,

Erik de Carpentier, Comte de Chagny

Then Erik took on the unenviable task of talking to Kaveh about their living arrangements.

"Kaveh, have you given any thought to your situation after I am married?" he asked his friend that night over a couple glasses of cognac.

Kaveh nodded. "I'm planning to go back to Provence; perhaps sell the cottage and look for a smaller one. I had also given some thought to staying here in Paris, perhaps look for another flat on the Rue de Rivoli." He glanced up and saw Erik's lips compress, just barely visible beneath the mask. "Erik, don't worry about us. We got by just fine without you once, and we'll do it again. Paris won't bother my health quite so much this time, now that I shan't be chasing you around those damp, dusty old cellars."

"Which I never asked you to do in the first place," Erik pointed out. "As to your situation, though... I wonder if you'd be willing to continue a slightly different arrangement?"

"What do you propose?"

"Well, you know that as the Comte de Chagny, I'm suddenly much better-off than I was two weeks ago. Christine tells me that I own not only the Paris flat she's living in now, but also the de Chagny summer home that I was born in, near Rouen. I also own the house in Sweden that she lived in with that little idiot, my cousin. There are several other chateaux cluttering up much of Europe as well; one in Britain, one in Belgium, one in Italy—you get the idea. Christine and I were talking about where we would live, and we came to a decision."

"And what is that? You want me to be caretaker for one of your grand mansions, is that it?"

Erik shook his head, leaning forward. "Oh, no, my friend. I don't want you to work for me. Christine and I would like you to come and live with us!"

Kaveh frowned. "Erik, this is a poor jest, even from you."

Erik shook his head. "It is no jest, Kaveh. We would be honored if you would be willing to become members of our household. Christine and I would be pleased to have you as our guest, for as long as you wish to stay."

Kaveh scoffed. "That's ridiculous, Erik! You and Christine will be newly married—why would you want to share your home with a stranger? I would have thought you'd prefer your privacy to be together."

"You'd be sharing our household, Kaveh, not our bedroom! I fail to see how your presence at meals and in the drawing room in the evenings would interfere with our privacy overmuch… and if it did, we could always leave."

"Fine, but what of me? You are seriously asking me to allow myself to be supported by someone else for as long as I wish? Are you mad? If I were a woman, I would think you wanted me as your mistress! What could you possibly mean by it?"

Erik gestured in the air, trying to explain his feelings—a difficult task for him, so used to hiding them over the years. "Look at it this way, Kaveh: after so many years of looking after me, giving me food to eat and a roof over my head, hounding me to take care of myself … when you get the chance to get a little of your own back, why not take it?"

"So you are suggesting that I allow myself to be a 'kept man' in exchange for having 'kept' you for the past five years?"

Erik nodded. "Exactly." He smiled.

Kaveh snorted at Erik's artlessness. "Well… since you put it that way, how can I possibly refuse?" His tone dripped with sarcasm.

Erik fidgeted. "The thing is, *daroga*, I owe you so much that I would never, ever be able to repay you. After several years of being in your debt for—well, for my very life, really, not to mention my bed and board—I am finally in a position to be able to do something for you for a change. I honestly intend no insult to you by offering my hospitality, only gratitude."

"Erik, you have no obligations toward me. I am not a duty that you must see completed. I did not keep you in my house because I ever hoped to get something from you; surely you must know that!"

"I do, Kaveh, and I thank you. But all the same, you're the second most important person in the world to me, and I would be pleased to finally be able to repay at least a part of your kindness. I know that if you lived entirely at my expense for the remainder of your life, I could never hope to fully repay you for all you've done for me. I owe you much more than money could ever buy.

"You're my best friend, Kaveh; my only friend, really. It would please me exceedingly if you were to allow me to express my friendship for you in such a way. Not to mention that I enjoy having you around, and would miss you sorely if you were no longer part of my household. And now that you've made me actually come out and say it, you must know that if anyone else ever asks, I'll deny it with my dying breath!"

Kaveh grinned. "Well! Erik, I had no idea of this great affection you have towards me!" he teased. "I can see now how rude it would be to refuse your generous offer, now that I know your reasons for it. I must insist on one condition, though."

"Which is?" Erik asked through gritted teeth. He might have known Kaveh would rib him a little for what he'd said.

"Allow me to earn my keep in some way." Kaveh's voice was firm.

Erik darted his gaze back to his friend's, puzzled. "How? You know I don't want you to work for me."

Kaveh shrugged. "Whatever way you could use assistance. You know my strengths, you know I'm quite good at making myself indispensable! I'm a very good detective, bodyguard (Madame de Chagny is going to be making many trips to and from the opera at all hours, is she not?), even politician. You must admit that

I'm much better at politics than you are; if you had been more aware of the political situation there, you might not have been threatened with execution by the shah! All I am asking is the chance to earn my bread and butter, because otherwise I shall feel like a parasite." He glared at the amused glint that leaped to Erik's eyes and growled, "*Don't* say it!"

Erik chuckled. "Very well, I won't. Your terms sound satisfactory. Unnecessary, as far as I am concerned, but satisfactory."

Kaveh nodded. "Fine, that's done, then. I am sure Darius will be pleased as well; he had been starting to sulk at the thought of breaking up our happy home. You and Mme. de Chagny have my thanks."

Erik smiled, relieved. "You are very welcome."

Kaveh held out his hand. "It's a generous offer, and I want you to know that I bear a similar affection for you, my friend." They shook hands solemnly, and then Kaveh cleared his throat and changed the subject. "Where are you going to take her for your wedding-trip?"

"Oh, I was thinking Mazenderan."

Kaveh choked on his drink and Erik cocked his head innocently. "Yes?"

"Do you want to get us both killed?" Kaveh sputtered.

Erik blinked. "I am teasing, Kaveh. Honestly, you must learn to relax, old friend. Otherwise, you're going to have an apoplexy one of these days."

"No thanks to you!" Kaveh retorted, wiping his mouth with his handkerchief. "I swear, Erik, you're going to be the death of me."

"Oh, good; if you're already resigned to it, then you shouldn't mind helping me out with a bit of mischief tomorrow, then."

"What 'bit of mischief' are you referring to?" Kaveh asked suspiciously.

"Oh, just a little problem of reclaiming some of my property, that's all."

# # #

Next morning, Erik had his answer from the priest. Yes, the old man would be happy to marry him and Christine on Friday morning, and yes, he would be very pleased with the gift of an organ. In the meantime, did Erik want him to complete any errands for him in Rouen?

Erik dashed off a reply directing Fr. Arnaud to please inform the staff in the Chagny estate

of his reinstatement of the title and his immi-
nent nuptials. He instructed them to prepare extra rooms for his wife and her son, not to
mention for his friend, his friend's manservant,
and four wedding-guests.

There remained the problem of how to get
Erik's organ out of the cellars. He solved it by
the simple expedient of putting on his rubber
mask and presenting himself and Kaveh to the
managers.

"Erik de Carpentier," he introduced himself
to M. Moncharmin and Richard. "Reinstated
Comte de Chagny. You probably remember my
friend, M. Tallis, who used to be much involved with the affairs of the opera—
specifically with my cousins Philippe and
Raoul, and the opera ghost."

"Of course, M. de Chagny. How can we
help you?" Richard was always eager to curry
favor with noble families.

Giving Kaveh a warning glance to keep him
quiet, Erik explained. "Five years ago, when
the opera ghost kidnapped Christine Daaé, my
cousin Raoul went into the cellars to try and
rescue her. You may not have known that M.
Tallis and I were both present as well. I am not
at liberty to say what happened, except that it

resulted in the death of the opera ghost and the escape of my cousin and Mlle. Daaé to Sweden."

"We thought things have been a little too quiet in recent years," Moncharmin muttered. "But what has this to do with us?"

"I am a musician, *monsieur*, and I recall seeing that the opera ghost had quite a fine organ in his house beside the lake. The same lake, you'll recall, where my cousin Philippe was found drowned on the banks. What I am proposing is that, in recompense for my cousin's death, I claim the organ—and possibly anything else of value that might still be down there."

Richard and Moncharmin looked at each other with eyebrows raised.

"But *monsieur*, we have never been down there. We do not know what condition the organ or the rest of the goods are in, and we have no idea how to even find the ghost's house!" Moncharmin protested.

Erik waved aside his objections. "Oh, that's of no consequence. M. Tallis and I are more than adequately familiar with the layout of the cellars."

The managers exchanged another skeptical

glance. Erik showed no sign of nervousness on his face, but Kaveh could see his fingers twitching against his leg.

Kaveh cleared his throat meaningfully. "Messieurs, I am sure that if you'll accede to the count's request, he might be willing to relinquish his claims to any *further* recompense."

Their glance was startled this time. "Oh!" Moncharmin exclaimed. "Uh, right. Well, sir, we might—"

"Might—might we have a word in private?" Richard interrupted. The mention of claims to further recompense had frightened him rather badly. It wasn't *their* fault that Count Philippe had gone down there after his love-struck brother and gotten himself drowned in the lake!

Erik assented, and he and Kaveh went in to the waiting room outside the managers' office.

"They'll agree," Kaveh said with confidence.

"Kaveh, that was brilliant! You have a positive talent for bullying and pulling rank!" Erik applauded. "I'm impressed. Wherever did you learn such a useful skill?"

Kaveh said nothing, but raised his eyebrows and gave Erik a flat look.

Erik flushed. "Ah." He probably *had* been

influential on Kaveh in that regard, back in Persia.

Kaveh grinned at his discomfiture and complimented him in turn. "I may have a talent for pulling rank, Erik, but you have an amazing flair for lying by telling the truth! What drivel you were spouting in there!" He affected Erik's posture as he quoted, "'My friend and I were present as well, but I am not at liberty to say what happened.' Indeed! Erik!" Kaveh shook his head slowly, in wonder and grudging admiration.

"Well, I'm not," Erik said pragmatically. "Not if I want to get my organ. And really, they don't need to know that I was present because I was the opera ghost!"

"But you did tell them that the opera ghost had died," Kaveh pointed out.

Erik spread his hands out in a look-at-me gesture. "Have you seen me haunting any operas since that night? And don't forget, there is a gravestone. There's even a coffin."

"An empty coffin, and an empty grave!" Kaveh expostulated.

"Well, of course they're empty. You didn't let me die."

Kaveh was about to give him a heated retort,

when the door opened and the two managers emerged. "M. de Chagny, M. Tallis!" Richard said. "My partner and I have discussed the matter, and we are quite willing to accommodate your request. When would you like the organ removed?"

"As soon as possible, as it must be fully installed in Rouen by Friday morning." Erik looked bored and fiddled with the ties of his cloak.

The managers exchanged glances. "Shall we see it done today, then, *messieurs*?" Moncharmin suggested. "Richard and I would be happy to provide a team of workmen to carry it out for you."

"Yes, please; I would appreciate that," Erik decided. "I shall arrange a conveyance for it to Rouen."

The managers, between them, were able to drum up six burly men to accompany Erik and Kaveh into the cellars. Erik did not falter; he led them unerringly down to the edge of the lake.

"God in heaven, how do you know your way so well, *monsieur*?" the leader asked, thoroughly confused and lost in the labyrinth of tunnels and stairways Erik led them through.

Erik exchanged amused glances with Kaveh,

who carried a lantern. "I have been here a few times before," he said dryly.

Kaveh coughed a little, to hide his chuckle.

"Might want to be careful about that cough," Erik teased in a low voice. "Unhealthy air down here, I've heard."

Kaveh's sarcastic rejoinder was swift. "You would know better than anyone." He smirked at Erik's glare, the yellow eyes reflecting the lantern light like a cat's.

By nightfall the organ was on its way to Father Arnaud's church in Rouen.

"You want to go with it, don't you, and make sure it's set up properly?" Kaveh asked Erik, seeing the man's longing glance as he watched the hired wagon rumble away.

"Of course I do. In fact I may yet. Arnaud said he would visit my house and set things to rights up there—I've already written to my house steward—but I would like to go up in person and make sure things are perfect for Christine." He cast a sideways glance at Kaveh. "Would you like to go with me?"

"Most assuredly!" Kaveh beamed. "Wouldn't miss the chance to see your childhood home."

Erik grimaced. "Yes, that seat of all happiness," he said sarcastically. "Very well. I will let Christine know tonight, then, and we will leave tomorrow."

When Erik and Kaveh arrived in Rouen, they hired a cab to take them directly to the church where Erik had met Father Arnaud. The priest was surprised, but welcomed them. Erik introduced his foreign companion as "the *real* Kaveh Tallis, former *Daroga* of Mazenderan."

"A pleasure to make your acquaintance, *monsieur*," Kaveh told him with a bow.

Arnaud grinned broadly, keeping a tight rein of control on himself so he wouldn't burst into laughter. Erik's impersonation of him had been flawless.

"And yours, *monsieur*. In some ways, I feel as if I already know you," he said, biting his lip to keep his composure.

Kaveh exhaled sharply through his nose, darting a quick glare at Erik. "Yes, I am told that you have, at least, been introduced to me before. Or someone who sounded like me, at any rate."

"True, true," replied the priest with a broad grin. "So, what are your plans now that you've arrived, my boy?" he asked Erik. "Going right out to the estate, are you?"

Erik nodded. "I'd like to inspect my organ first, of course."

"Certainly, certainly. Mind if I go along with you to the house, though? Make sure they're doing what I told them you wanted done?"

"Not at all," Erik replied, already distracted by the sight of his organ. He went over and ran his fingers over the keys with longing. He slid onto the bench and began to play.

Father Arnaud's jaw dropped as he listened. "I had no idea...!" his voice trailed off and he shook his head.

"Yes, he's very good," Kaveh admitted. "But then again, living below an opera house, he should be."

Arnaud chuckled and went closer. "Has it been installed to your satisfaction, then, my boy?" he asked Erik.

Erik nodded and went on playing till he'd finished the piece. He slid off the bench a little regretfully, and caressed the side of the organ. "You promise I'll be able to come and play whenever I wish when there is no mass?"

Arnaud nodded. "You have my word, son, and my gratitude. It's a fine instrument."

Erik lifted his chin. "Of course it is!" He

sounded affronted at the suggestion that he would have owned a lesser-quality organ.

Kaveh cleared his throat. "Erik, we should be going."

The priest, for all he was so old, was still a very good horseman. He scoffed at Erik's suggestion that they hire a carriage to take them to the estate, and soon the three of them were cantering on horseback toward the house.

The house steward met them at the door, bowing obsequiously as he gestured for a stableboy to take the three horses. The steward was a small, slender little man with a tiny dark moustache. He introduced himself (his name was Guillaume) and welcomed his master, fawning on him a little until Erik stopped him with a ferocious glare. Subdued, he backed off and quietly introduced the rest of the staff.

"I'd like a tour, please, beginning with the rooms I've ordered prepared," Erik requested.

"Very well, *monsieur*," the man replied smartly. He brought them upstairs first and down a long corridor. He proudly threw open the door on the end. "The master bedroom, *monsieur*."

It was very masculine in décor, with dark red bedclothes and draperies. They were closed, and the room felt stuffy, dark and tomb-like. Erik grimaced. "Might as well have stayed in the cellars," he muttered an aside to Kaveh. "Guillaume, open these curtains. Open the windows as well. If I wanted to live in a tomb, I would have stayed—well, just open it up in here, that's all."

The steward leaped to obey, ignoring the fact that it was the housemaid's job and not his. Erik nodded in approval.

Then the man led them to the next room. "And here is the bedchamber of the mistress," he announced.

Remembering his argument with Christine, Erik pursed his lips in thought. The room was more feminine, decorated in paler shades. It looked altogether lighter and more airy than the master's, though, and there was—"Is that a connecting door?" he asked, pointing.

Guillaume nodded. "Yes, sir."

Erik nodded, satisfied. Perhaps he and Christine could sleep in one of the rooms to-gether and use the other for a dressing room. As long as there was a connecting door, she shouldn't mind, and he wouldn't have to feel like a thief stealing down the hall in the middle of the night to spend time with his own wife!

Kaveh's room, on the same floor but down a different corridor, was clean, well-appointed, and good-sized. They exchanged satisfied nods. The nursery was upstairs from the master bedrooms, and to Erik's untutored eye it looked perfectly satisfactory. There were still some toys in it, mostly dolls, and he realized suddenly that these were the toys that his own sisters had played with.

He turned away from the door sharply. "Get all that rubbish cleared out," he ordered harshly. "My stepson has his own things, and I don't want him haunted by things of the past."

Kaveh happened to catch the eye of the priest and they shared a knowing glance. It wasn't the stepson who was haunted by the past!

Guillaume took them all through the rest of the house—and lastly, through the furthest wing of it. This was what Erik remembered; this was the place he had spent his first decade of life. He averted his eyes from the staircase where his nanny had fallen and died when she tried to strike him. He got more and more restless as they walked through the whole wing, until Father Arnaud reached out and took his arm.

Erik glared at him, but the old man smiled, unperturbed. "You don't mind, do you, son? I'm a little tired; this is more walking than I'm used to."

Erik grumbled a little under his breath, but he found the old priest's presence strangely comforting. It reminded him that he had, in fact, confessed and been forgiven for that accident, and that part of it had been the old woman's fault in the first place for thinking he was a demon and trying to kill him.

All the same, he was glad when they went back into the other part of the house. He wished he could just tear down that entire wing, so that he'd be able to live here with Christine in peace without being haunted by thoughts of his isolated childhood and his first killing.

Wait a minute. He owned the place. He could tear down the entire wing if he wanted to! And he could even design a whole new wing while he was at it. Suddenly brightening at the thought, he realized what the priest had done and nodded ruefully at him. "I think you'll find your legs much improved now, Father," he said dryly.

Noticing that Erik's mood seemed much improved by leaving the old wing, the priest grinned and nodded. "I think you're right, son. My thanks for the support."

"Glad to help," Erik replied, trying not to smile at the irony of the priest's thanking him for the support, when it had been the other way around.

# # #

Erik's letter offered Christine the choice of whether to stay in Paris and teach for the rest of the week, or join Erik and Kaveh at the Chagny estate in Rouen three days before the wedding. Christine lost no time in telling her students that she would be unavailable for lessons "for the foreseeable future," and that she would contact them once she got back to town.

She did go to the opera briefly to deliver her notes and to see Mme. Giry and little Meg. She asked them both to come into a private practice room with her, and then closed the door.

"What is the big secret, Christine?" Meg demanded eagerly.

Her mother smiled comfortably. "I'll wager I know what it is, now that he's returned."

Christine giggled, a little self-conscious, and said, "I called you in here because I should like to invite you both to my wedding on Friday morning."

Meg shrieked in excitement, and *Madame* Giry just gave a knowing laugh.

"Your wedding? Christine! Who are you marrying? Do I know him? Why did I not know you had a suitor? You've been keeping secrets from me!" Meg accused and demanded, all in one breath.

"Friday morning, *madame*? My, this has happened quickly, has it not?" *Madame* Giry teased gently. "I first saw you with him barely a week ago!"

"What? Who is it? Is he handsome? Tell me, Christine, do! I must know!" Meg pleaded.

Christine, eyes sparkling, gave in and told her young friend what she wanted to know. "His name is Erik de Carpentier. We met years ago and were friends, but we have only recently found each other again. He is not at all handsome," she said candidly, "but he is a brilliant man and I love him dearly."

"Ooh!" Caught up in the romance of the moment, Meg clasped her hands over her heart and let out a rapturous sigh.

Madame Giry held out her hand and Christine took it. "I wish you the very best, my dear." Not wishing to reveal the Opera Ghost's secrets to her daughter, she said only, "It is nice to finally find out the gentleman's name at last. I hope you and he shall be very happy."

"Erik? Your fiancé's name is Erik? Did you name Erik-Daaé after him, then? You said you knew him years ago. How did you know him?" Meg's curiosity was unquenchable.

Christine laughed. "Our story is so full of co-incidences, Meg, that you wouldn't believe even half of them if I told you! He was my voice teacher years ago, a very great and talented man. He was in poor health, though, and I had heard that he'd died before I left Paris with Raoul. It turns out he hadn't, and in fact had regained his heath. We met again when he visited Paris recently, and, well…" she gestured helplessly. "We're getting married on Friday morning in Rouen, and would love for the two of you to be our guests for the wedding."

"Oh, isn't it romantic, *Maman*!" Meg exclaimed.

"Absolutely it is," Mme. Giry agreed. "It is wonderful that you and the gentleman are going to be happy together after being apart for so long, Madame. Yes," she nodded decisively. "We would be delighted to come."

"Ah, wonderful!" Christine cried. "We had hoped you would! Erik has arranged for you to pick up your train tickets when you leave on Thursday morning, and you shall be our guests at his estate in Rouen until Saturday."

"He owns an estate in Rouen?" Meg asked, dark eyes wide.

"Actually," Christine said, "He owns *my* estate in Rouen. That's one of the strange coincidences. It turns out that Erik is the rightful heir for the title of Comte de Chagny; apparently, it never should have gone to Raoul's branch of the family." She stepped back and frowned. "You'll have to remember, though, not to remark on his appearance. Erik's looks are rather distinctive." She impulsively hugged her friend. "Just wait till you meet him, though, Meg. You'll see how happy we are!"

Meg laughed. "I surely will! *Maman*, do you think *Messieurs* Moncharmin and Richard will let us go?"

Christine chuckled. "I'm sure they will. Erik has written to them already." She waved to them both and hurried off to find Sorelli and deliver her invitation as well.

The managers both had very odd looks on their faces when the Girys went to talk to them about taking the weekend off to attend a friend's wedding. "Who—who is this friend?" Moncharmin asked.

"Christine de Chagny, née Daaé," Mme. Giry answered.

Richard swallowed convulsively and picked up a letter from his desk. It was written in black ink, but bore a stilted and all-too-recognizable hand, as if it had been written by a child who had not yet learned cursive writing. "And *Madame* de Chagny is planning to marry the writer of this letter?" he asked in a horrified whisper.

"If the letter was written by a man whose Christian name is Erik, then yes," Meg piped up.

The managers looked at each other in horror. "Could it be… he?" Moncharmin gasped.

Richard brandished the letter in his face. "I would recognize his hand anywhere, Moncharmin! It is he! It has to be! And to think, we had him right here, just two days ago…" He threw the letter down on his desk and began to grind his teeth. "We helped him remove his belongings, for God's sake! From his own house!"

Moncharmin groaned and sank down into his chair, resting his head in his hands. His fingers made circular motions on his temples. "Oh, God, what are we going to do?" he moaned.

Mme. Giry cleared her throat. "That is what we're here to find out," she reminded them, "...whether you're going to let my daughter and me attend the wedding or not."

"Oh, God!" Richard muttered. "As if we could refuse! If we couldn't refuse him before when he was haunting the place, we can refuse him even less, now that we know his social status! Yes, Madame, you may go. Yes, your daughter may go. But please, please, don't let him start up with his old tricks, I beg you!"

"What do you mean, 'haunting the place'?" Meg wondered.

She hadn't thought it possible for Moncharmin's face to get any redder, but it did. "What do I mean?" he bellowed. "What do I mean? Her friend is marrying the Opera Ghost, and she has the nerve to ask me 'What do I mean'?" He finished with an incoherent cry of rage and stormed out.

Richard fixed both Girys with a pale-faced glare. "If that was all…?"

"Yes, *monsieur*," Mme. Giry said promptly, with a curtsey. "Come, Meg." She closed her daughter's gaping mouth, grabbed her arm, and hustled her out of the office.

"*Maman*," Meg said quietly as her mother dragged her through the corridors of the opera. "*Maman*?"

"Not now, Meg, and not here," Mme. Giry ordered.

"But Christine... and the Opera Ghost?"

"I said, not here!"

# # #

Christine went from the opera to Sorelli's house, but learned from the landlord that the entire Picard family had left town for the week. Disappointed, she did a little shopping for some wedding-clothes and other essentials that she would need to bring to Rouen with her...and on her honeymoon.

Christine was examining some hats and musing about where Erik would take her for their honeymoon, when she heard a woman's voice say, "Oh, look, isn't that Christine, right there?"

She glanced up to see Clémence and Martine, Raoul's two older sisters, standing a few meters away. One was dark like Philippe and the other fair like Raoul, but both were very stylishly dressed. Apparently they had both married well. Christine had never met their husbands.

Neither sister had supported Christine's marriage to Raoul—not that she blamed them, as it was a significant step down for a count or even a viscount—and Christine still remembered their visit to Raoul in Sweden. They had shouted at him for the better part of an hour, calling Christine a fortune-hunter and a poxy whore. Raoul had sent them on their way and they had never talked about it.

Since Raoul's death and Christine's return to Paris, the two women had contented themselves with sending Erik-Daaé a birthday gift, and visiting him and his mother on an annual basis. Christine had seen them exactly twice since she had moved back.

She greeted them politely, but with her heart sinking within her. "*Bonjour*, Martine. *Bonjour*, Clémence. How are you both?"

Martine began, "Oh, we're fine, thank you—"

"—But we were a bit worried about you," Clémence cut in. "We received some rather odd letters from M. Coté yesterday and resolved to come into town to see you and see if what he said was true. We thought it couldn't possibly be, as you've only been widowed for a few—"

"That is to say," Martine interrupted in her turn, with a quelling glance at her sister, "We felt it best to offer our congratulations in person and find out more about this man."

"This is about my remarriage, then," Christine surmised.

"Among other things," Martine replied. "Might we go somewhere for a few minutes, to talk about it in private?"

The three women were soon comfortably ensconced in Christine's carriage, with the driver under orders to keep circling the park until he heard otherwise.

"There, now. What is all this business about this man you're marrying being a Chagny? We have never heard of him, have we, Martine?" Clémence introduced the subject quickly.

"It is true, nonetheless," Christine explained. She told them the bare minimum that she could, but they were family; they did deserve to know the truth about why they were suddenly no longer the daughters of a count. "He is the eldest child of your uncle, old Count Erik. Due to his appearance of ill health, he was kept out of sight and people were told that he had died at birth. Count Erik always expected to have another son, a healthier one, but had only daughters. When your uncle died, he passed the title to your father, Count Philibert, when it should rightfully have gone to Count Erik's son." Christine felt that "appearance of ill health" was the literal truth of the matter, but gave the perception that the child had been weak and sickly. She knew Erik wouldn't want these two biddies knowing about his deformities.

"It is a fantastic story," Martine responded with a frown, "but how could we not have known?"

Clémence scoffed. "It is a fantastic story, yes; but if you ask me, it's too fantastic to be true! Christine has made it up because she misses having a husband who is a count!"

"Hush, Clémence," Martine told her. "Christine, why did he not come forward with this story before? Why wait until now? He must be in his early forties at least."

"Late forties," Christine clarified. "He is older than your brother Philippe, rest his soul. My fiancé did not know any of this until recently. He had been very ill the last time I saw him, years ago; I was unaware that he still lived, and he had not known that I was widowed. After we met up again recently, he asked me to marry him but thought he had no true name to give me. That is when he went to Rouen and discovered the family connection."

"What about Raoul, then?" Clémence demanded. "Now that you ruined his life through an alliance with an opera singer, I would hope that you would at least be faithful to his memory."

"Clémence!" Martine remonstrated, laying a mollifying hand on her younger sister's arm.

Christine had had enough. "Clémence, I did not ruin Raoul's life, nor was I the faithless one! That is enough, now. I had been going to invite the two of you to my wedding, but considering how you feel about me I may forego it!"

Clémence snapped her mouth closed, shocked. Raoul had been faithless? Her innocent, naïve baby brother had deceived his wife? She would never have thought it of him; she and Martine, together with their aunt, had taken great pains to raise Raoul as a devout Catholic with the conscience of an angel. To hear that he had sinned against his wife, even if she was only an opera wench, was disheartening.

Now Martine was speaking, leaning forward to clasp Christine's hand. "Please, pay no attention to my sister. It is a family joke that someone named Clémence can be so merciless. I beg you, Christine: forgive her. We would love to come to your wedding and meet this long-lost cousin of ours."

Christine's eyes were still hard. She did not remove her hand from Martine's, but neither did she clasp it in turn. "Before you beg such a thing, dear sister," her tone was grim, "you should probably know that my fiancé is a musician and we are both planning for me to go back onto the stage after we are married."

Martine blinked at the startling news, but left her hand where it was. "Then he must be very good," she said smoothly. She waited.

Finally Christine relented. She nodded and smiled at the woman. "Yes. He is the finest musician in the world!"

Clémence, still sulking in the corner of the carriage, finally raised her gaze to meet Christine's. "I apologize for my thoughtless remark," she said stiffly. "Do forgive me."

It sounded a little perfunctory, but Christine let it pass. "Very well," she said. "If the two of you would like to attend our wedding, you are welcome. Friday morning at eleven in Rouen, with Fr. Arnaud presiding."

Both women promised to be there, but Christine held up a hand to stop them in mid-sentence. "I know what you both think of me," she said bluntly. "I don't care about that, but I do want to say that if either of you does or says anything that makes my fiancé feel uncomfortable, I will have you removed. Do you understand? Neither of you is to remark negatively upon his appearance, his title, or even his choice of bride, without serious repercussions." She gave them a chilly smile as she clarified, "My fiancé has a short temper, and no reason to be fond of you. He has not always been a gentleman."

Clémence's eyes widened, but Martine began to smile. "I think we can do that," she replied evenly, elbowing her younger sister pointedly in the ribs. She glanced out the window. "Now I see that we have come full circle around the park and are back where we started. We shan't keep you from your shopping any longer, Christine. We bid you *au revoir*, and will be delighted to see you on Friday at your wedding."

The driver helped them out, and Christine

grinned inwardly as she resumed her shopping. It had felt so good to stand up to those two that she wished she had done it years ago!

# # #

Christine rose early the next day and boarded the train with Erik-Daaé and his nurse, Anneke, and Darius. Kaveh had thoughtfully left behind his own servant so that Christine would be able to travel in safety. Erik was there to meet her at the station; she opened the door almost before the train had stopped and threw herself into Erik's arms.

"Oh, I missed you!" she whispered in his ear.

He held her close for a moment, and then released her with a brief touch on the cheek. "And I, you. But I'd prefer the privacy of the house before I show you just how much."

Christine laughed, a little self-consciously, and agreed. "Besides, I want to see the house! Raoul never brought me there, so I've never seen it." She beckoned to her son to come to the door.

The nurse gave him a little push, and Erik Daaé came out. He made a beeline for Christine and clung to her skirts, refusing to show his face. He'd barely said a word for the whole train trip, but had clutched his mother in panic for the past three hours.

Erik squatted down to talk to him at his level. "*Bonjour*, young master," he greeted the boy gravely. "I hope you don't mind that I've brought some new toys for you; I didn't know if you had enough to be able to put on a whole opera, and my new house has quite a large nursery. You don't mind the new toys, do you?"

Erik-Daaé regarded Erik with unblinking dark blue eyes. He shook his head in silence.

"That's good. I hope we have enough with what you brought; that battle scene I was telling you about requires a lot of extras. We may have to get a few more." Erik spoke very seriously, as if he were talking to another adult, discussing politics or something equally profound.

Erik-Daaé blinked. "Can... can we get a bull?" he asked shyly.

"A bull?"

The little boy nodded vigorously. "Yes. I don't have a bull. For Escamillo to fight."

Erik hung his head and stifled his groan.

Carmen again. He sighed. "Yes, young Erik-Daaé, I suppose we can get a bull. But right now, I'd like to take you and your mother back to our new house and show it to you. *D'accord?*"

Erik-Daaé nodded. "*Oui!*" He held up his arms for Erik to pick him up.

Christine, alarmed, held out a restraining hand. "Oh, Erik-Daaé, sweetie, *Monsieur* Erik might not want to carry you."

"It's all right, Christine," Erik said quietly. He reached down and swooped the boy up in his arms. Erik-Daaé's arms went around his neck quite naturally, and Erik marveled to himself at the child's acceptance. It felt distinctly odd to be holding a small child (and not hearing any terrified screams), but it felt even stranger to look at the child and see no revulsion, nothing but somber interest on his face.

Erik enjoyed showing Christine around the house that he now owned. They went to the nursery first, as Erik-Daaé was eager to see what toys his new friend had bought for him. "Oh! *Maman!*" was all he could say when he saw the assortment of animals, toys, and old stage props that Erik had carried from his old home and brought here for the little boy. "Oh, *Maman!*"

"I think he'll probably be quite happy here," Christine observed in a classic understatement.

"That was my hope. And now, shall I show you the rest of the house, then?"

Christine's jaw dropped as she walked through the rooms, noticing the rich but threadbare wall hangings, the luxurious velvet furnishings with most of the nap worn off them. "Oh, Erik, this is so…" She shook her head, not knowing what to say.

"Overblown? Ostentatious? Showy? Pretentious? Grandiose?" Erik suggested with a snort of disgust.

Christine giggled. "You sound as if you've swallowed a dictionary. It is very… 'old money,' isn't it?"

Erik shrugged. "Aside from what I already had, that seems to be the kind we have, my dear. Apparently old Count Erik bought the furnishings when he first became a count, more than fifty years ago. After that, no one bought, replaced, or even—" he scuffed his foot over an area of the carpet that had worn all the way through, "—bothered to repair anything. Fret not, though; I'm planning to redo nearly every room in the place even if it takes me a year. And I'll be starting with this one," he said with disgust, opening the door to the master bedroom.

Christine went in and looked around. She grimaced. "It is a little dark, isn't it?" She turned twinkling eyes on her fiancé. "Your coffin would look perfectly at home in here!"

Erik closed his eyes. "My coffin," he informed her deliberately, "is going to stay at my grave, where it belongs. This room, on the other hand, is eventually going to be remade into one that we can both share and be happy in."

Christine put her arms around him and gave him a quick hug. "That strikes me as a very good idea," she smiled. She pointed to the connecting door. "What's through there?"

Erik went and opened the door. Sunlight streamed in through the open door and illuminated the darkened master bedroom. "This will be your room until Friday," he said quietly. "Friday night it shall be *our* room." He fixed his eyes on the far wall, to hide his discomfiture. "The connecting door shall be locked until then of course."

Christine said nothing, but lifted up his mask and placed a gentle kiss on his cheek. "And then?" she asked, a little flirtatiously.

"And then it shall be unlocked," Erik replied, "until Saturday."

"What happens Saturday?"

"Saturday is when we shall get on a train and leave for our honeymoon," he told her.

"And where shall the train be headed?"

"Paris, first; I thought you might like us to accompany Mme. Giry and little Giry back to the city, since it's on our way. After that, Provence."

"Oh!" Christine exclaimed. "Shall I get to see your cottage, then?"

He nodded. "I suppose I should take you to some exotic place—Italy, Greece, perhaps—but the truth is, I've been all over Europe and half of Asia, and so far that little village in Provence is the most beautiful spot I've ever seen. While we're there, I've arranged for some of the improvements to be done to this house."

"Oh? Besides the décor, you mean?"

He nodded grimly. "I'm having one entire wing knocked down, so I can replace it."

Christine's eyebrows lifted. "Which wing? Is there something wrong with it?"

In a strange tone, he replied, "There is nothing wrong with it except for one thing." He met her eyes with a blazing stare. "It is the one I was kept in."

"Ah. I don't blame you, then."

Chapter 16
An Early Visitor

The day before the wedding, Erik rose early and went to the music room to put the finishing touches on the music he had written for his nuptial mass. He was interrupted by the house steward after an hour or so.

"Sir, there is a lady to see you," Guillaume hesitated a moment and then clarified. "Mme. Sylvie de Chagny. I've put her in the library."

"Sylvie?" Erik asked. "Which one is that?" He'd been hoping to avoid any confrontations with his new relatives until after the wedding; he disliked all the Chagnys on principle, and had no desire to have one of them storm his house and berate him for being an interloper. He sighed. All the same, for Christine's sake and the sake of her son, he was bound to at least be civil to the Chagnys whether he wanted to or not.

"I am not sure, sir; I am sorry. I was not appointed to this post until a few years ago," the steward apologized.

"Well, I'm busy right now, and can't be bothered to go to her. You'd better show her up here, Guillaume," Erik decided. "Stay close, though; I have a feeling you'll be showing her right back out before long."

Guillaume bowed and backed out into the hallway.

The lady in question was slender and quite tall, with a graceful way of moving. Her black hair was shot with a few strands of silver, and her eyes were wide and golden-colored. When she heard Guillaume come into the library she turned to him. Her eyes gazed at a distant point somewhere over his left shoulder as she asked, "Will he see me?"

"Yes, *madame*. If you'll follow me." Guillaume was too well-trained to glance over his shoulder to see what she was focusing on.

She followed him slowly, with a frown of

concentration furrowing her clear brow. Guillaume showed her into the music room where Erik was glaring at the piano keyboard as if it had personally offended him.

"Mme. Sylvie de Chagny, sir." Guillaume went back out and stationed himself across the hall to wait.

Erik rose. "Mme. de Chagny, to what do I owe the pleasure so close to breakfast?" It wasn't even eight in the morning yet; her arrival was scandalously early.

"Sir, I wanted to talk with you about your claim on the count's title. Forgive me for coming so early, but I wanted to make sure I got to you before you began your day's obligations."

Erik frowned. "It's too late for that, actually; you interrupted my first obligation already, which was to this piece of music. But no matter. Sit down, and say what you need to say about my claim." He expected outrage and denunciation; he was surprised when the woman sat down and reached into her reticule that hung on her wrist to pull out an aged sheet of paper. It had been folded and unfolded many times. She flattened it out on her lap.

"How much do you know of your birth family?" she asked.

"Little," Erik replied shortly. "I know my parents' names and the circumstances surrounding my birth and childhood. I know there were a couple of younger sisters, but I know nothing of them; not even their names. Why?"

"What were your parents' names?"

"Erik and Marie-Therese de Carpentier. Erik was the first Comte de Chagny."

Sylvie blinked rapidly, but was not quick enough to catch the tears that welled up in her yellow-brown eyes. "It is true, then," she whispered. "I always wondered!"

Erik frowned. "What is true?"

"And pray, what is your Christian name?"

"Erik, after my father, even though he refused to acknowledge me. And now you'll begin explaining yourself, *madame*." Erik's tone would brook no more questions.

"Sir, I am your sister," she said simply.

Erik stood up and walked to the other side of the room. With his back to her, he asked, "What do you want from me, then? Money? Want me to renounce the count's title? What?"

Sylvie lifted her chin at a haughty angle and turned her head toward Erik's voice. "Well, since you asked, I want you to sit back down and listen to me." Her tone was every bit as as-

sertive as Erik's, and he noticed the similarity.
"Nothing else."

"Very well." He seated himself again and
stared at her. "I am listening."

"I don't know where to begin. I wish to ask
about your childhood, but I don't wish to pry. I
had some small bits of information from Father
Arnaud, but most of what I know is in this letter." Her expression was thoughtful, but her
gaze seemed to go right through him; her eyes
seemed focused on something immediately behind his shoulder blades.

Erik glanced over his shoulder, but could see
nothing of note. She must be staring past him
like that to avoid looking at his face, he decided. Might as well get the worst part over
with right away. He asked her bluntly, "Aren't
you going to ask me why I'm wearing a mask?"

She blinked. "Actually, no, I wasn't. I was
unaware of your mask. I'm blind."

Erik's jaw dropped. It wasn't often someone
could take him by surprise like that, but she had
seemed so surefooted and confident that he'd
had no idea. He reminded himself that she had
grown up in this house, and that nothing had
changed in it since she'd left. This also solved
the mystery of what she was looking at over his

shoulder; she simply couldn't see where his eyes were.

She went on speaking just as if she hadn't just astonished him into silence, and smoothed out the letter. "If you do wear a mask, I am assuming it's because of the deformity of your face. Mother wrote about it in a letter to me just before she died. That's why I came here; I thought you might wish to read it." She handed it over.

Erik took it in a trembling hand.

"Would you..." Sylvie began, and swallowed. "Would you mind reading it aloud? It has been many years since I have been able to read it for myself, and it is not something I could ask another to read for me. Please."

Erik cleared his throat and began.

My Dearest Sylvie,

I know I am dying; the doctor tries to hide it from me, but I know the truth. I don't mind; I hardly want to live anymore, eaten up from the inside as I am by the secret knowledge I carry. I have lived a lie for the past twenty-five years, and I must unburden myself to someone before I die or else I shall never have any rest.

Sylvie, you are not my eldest child. I know

that the older servants may have gossiped about my having had a son two years older than you, who died at birth—but the truth is, he did not die. I am so ashamed to admit this to you, Sylvie, who always loved and looked up to me. But I cannot go to my grave with this lie still between us.

You are so beautiful, my dearest girl; when you were born I wept with joy at how lovely you were even then. The midwife was a little shocked at how I exclaimed over your beauty, but she had no way of knowing the truth behind my exclamations.

You see, your brother was born very much alive, but badly deformed. His face—I have never forgotten it. It looked like paper-thin, greyish-yellow skin stretched over a skull. There was no nose, and the eyes could hardly be seen, they were set so deeply in that horrible skull. The blue veins showed clearly at the temples and the cheeks had no flesh at all; they were spread out tightly over the very bones.

The rest of his body was the same; skin stretched taut over bones. He was so very ugly, Sylvie, that I shrieked when I saw him, thinking that he had died and started to rot even within my womb! But then he opened his mouth and cried, and I screamed even louder at the thought that something that looked this dead could actually live and breathe.

I can hardly write, now, for the tears of shame that obscure my vision and drop onto the paper. There are so many things I did wrong with that child, Sylvie, that if I go on to glory when I die, I shall be quite surprised. Oh, if only I could see him now, one more time, and tell him how very sorry I am for everything! But apologies are probably meaningless after so long.

You see, after I recovered my wits, I realized that your father would never acknowledge a son who looked like nothing so much as a tiny corpse. He might even try to have the child killed, especially if no one else knew about him except the midwife and me. Deformed and hideous the baby might be, but he didn't deserve to die for it! I conspired with the midwife to send for the priest. It was young Father Arnaud; he came to the house and saw how matters stood, and then the two of us went together to discuss things with your father.

Your father was furious; I had been right in thinking that he would have tried to kill the child. He blamed me for the baby's deformities, but was swayed from violence by Fr. Arnaud's presence. The priest could not, however, influence your father to acknowledge your brother as his, or name him as heir. Fr. Arnaud acknowledged him on your father's behalf, though, by baptizing him "Erik" as well. (Secretly, I think Fr. Arnaud rather enjoyed that part! I remember him smiling as he did it, and the midwife chuckled.) After that, he and I made all the arrangements to have the child raised in secret, way off in an unused section of the house. Fr. Arnaud even sent over a nanny for him, who would not betray us about little Erik's existence or appearance. I made sure the baby was masked before she even got there; she would have to see his face to bathe him and feed him, but there was no reason she should have to look at it all the time.

You were born when Erik was two, and we chose not to tell you of him; your father said the fewer people who knew about him, the better. This is another decision I regret going along with. I did worry for Erik's life again when you were born; I was very glad you were a girl, as I am sure your father would have had Erik killed if you had been a boy.

I feared that my next child would be a boy,

so I took steps to protect Erik. With Fr. Ar-
naud's help, I sent a letter to M. Coté Sr., the
family solicitor, with information about Erik's
birth. I requested complete confidentiality on
the matter until my husband's death, when I
had planned to introduce Erik as our son and
heir no matter what he looked like. (I also told
my husband of that letter, which would stay his
hand and keep Erik safe even if we did have
another son at some point.)

There was an accident, though, some sort of
scuffle between him and his nanny when he was
nine. We found her lying dead at the bottom of
the stairs, and Erik had completely disap-
peared. We think the band of gypsies that were
in the area at the time may have kidnapped
him, but my husband forbade me to pursue the
matter. "Good riddance," was his thought—not
to mention he was safer now that his dirty little
secret was no more.

After that, to my shame, I tried to forget that
I ever had a son. I never can, though, and it
wasn't until recent years that I realized I loved
him. He was horribly ugly, Sylvie, but he had
the most beautiful voice I have ever heard. He
loved music and sang like an angel. I always
thought that all the beauty that was absent in

his face was multiplied in his voice.

I have no idea what ever became of him; I have heard nothing of him since he disappeared at age nine. I don't know if he is living or dead, but Sylvie—somewhere out there, your older brother may yet live. If your paths should ever cross, I beg you to tell him of my regrets, and let him know that I am deeply sorry for every wrong thing I ever did to him or allowed others to do.

Tell him I loved him from the day of his birth to the day of my death. If only I could see him now, I would clasp him in my arms and beg his forgiveness for what we, his parents, did to him!

Sylvie, you and Cécile have been my saving grace, and I am glad that God allowed me to have a second chance raising children. Your father and I have not been terribly happy together, but the two of you have given me more joy than I ever deserved. I love you both just as much as I love Erik, and I pray that he may someday come into his own. I pray that someday you may have a daughter who brings you as much joy as you have brought me. Thank you for reading this, Sylvie; you may show it to Father Arnaud if you wish to verify the infor-

mation; also, the Messrs. Coté should still have my letter in their files.

My dearest Sylvie, I don't think I shall live much longer; this secret has eaten away at my inner self for so long that it will be a relief to finally lay it down. I bid you au revoir, and ask God's blessing on you and Cécile. May you find good husbands, raise many children, and have happy lives.

With much love,

Maman

When Erik finished reading the letter, Sylvie was weeping openly. Erik cleared his throat again and asked quietly, "What became of Cécile?"

Sylvie gulped and responded after a moment, "She died in childbirth, eighteen years ago or so. Her husband is no longer living either."

"And yourself?"

"I was ill when I was about twenty-three, and went blind at that time. I have never married."

"And so there have been no other sons in this family for the title to be passed to," he concluded.

She nodded.

He did not speak for several moments; his throat closed up each time he tried.

Sylvie spoke first. "May I call you Erik?"

Erik coughed. "Yes, of course. You are my sister," Erik hesitated, and then added, "Sylvie."

She smiled sadly. "There is no 'of course' about it, Erik; you have little enough reason to like anyone in your family."

Erik smiled ruefully. "That is true; however, thus far you haven't proven as much of an annoyance as I had feared."

Sylvie laughed in surprise at the cautious teasing. "Isn't it a little sister's job to be annoying?" she teased back. Then she sobered. "Erik, I have a favor to ask, but I will not mind in the slightest if you say no."

"How fortunate," Erik replied drily, "as I am unused to granting favors to a Chagny. What is it?"

"I would like to 'see' your face," she said. She lifted her hands to demonstrate how she planned to do it.

"Why?" His voice sounded wary.

"You seem so unreal to me," she admitted. "For the past twenty years I have known that I have a brother, but I never expected to meet you. Mother's letter speaks much of you as a baby, and so you are locked into my mind as a deformed infant. I would like to become acquainted with my brother as he is today—if you are willing. I don't blame you if you are unwilling, though."

Erik thought it over; he hoped that his face would not be quite so shocking to touch as it was to witness. Sylvie had shown him nothing but kindness so far; she seemed to be taking her mother's words to heart. He nodded to himself and stood up.

"Very well; come closer."

Sylvie rose and approached him slowly; He untied his white silk mask and laid it down on the end table. As she neared him, he took her hands and lifted them to his face.

He stood stock-still as her long, slender fingers—so like his own—roamed over his bony cheeks, his overhanging brow, his nearly nonexistent nose. He closed his eyes, feeling her butterfly-like touch on his deep-set eyelids. She brushed over his temples, reached up to feel his sparse black hair, and then moved down to touch his chest and shoulders.

"You're very thin," she whispered.

"Yes," Erik replied. "I used to be much thinner."

She moved her hands around his ribcage to his back, so she was almost embracing him as she felt his bony, bird's-wing shoulders. Tears welled up in her golden-brown eyes again, and she smiled when Erik silently reached up to wipe them away.

Then it turned into a real embrace, and she turned to kiss his gaunt cheek and rested her head on his bony shoulder.

Erik's throat closed up entirely, and he let his own tears fall as his arms went up to hold her in return. This was his family, the daughter of the mother who had loved him even though she realized it too late.

He heard a sound and glanced up to see Christine's back as she left the room. She must have seen him with his sister and decided not to interrupt them. He smiled; they'd had an argument the night before, about how he should behave toward the Chagnys. She must be pleased to see him hugging Sylvie instead of berating her and throwing her out.

Sylvie spoke quietly in his ear, not letting go of him. "What color are your eyes?"

"Gold. Rather like a cat's. Like yours, but lighter."

"You don't have much hair," she observed, sliding one hand up to touch his scalp again. "What color is that?"

"Black."

"Like mine, too."

"Yes, only I don't have any greys yet."

Sylvie stiffened in his arms and stepped back. "I have *greys*?"

She sounded so outraged that Erik laughed aloud. "Not many," he assured her, "and the contrast is lovely."

She sniffed. "Flatterer." She reached to touch his face one more time. "I know you shall probably never allow this again, and I want to fix your appearance in my mind." His cheeks were wet, and she smiled warmly at him as she wiped them without comment.

"Why would you want to do a silly thing like that? My appearance is not exactly a handsome one."

She shrugged, dropping her hands. "It's you, Erik. This is nothing more than a miracle that I'm even meeting you at all! I know you're getting married soon, and I don't know if you'll ever want to see me again; I'm somewhat an embarrassment to the rest of the family because of the blindness and the circumstances in which I live. This may be my only chance." She spoke matter-of-factly, and Erik was impressed. It was obvious she wasn't just trying to curry favor with the new head of the family.

He scoffed. "If you think *you're* an embarrassment, you should try being me."

She laughed.

He went on. "It's true; deformed as I am, I am getting married tomorrow to an *opera singer*, my former vocal student, who shall continue being an opera singer even after our marriage. I somehow suspect that the Chagny family hasn't even *begun* to be embarrassed yet!" He helped her back to her chair and took the one opposite her. "If you are not too ashamed of us by now, would you like to meet my bride?"

Sylvie's smile was very real; no shame to be seen. "I would love to, Erik. But would you mind first…"

"What?"

"If you're a musician, good enough to teach an opera singer, would you let me hear you play or sing something? Singing, especially; your speaking voice is beautiful, and I would particularly enjoy hearing you sing."

Never proof against flattery of his talents, Erik smiled and sat down at the piano. He chose part of the opening aria from *Orphée et Eurydice*, and started singing.

Chapter 17
A Mystery, A Mistress, and a Misunderstanding

Christine had slept a little longer than she'd been used to, and woke up feeling wonderful. She stretched luxuriously and thought with a *frisson* of pleasure that two mornings from now, she would be waking with Erik beside her. It was nice having him on the other side of the door at night—certainly better than Raoul's being at the far end of a long corridor, when she'd been married—but she couldn't wait until she and Erik could begin to share a room, a bed, and a life together.

Anneke must have been waiting outside for some sounds of movement, for she came in right away and helped Christine to dress. "Thank you," Christine said as the maid put the finishing touches on Christine's hair. "And where is M. Erik this morning?"

"In the music room, Madame," Anneke replied. "M. Guillaume, the house steward, says he had an early visitor."

"A visitor?" Christine mused. "It must be Fr. Arnaud. I shall go say hello."

She made her way down to the music room and pushed the door open quietly.

She stopped dead in the doorway, shocked. Erik was standing very close to a tall, black-haired woman, facing her. She was close to Erik in age, Christine thought; rather striking, with a proud bearing.

As Christine watched, Erik untied his mask and reached for the woman's hands, placing them on his naked face. The visitor touched him willingly, caressing his face with a tenderness that made Christine's heart fill with a hot rush of jealousy. He even leaned down a little bit, so the visitor could reach his brow, to stroke his hair. Christine's eyes widened as she watched the stranger run her hands over Erik's upper body, finally drawing him into an embrace. When the woman pressed a kiss to Erik's withered cheek, Christine swallowed back the sick feeling in her stomach and forced herself to withdraw. She closed the door quietly behind her. Blinking back a tear or two, she hurried to her room.

Who was that woman?

She was sure Erik wouldn't be cheating on her; he loved her too much for that. But at the same time, he had been up here in Rouen before without her, and before that he had been alone for five years. He could have met anybody.

But he took off his mask for her!

Christine had no illusions about Erik's looks. She knew that her fiancé's face was utterly gruesome to most people. All the same, she took it as a compliment that she was the only person who was allowed to see it regularly. He did not unmask himself even in front of Kaveh or Darius very often; he would do it for Christine, though, every time they were alone together.

Apparently he was willing not only to unmask himself for this stranger, but to let her run her hands all over his body and his naked face.

Maybe she was an old mistress, come to say goodbye. Christine was no longer naïve about such things as mistresses; being friends with Sorelli had disabused her of many of her pre-conceived notions about men's behavior. That must be it; Erik was saying goodbye to his for-mer mistress the day before his wedding. He wouldn't be dishonorable enough to maintain relations with her after he was married, so per-haps he had invited her here to break off their relationship.

Christine perched on the edge of her bed, unsure of what to do about the woman, and wondering why Erik had never told her. Her heart sank within her at the thought that while she'd been married, Erik had found someone else. She scolded herself for feeling so; after all, she had been with someone else, so why not Erik too? It was no use— there was no room in her mind for him to have ever been with any-one else. Erik was hers, had always been hers, and tomorrow would just formalize the way things had been since the beginning.

The visitor was taller and slenderer than Christine was; she had probably never borne a child. Her demeanor was poised and elegant. Her hair was dark, sleek and straight, quite a

contrast with Christine's riot of blonde curls.
Christine had borne two children, and her figure—though still slender—showed evidence of
it; her hips were broader than they had been,
and her breasts lower and fuller. For all that she
was a countess, Christine felt like a peasant in
comparison to the visitor's poised, almost regal
beauty.

Did he love this woman? Was it possible?

Had Erik become tired of loving a child?
Christine knew how immature and naïve she
had been five years ago. She knew that compared to Erik she was probably immature even
now! Was that it? Was she too "young" for him
to really be able to relate to, except musically?
Had he found a woman closer to his own age to
assuage his loneliness? One whose affection he
could depend on, who wouldn't go charging off
into the arms of a handsome young rival as she
had done? One who wouldn't keep changing
her mind about him like Christine had done,
five years back?

Considering how she had behaved back
then, she didn't blame Erik in the least for having found someone else. She just wondered
why he was still going to marry *her* when he
could have that poised, elegant lady in the mu-

sic room. She tried to swallow the lump in her throat. She herself probably couldn't measure up to a woman like that. For the first time, she began to feel inadequate in Erik's eyes.

At least—Christine comforted herself with this thought—at least the other woman probably didn't sing as well as Christine. That was something she and Erik had shared that no one would be able to take away. The other woman may have had his heart and his body, but at least Christine had his music. She was reasonably sure that Erik would never share his music with anyone but her.

No sooner had she had that realization, than she heard the faint sound of Erik's singing. He had chosen part of Orphée's love song about Eurydice, to sing to his guest.

Christine lost the remnants of her self-control then, and wept.

She had no idea how long she sat there shaking and sobbing, when she heard a knock at the door.

"Christine? Are you in there, *ma douce*[11]?" Erik.

Quickly she wiped her eyes and swallowed. "Yes, Erik," she replied, hoping that he didn't

---

[11] My sweet

notice the slight thickness that she was unable to keep out of her voice.

Outside the door, Erik frowned. She sounded strange, as if she had been crying. "Are you all right, love? Will you open the door?"

He heard her cough a little, and then, "Actually, I'm not feeling very well right now, Erik; I'd rather not see anyone if you don't mind."

"Shall I call a doctor?"

"Oh, no; it's just a bit of a headache, that's all."

He could hear the forced cheerfulness in her voice, and shook his head. Something was wrong. Slowly he replied, "Very well, then; there was someone I'd wanted you to meet, but she can easily wait until later if you're not up to it."

Inside the room, Christine's mouth dropped open. He'd wanted her to meet that tart? He had wanted to introduce his mistress to his fiancée? What on earth was he thinking?

No matter; she had to get rid of him, get control of herself, and then go out and have a talk with him as soon as she was sure she could maintain her composure. She would maintain her dignity as she asked Erik who the woman was and why he was singing to her; she didn't want to break down into desperate sobs in the middle of the conversation and beg him to come back to her instead.

"Yes, I'm sure tomorrow will be fine. I'll be all right, Erik; you don't have to stay. You ought not to neglect your guest."

On the other side of the door, Erik frowned. Something was wrong; she was trying to get rid of him. "Very well, then; I'll see you when you're feeling better."

He left and returned to the music room, moving with the stealth that he had never lost when he left the opera, but Sylvie still glanced up when he entered.

He chuckled. "If we had met six years ago, you would have given me trouble with that sensitive hearing."

"Oh? Why is that?" she smiled.

"My previous profession required me to be able to move about quietly. I may tell you about it someday." Erik changed the subject, feeling foolish for having mentioned it at all. "I am sorry; Christine is indisposed at the moment. Perhaps we might call on you a little later in the day, if she is feeling better?"

"Yes!" Sylvie agreed eagerly. "Yes, that will

be lovely! My address is on my card."

Erik called for Guillaume to show out their guest, and then he went back upstairs.

He crept silently to his own room. He went in and listened through the connecting door.

Sure enough, Christine had started crying again, with loud, gasping sobs that she must have been stifling during their talk. She continued weeping noisily, and Erik's eyes filled with sympathetic tears as he listened. He deftly picked the lock on the door and swung it open.

She didn't even hear him come in. Her swollen eyes flew open and she gasped in surprise when he leaned down and scooped her up in his arms. He carried her over to the armchair and sat down, placing her on his lap. He pulled out a handkerchief and handed it to her.

"I thought so," he said quietly. "You *were* avoiding me. If you're upset, my darling, you should have come to Erik first. Whatever the problem is, he'll fix it. He can fix all kinds of problems." His speaking in the third person for once held no undertone of mocking himself; it was more as if he were speaking to a small child.

She shook her head mutely and would not meet his gaze.

Ah. That was it. "I see. Erik is the one

you're upset with."

A pained glance was his only answer, followed by more crying. Christine tried to sit up, to get off his lap, but his slender arms held her firmly as he shook his head. Mystified at what he could have done to upset her, he said, "Oh, no, my dear. Not until you talk to me. What have I done, love? You know that whatever it is, I shall make it right. I cannot bear to see you cry."

She stiffened and turned her head away. "Oh, Erik, it's too late to make it right," she told him in a quavering voice.

His voice deepened as his heart sank. "Is it?" It probably was. He knew there would be no atonement, no reparation for the way he had treated her five years ago when he'd been at the lowest point of his physical and mental illnesses. Not to mention for all the atrocities he had committed before he even met her. Was she about to break off their engagement, the day before the wedding? He didn't blame her, but he knew his heart would never mend.

She nodded without lifting her head. "Yes. You see, all these last couple of weeks that I've known you were alive, I never gave any thought as to who else you might have met or spent time with when we were apart."

Erik tilted his head, perplexed. "And this drove you to tears?"

"Well," Christine began uncomfortably. "I never gave any thought to any... other women... that you might have spent time with."

"What? Why *would* you?" Erik was bewildered. No other women had ever been interested in him; a few had been intrigued by the thought of what might lie behind the mask, but he had frozen their curiosity right out of them. If they weren't Christine, he wanted nothing to do with them.

Christine took it the wrong way. "I know," she said miserably. "There I was, happily married—for the most part, anyway—and it would have been only natural for you to seek other... companionship. Men do it all the time; for that matter, Raoul may even have done so. It is probably selfish of me not to have thought about that before, but Erik," she continued, sitting up and facing him. "I am not going to share you. Just because I shouldn't begrudge you your mistress doesn't mean that I should have to meet her or socialize with her. If you haven't ended it for good, then I will not marry you."

"My *what*?" Erik said, leaping up and almost dumping Christine on the floor. He righted her swiftly. "Did you say…?"

"Your mistress. The woman downstairs." Christine swallowed painfully and pressed on. "She is quite beautiful, Erik; I wouldn't blame you if you did love her. The way she was touching you, even your face, it looked as if she loved you too. If—" And here the tears started welling up again. "If you would rather be with her, then I'll understand. You don't have to marry me; after all, we did move rather quickly, considering that two weeks ago I thought you were dead. Maybe it was too fast?"

Erik took two steps backward, his jaw dropping in shock; Christine could see it trembling below the edge of his mask. He was stopped short by the tall bedpost, which he immediately clutched as if he needed the support. "Wha— what?" he stammered in alarm.

Suddenly the pieces began to come together. Christine was having second thoughts. She must have known who the visitor was. She had probably even met Sylvie before, along with Raoul's sisters. She could not possibly think that any other woman would consent to be Erik's mistress. A false accusation, coupled with the embrace that she had seen, would be enough to obtain her freedom and exonerate her in the eyes of the world.

He clenched his eyes shut and leaned his head back against the post. If she left him now, she would crush him—but he was determined that this time, he would not let her know. He would take her rejection as a man. No more crawling and pleading for him—not this time!

He decided to test her. He spoke coolly to mask his despair, and didn't bother to open his eyes. "Or perhaps you have come to your senses, and are using this as an excuse to avoid marrying me. You could have just told me, Christine; there was no need for all this hysteria over my supposed 'mistress.' Not that I blame you; who would want to be saddled with a living corpse all their days?"

"'Supposed' mistress?" Christine exclaimed sharply. "Oh, no, Erik; from what I saw there was no 'supposed' about it. You let her look at your face; you let her touch you; Erik, you even sang to her. I heard you!" Her voice was getting shrill, but she pressed on. "I hate the thought that someone else had your heart, and even your body—even though I was married and hardly in a position to claim them. But to share your music with her feels like the worst betrayal! I know you are perfectly within your rights to do so, but Erik, it hurts! Why would you do this to me?"

She took a deep, shivering breath and continued in a softer tone, "I had grieved your death; I had finished my mourning for you. Why did you even let me know you were still alive, if you would rather be with her? It was unkind, my love. More than that; it was cruel!" Her tears claimed her again as she sank down into the chair and buried her face in her hands.

Erik studied her, trying not to let her weeping affect him. Was it possible she was telling the truth? Her theatrical skills were superb; he knew, because he had taught her himself. Her devastation looked genuine, though. "Christine," he said. She sobbed harder. Brow furrowing in concern, he stepped forward and went to his knees in front of her. He took her wrists and gently pulled her hands away from her face.

"Christine, look at me." She kept her face turned away. "Please," he pleaded. His voice broke on the word, and she turned back and opened her eyes.

"Are you sure you're not just saying this to get out of marrying me?" Erik asked, trying to keep his voice steady. If she wasn't acting, he was going to feel like a cad.

"Are you mad?" she demanded angrily. "I've spent the last five years falling in love with you and feeling my heart break a little more each day because I thought you were dead! You're the one who is trying to get out of it, downstairs alone in the music room with that *fille*, the lovely Madame Hands-all-over-you!"

Hope was starting to sing in his heart again, and a detached part of Erik's mind was amused at Christine's nickname for Sylvie, but he still needed more reassurance. "You still mean to marry me tomorrow, then?" Erik pressed. "Do you swear it?" His voice came out rough with emotion. He was hard-pressed not to crumble in the face of her tears as he had before; this was too important, though, for him not to make sure.

Christine blinked and pulled one hand away from his to swipe angrily at a stray tear on her cheek. "Yes, Erik, of course I do. On my hope of heaven, I swear it! I want nothing more than to be your wife, but you should know right now that I will not share you with another woman." Overcome at the thought, she pulled her hands away from Erik and wiped her eyes.

Erik closed his eyes and breathed a deep sigh of sweet, blessed relief, coupled with shame. She hadn't been acting. She *did* still want to marry him! Opening his eyes, he winced at the sight of her pale, miserable face. He bent his head to kiss her knuckles.

"Christine, in all my life I have loved only you. I give you my word."

Christine looked away. "So you don't love her. That means little. I know that men frequently 'have' women they do not love."

Erik made an impatient, dismissive gesture. "I have never 'had' any woman in my life in that way. That woman has never been any mistress of mine; I thought you would know that when you saw her."

"How could I possibly know that, when I walk in and see her doing this to you?" She briefly mimed Sylvie's stroking Erik's chest and shoulders. Her tears had mostly dried now; she went from despair to righteous anger. "And then the embrace—she kissed you, Erik. I saw it!"

Erik hung his head, now thoroughly ashamed of his misapprehension. "I am sorry, my love. I thought you knew her."

Christine was still suspicious. "Why would I

know her? I have never been to Rouen before."

Erik caught her hands again and held them firmly against his chest. "Her name is Sylvie de Chagny. She is your cousin... and my sister."

"Your sister?" Christine responded, dumfounded. She'd had her mind firmly wrapped around the concept of "mistress," and this was not the answer she'd expected. Her reaction was predictably inane. "I didn't know you had a sister."

"Neither did I, before this morning. Apparently I used to have two, but Cécile is dead. The remaining one would be Sylvie. She is blind; I was allowing her to see what I looked like."

Stunned, Christine opened and closed her mouth a few times as if she didn't know what to say.

Erik took advantage of her silence to straighten things out. He pressed one of her hands against his silk-covered cheek. "Christine—my dearest love—don't you know there's only one woman in the world for me?" He turned his head slightly and kissed her palm through the thin silk that covered his mouth. "Even if I looked like a normal man, why would I ever want to find anyone else?"

"But... I was married, and you were alone, for five years!" Christine gave a final, half-hearted request for reassurance.

Erik shook his head firmly. "I've been alone for more than forty-five years. I would rather stay alone forever than be with someone else, to give myself or share my music with someone who wasn't you. Please, never doubt that, my love."

"But Erik, you were singing for... for Sylvie. You showed her your face."

Erik lightly stroked her hand as he explained. "Our mother, on her deathbed, had written Sylvie a letter telling her about me—what I looked like, the circumstances of my birth, everything—and Sylvie brought the letter to me this morning, for me to read. It was..." he stopped and swallowed, continuing with difficulty. "It was most affecting to read, to see what my mother thought and how she felt about me. She said she loved me! And then Sylvie asked to see for herself what I looked like, to touch me with her hands, so I let her. She said she had never expected to meet her brother, so she wanted to know as much about me as she could. She was crying, Christine. She actually wept over me. It seemed natural to sing for her when she asked me to."

Christine leaned forward and untied his mask so she could see his face. She studied his expression for a long moment. He looked intense and emotional, his deep-set eyes glistening with unshed tears. "I believe you," was all she said.

Erik closed his eyes and inhaled a deep breath. He let it out, bending to rest his head on her lap where he still knelt before her.

She smiled tenderly and stroked his hair. "I've wept over you, too, my love. I shall have to meet this sister of yours; it seems we might have a meeting of the minds after all."

His shoulders twitched a little and she realized that he was chuckling there in her lap. "It seems you might, at that," he replied, his voice muffled in the folds of her dress. He glanced up at her. "My singing for her was certainly never meant as any sort of betrayal; after all, you hold my heart. Compared to that, a little song didn't seem like that much to give her. She's certainly received precious little else from this family. She seems to expect that we won't be receiving her again; apparently she's somewhat of an embarrassment to the rest of the Chagnys."

"Oh!" Christine thought a moment. "I recall

one time Raoul mentioned a distant relation named Sylvie, but he spoke as if she had disgraced the family somehow. Is that the same Sylvie?"

Erik shrugged. "She seems respectable to me; I think the Chagnys just had some odd ideas about what constitutes disgrace." He grimaced; Christine smiled at the sight, still not used to seeing his open expressions. She wondered if he even knew how transparent he was, unmasked.

"I suspect her blindness is what shamed her in the eyes of the family," he went on. "Not to mention that when the title passed to my uncle instead of me, the majority of the family fortune went with it. Sylvie has never married, and has no way to support herself. Instead of providing her with an adequate income, it seems her estimable cousins merely left her to fend for herself."

In record time, Christine went from being outraged at Sylvie's behavior to being outraged on her behalf. "Oh, those lying leeches!" she exclaimed. "I should have known they'd be so caught up in their own affairs they'd never give a thought to their poor cousin!"

"To whom do you refer, my sweet?" Erik

asked, amused. "Your former husband and his brother?"

"And his sisters. I told you last night about what happened when I met them in Paris."

"You did. It was rather entertaining."

"I ended up inviting them to the wedding tomorrow, though."

Erik said nothing, but gave her an incredulous glance. She shrugged ruefully and blushed. He shook his head, smiling, and stood up.

"Come here," he said, lifting her to her feet. He took her in his arms, kissing her hair. "I do love you," he told her fervently. "Oh, my Christine. Only you, now and forever."

Christine rested her head on his shoulder. "I know," she affirmed. "I love you too, Erik." She looked up and smiled impishly. "*My* Erik." The smile faded and she looked away, abashed. "I am so very sorry for doubting you, and for thinking the worst of you when I saw you and Sylvie together. Can you forgive me?"

"Of course," Erik teased, "but it was very silly of you, you know." He kissed her tenderly, to take out any possible sting from his teasing. "Thinking that I could possibly love someone else, when you've owned my entire being ever since the first time I ever heard you sing?" He kissed her again. "Shame on you, my dear." Another kiss. "Let me not hear you say anything like that, ever again." One final kiss, and he rested his forehead against hers and smiled.

She grinned. "With a reprimand like that, my love, you're only tempting me to misbehave again!" She went back into his arms and kissed him in turn. "Scolding me like that isn't exactly a deterrent, you know."

He laughed, and she rejoiced inwardly to hear it. "I shall have to make sure to be even nicer to you when you're not naughty."

"I like the sound of that," Christine mused, "but somehow I think that should probably wait until after tomorrow morning."

Erik nodded, turning a little pink at her implication. He cleared his throat and changed the subject. "As to that... would you be interested in calling on Sylvie this afternoon? And then on the way back we can go to the station and meet *Madame et Mademoiselle* Giry."

Christine nodded eagerly. "Now that I know Sylvie is your sister, I'll be able to admire her without reserve!" she teased. "She seemed quite handsome, but I was too jealous earlier to let myself notice. Oh, and I'll be able to see if she resembles you at all."

Erik snorted. "I think it safe to say she looks nothing like me. She is, as you say, rather fine-looking."

"We'll see," Christine said. "And now, I think my dramatics have taken us almost till lunchtime. Shall we go down?"

The visit with Sylvie that afternoon went smoothly; she and Christine got along very well, and Christine did indeed think that Sylvie resembled Erik. Erik argued with her good-naturedly about it all the way home. He saw no resemblance at all. He saw her as his exact opposite: Sylvie had a nose, a lovely face, and a shapely figure. He had no nose, a gruesome face, and a skeletal figure. Christine on the other hand saw a strong resemblance: both siblings were tall and slender, with black hair and golden-colored eyes. They both had a graceful way of moving, a proud, almost regal bearing, and similar-sounding speaking voices. Erik spoke a more cosmopolitan style of French whereas Sylvie had a stronger regional dialect, but both voices were low, expressive, and musical.

Erik also began wondering aloud on the way home how well Sylvie sang; if both of them shared the same lineage, perhaps they shared the same talents as well? He decided to ask her to sing for him, sometime after they returned from their honeymoon.

Christine laughed at that thought. "Just think of how we would embarrass the rest of the family then! Not only a count who is a composer, but a countess who is an opera singer—and a sister who also sings! Clémence and Martine and their husbands will be mortified! They may never recover."

Erik chuckled evilly. "That does it, love; you've convinced me."

Christine laughed. "Erik! Now who's being naughty?"

He reached out an arm and hauled her closer to him in the coach. "Do I get a scolding like the one I gave you earlier?"

"I should think so! You've earned it." She kissed him soundly as the coach pulled up outside the train station. "Now let that be a lesson to you."

Christine looked forward to seeing her opera friends again. She giggled at the thought of Kaveh and Mme. Giry meeting each other. Kaveh so enjoyed goading Erik that one would think he would join forces with anyone else who also irritated Erik. Such was not the case, however; she had found the Persian to be staunchly protective of his friend, as if he were allowed to harass Erik but no one else was.

Mme. Giry was always so deferential to the "Opera Ghost" that Christine was betting her obsequiousness would get on Kaveh's nerves in record time. She looked forward to her friends' visit being very entertaining.

Meg flew at Christine and hugged her, while her mother gave Erik a deep curtsey. "Oh, *monsieur*, may I offer my most heartfelt congratulations!" she exclaimed. "We were so happy when Madame de Chagny told us her good news!"

Erik bowed in return. "Thank you, *madame*. I appreciate your coming such a long way to share in our joy."

Mme. Giry chuckled. "Oh, it was no trouble, *monsieur*, not after your letter to the managers. I'm afraid your secret is no longer your own, though. They recognized your handwriting, from when you used to send them notes all the time."

Erik gave his standard one-shouldered shrug, with the barest hint of a smile for his old friend. "And who would they tell? Who would believe them? I doubt I am in any danger from them—

and if they believe they're in danger from me, it will make them that much more amenable to my suggestions regarding the opera."

Meg was hanging back, staring at Erik with wide, fearful dark eyes. Christine saw the look and smiled. "Come and be introduced," she murmured, catching her friend by the elbow and pulling her over to Erik.

"Erik, may I present Marguerite Giry, the prima ballerina of the opera? Meg, this is my fiancé, Erik de Carpentier, Comte de Chagny."

Erik noticed Meg's apprehension and nodded to her. "I've seen you around the opera, of course, *Mademoiselle* Giry," he said. "And I know you must have seen me from time to time as well," he said sarcastically, referring to the countless times when little Meg and little Jammes would catch a glimpse of the opera ghost and run away in terror. "It is a pleasant change to make your acquaintance." In a lower voice, he added, "Without all the screaming."

"Y—yes, *monsieur*," Meg nodded nervously. Bravely she offered her hand, giving Christine a relieved smile when Erik merely bowed over it like any gentleman. "May—may I offer my congratulations to you, Monsieur de Carpentier?"

"You may, and I thank you." Erik turned abruptly and led the way toward the coach.

Supper that night was mildly comical. Christine had accurately predicted Kaveh's reaction to Mme. Giry's admiring and deferential manner towards Erik. Kaveh sniffed audibly the third time Mme. Giry addressed Erik as "Monsieur Ghost" in a deeply respectful tone, and he began talking loudly to Erik to try to drown the old woman out. Darius was the only servant serving them, and more than once Christine noticed him biting back his smile.

Meg soon relaxed; Christine's easy manner with her tall and intimidating fiancé helped to accustom Meg to him as well, and soon she was chatting quite amiably with the both of them.

Erik's manners began stiff, but the combination of Christine's sweetness and Meg's vivacity eventually wore away his reserve. Mme. Giry's attitude of awe, combined with Kaveh's subsequent jealous chatter were the icing on the cake. It amused him no end, to have his best friend and his box-keeper making a show of jealousy over him. Every so often he would get in a sly dig on one of them or the other, and then sit back and smirk behind his mask as they started up again. He could have kept it up all night, but then Christine—who knew exactly what he was doing—kicked him in the ankle and hissed for him to stop it!

He happened to catch Meg's eye right then, and she was surprised that such burning yellow eyes as his could also twinkle with sardonic humor. She grinned at him suddenly, her teeth very white in her swarthy face. The slight lightening of his eyes behind his mask told her he was smiling back, and all at once her fear of the opera ghost disappeared. Why, he was just a man, she told herself. Just a man like any other, albeit with a stranger history and appearance than most.

And he was a count, too! Christine had done very well for herself, not just once, but twice! Meg had to ask. "Christine, I must know: how did you happen to find two different Counts de Chagny to marry? I could have sworn that usually there's only one at a time! You said it was a long story, but we have all evening; won't you tell us?"

"That's really Erik's story to tell," Christine said, looking at him with smiling blue eyes. "Shall you tell it, then, my love?"

Erik glanced around the table, considering.

Christine and Kaveh he would trust with his life and his secrets both. Mme. Giry had already kept his secrets for years. Meg was the only unknown factor.

He addressed her directly. "Mlle. Giry, my story is not such as I would wish made known when you return to the Opera. If I tell it, then you must swear to me never to share any part of it with anyone except the people in this room. Please believe me: the safety of your friend and her son depends on my continued anonymity."

"I understand, sir," Meg replied breathlessly, with two bright spots of color on her cheeks. "I give you my solemn word. I swear on my father's grave, *monsieur*, that I will not tell anyone else your story."

"Very well." Erik launched into a skeleton version of his life-story, glossing over both his ill-treatment from others and the horrors and atrocities he had committed against them. He briefly mentioned he and Raoul being rivals for Christine's affections, and he gazed at her fondly when he told of how he had sent her away to be happy with the boy, as he didn't feel himself long for this world.

That's when the story got good. Erik described in detail how Kaveh and his servant had dragged him bodily from his house, forced him to seek medical treatment against his will, and transported him willy-nilly to Provence. There, they had ruthlessly compelled him to go sea-bathing, work outdoors in the sun, and interact with other people even in spite of his mask. His manner of storytelling was dry and understated, and Meg and her mother found themselves in fits of giggles more than once.

Kaveh's color rose and fell several times during the recitation, but then he noticed Mme. Giry's eyes on him with an expression of... could it be admiration? Oh, dear. He slouched down a little in his chair, not meeting Darius' gaze. He knew he'd never hear the end of it from his servant.

Then Erik told them about searching for his past, and how he had stolen Kaveh's hat, name, voice and accents, so that he could question people undisturbed. He imitated Kaveh's voice and accent again to tell about his encounters with both the town clerk and the priest. Darius could not keep the broad grin from his face as he served. Meg, Christine, and Mme. Giry laughed without restraint, their mirth ringing through the large dining room.

"Then after I made my confession to the priest, he told me the missing pieces of my story," Erik finished in his own voice again. "My father, when he died, declared his brother to be his heir instead of his son. His brother's sons were Philippe and Raoul de Chagny. So there it is—my long-hated rival turned out to be my own first cousin. It was my title that he inherited, but now I'm inheriting it from him—and tomorrow his widow will be my bride." He reached across the table, and Christine took his hand.

"See what I mean, Meg, about all the coincidences?" she said, looking at Meg but keeping a firm grip on Erik's hand. "So what do you think of his story?"

Meg had tears in her eyes. "It's the saddest, most beautiful, and the nicest story I've ever heard," she said. "Oh, I'm so glad for you both!"

Erik, charmed by the sincerity of her wishes, bent his head. "Thank you, Mlle. Giry. Thank you indeed. And you, Madame?" he leaned toward Meg's mother. "What do you think?"

"Monsieur, I always knew you were a gentleman, even when I thought you were a ghost. To discover that you're a noble surprises me none. But isn't it funny, how things sometimes work out for the best?" Mme. Giry was feeling philosophical. "As you were talking, I couldn't help but think, *mon Dieu*, what an opera this would make!"

"Indeed?" laughed Erik. "I had never thought of that."

"Well, it would, Monsieur Ghost, so the next time you get the urge to start making up your compositions, why don't you try composing something like this? And as for you, M. Tallis," she said, turning full on to Kaveh. "I must thank you."

"Thank *me*, Madame? Whatever for?" Kaveh's discomfiture grew when faced with Mme. Giry's customary brusque candor.

"Well, sir, I used to take care of Monsieur Ghost's box, back there at the opera. Always kind and polite to me, he was, and I used to like to think that in a way I was taking care of him as well. Well, when Mlle. Daaé left with her little vicomte, the ghost disappeared also, and I was worried about him. I used to wonder how he was getting on, and who was looking after him, and I never expected to find out. And now I finally know that it was you who was tending him! And I just wanted to thank you, Monsieur, for taking such good care of the gentleman ghost, once he left my charge."

Kaveh grinned, completely unembarrassed now that he saw a chance to tease Erik. "You are most welcome, Madame Giry. It is good, is it not, that Monsieur Ghost has been surrounded by such good friends that he never needs to worry about who is looking after him?"

"It is, sir, it is indeed." Mme. Giry bobbed her head several times; each time she did it, her chignon looked to be in danger of falling off the top of her head.

Erik cleared his throat. "I assure you, Monsieur Tallis, that I am perfectly capable of looking after myself," he said flatly.

Mme. Giry leaped to Kaveh's defense, just as the Persian had been hoping. "Ah, but during all that time when you weren't able to care for yourself, it was nothing less than a blessing from God that M. Tallis and his good servant were there to tend you. Surely you must admit this, M. Ghost."

Erik sighed. It would be pointless to lose his temper with Mme. Giry; she wouldn't notice anyway. He inhaled through his gritted teeth and agreed. "It was surely a blessing." His voice dripped with sarcasm.

"Oh, please, Erik, don't mention it," Kaveh said with a grin. "I don't expect any thanks; it was the same as any good friend would have done for you."

Erik glared at him, and Kaveh's grin got wider. Watching them, Meg's eyes grow very big indeed: was it possible that M. Tallis was actually provoking the Phantom of the Opera? Goading him? Mocking him, even? She was shocked and a little fearful for Kaveh's life.

And yet there was a subtle undertone of affection there, as if neither one was actually offended by the other, despite all the glaring and posturing. She shook her head, not knowing what to make of it.

Men had such strange sorts of friendships.

Chapter 18
An Irrevocable Pledge

Erik didn't sleep well that night, knowing that the next day was his wedding-day. He had laid awake for much of the night asking himself if he were really such a beast as to actually tie an angel like Christine down to a devil like himself for the rest of her life? His thoughts spiraled around, growing blacker and blacker, until it was all he could do not to flee out the window in a panic, or burst through the connecting door into her room and tell her he loved her too much to marry her! He got up, planning to dress and go out, but then his eyes fell upon Christine's jewelry box, sitting there on his dresser.

He had only read her letters the one time, preferring to conduct his interactions with Christine in person now that they had found each other again. He picked up the stack and started reading, beginning with the death of her foster-mother and continuing to the end. His eyes filled with tears as he read of her loneliness and despair at having realized her love for him too late; he realized that as selfish as it might be for him to go through with this marriage, she would be devastated if he backed out. Not to mention that he was *still* curious about that dream she had written to him about!

Soothed by the loving words of his fiancée, even if they were addressed to a dead man, he smiled and went back to bed for the few brief hours before dawn.

When he woke a second time, he felt much better. He rang for Guillaume to send up a servant with fresh water. Disdaining the services of the valet, he bathed, and carefully shaved his chin (it being the only part of his face that ever needed shaving; his sunken cheeks and his twisted upper lip had always stayed smooth). He dressed in a dark blue morning-suit, white shirt, and waistcoat of medium blue velvet. He put on his rubber mask, and then tied the white silk one on over it.

He went down to eat breakfast alone, only to find that it stuck in his throat; he had to take a big gulp of juice to wash it down. He finally gave up eating as a lost cause, and stood up.

His nerves got the better of him, and he paced. From one end of the dining room to the other and back again, Erik strode, frowning furiously. He heard a step at the door and spun around.

Kaveh came in, yawning and knotting his cravat. "Good morning!" he greeted cheerfully.

Erik growled at him with a black glare.

Kaveh laughed. "Glad to see you're in such a good mood on your wedding-day," he teased as he filled his plate at the sideboard.

Erik took out his watch and flipped it open pointedly. "You're late," he accused his friend. "Must you take the time to fill your face at this hour?"

Kaveh calmly spread marmalade on his toast. "It's eight o'clock," he said.

Erik shrugged impatiently.

"Your wedding is scheduled for eleven."

"Your point, *daroga*?"

"It's only a fifteen-minute trip to town in the

carriage. Ten, if we ride. Why the rush?"

Erik sighed, a deep and longsuffering sound. "Kaveh, how long has it been since your own wedding?"

The Persian stopped and thought a moment. "Twenty-three years."

"Then in your dotage, you've probably forgotten what it's like," Erik said. "And how you felt, the morning of your wedding. I'd wager you weren't all that calm either!"

"Frightened half to death," Kaveh returned promptly. "But the difference is, I hadn't yet met my bride by that point."

Erik grinned, the barest curve of his lip showing beneath his white mask. "Ah, so your biggest fear was that she'd be ugly, then?"

"Among others," Kaveh replied dryly. "At least that's one fear you don't have."

Erik made an amused noise deep in his throat. "No," he agreed. "My bride is definitely not the ugly one."

Slightly surprised to hear Erik speak of his looks so calmly, Kaveh decided to follow his lead. "She's already seen you as well. There won't be any nasty surprises there."

Erik coughed and seemed to relax a tiny amount. "True. Although hideousness like mine probably comes as a shock every time, no matter how often you see it! But Christine either isn't shocked, or hides it well." He shook his head in awe, eyes shining fondly. "She's such a good girl. God bless her for marrying a corpse like me."

"Erik," Kaveh remonstrated. "You know she doesn't like to have you say such things about yourself."

"She's not here, though."

"But is it respectful to her, to say things in her absence that you would not say in her presence?"

Erik turned away abruptly, and there was a brief pause before he said irritably, "You know, Kaveh, sometimes I really don't like you."

"I know, I know," Kaveh replied, not without sympathy. "Every time I'm right. Right?"

Erik scowled at him and Kaveh grinned and stood up, shaking crumbs off his napkin. "I've finished. Shall we go, then?"

Erik rang for a servant to arrange for their horses to be saddled. He continued pacing impatiently until the servant returned to tell them that their horses were ready, and then he was out the door in a flash. Kaveh followed at a more sedate pace, shaking his head and chuckling to himself.

Father Arnaud was kneeling at the front of the church when they got there, but he rose when he heard them. "Erik, my boy! Welcome, and M. Tallis—it's nice to see you again, sir."

Kaveh bowed. "And you, sir."

Arnaud grinned affectionately at Erik. "And you, young man... you're just bound to be difficult, aren't you?"

"In what way?" asked Erik with dignity.

Arnaud nodded amiably at Kaveh. "You're not only unconfirmed as a Catholic, but you're having a Musselman as your attendant."

"And another as a wedding-guest," Erik added. "M. Tallis' servant, Darius, shall be attending as well. And you told me that my not being confirmed would not be a problem."

"No more it shall be," Arnaud agreed. "Although I would like to have a chat with you about that at some point."

Erik sighed. "I suppose it is probably unavoidable."

"Completely unavoidable, son, I promise you that! But about the wedding today; as you're unconfirmed, I shall perform only the nuptial part, and leave out most of the actual mass. And then we shall see about getting you confirmed, sometime after the wedding. I see no point to delaying your union until then. Will that be acceptable to you?"

Erik nodded. "I shan't mind the deficiency," he replied. "And I suspect my bride will not either." Erik went over to the organ. He ran silent fingers over it in greeting.

"Shall we have the pleasure of hearing you play, Erik?" Father Arnaud asked.

"Most assuredly. I would not trust anyone else to play the piece I wrote for my nuptial mass," Erik replied haughtily.

"Ah, good! I shall look forward to it. Now, then, where shall it fit in?"

They decided to place the music at the end, in place of the rest of the mass. Erik slid onto the bench and began playing quietly, just as a warm-up. Kaveh had gone outside to smoke his pipe, and Fr. Arnaud knelt at the altar, praying. Therefore, when Clémence and Martine came up the aisle together looking grim, the only people they saw were the priest and the slender man they thought was the church organist.

Clémence cleared her throat pointedly. Martine sighed and greeted the kneeling priest. "Good morning, Father."

Fr. Arnaud rose. "Mesdames! How nice it is

to see you both after so long. Have you come for confession? I do have a wedding to prepare for, though."

"Thank you, Father, but we have not come to confess. We have come to—"

"—To ask how can you go through with this farce?" Clémence interrupted.

He raised his white eyebrows in a bland expression. "Now, what farce would that be?"

"To this... this..." Clémence sputtered.

Martine intervened smoothly. "My sister speaks of the marriage you are going to perform this morning, as a farce. She feels it cannot go on."

"Oh? Why is that?" Arnaud noticed that Erik was now using the soft pedal; he suspected the man could hear every word they said. He glanced over at him, hoping his new friend's temper wouldn't get the better of him.

"We feel," Clémence began, with a pointed look at her sister, "that it cannot possibly be a legally binding marriage: my brother's widow with an imposter calling himself the Count de Chagny. You're a respectable man of the cloth, Father; how can you conduct the marriage of that swindler?"

"Swindler? Oh, you mean the rightful and

documented Count de Chagny? I'm only conducting his wedding. He'll have to conduct his
marriage himself." Arnaud heard a snort from
the direction of the organ, and smirked inwardly.

Momentarily speechless, Clémence blinked
and her mouth dropped open in shock. "D-d-
documented?" she stammered, flustered.

"Well-documented, naturally," Fr. Arnaud
assured. "You didn't think I'd perform a wedding for someone who wasn't who he said he
was, did you? No, no, his claim to the title is
legitimate and verified."

"What, exactly, are the documents, Father?"
Martine asked, once again covering for her
younger sister's explosive nature.

The priest nodded toward the office door.
"His baptismal records, to start with."

"How do you know they aren't forged?"
Clémence demanded.

He fixed her with a mild look. "I baptized
him and filled them out myself." He smiled at
her and went on. "There are also some letters
from his mother in the possession of M. Coté,
your family solicitor. You may ask him about
them yourself, later on; I believe he was invited
to attend."

"Indeed he was," Erik offered as he approached them from the organ. "Your pardon, Father; I accidentally overheard your discussion with these *women*." There was a hint of a sneer on his face as he emphasized the last word; the fact that he hadn't called them ladies was not lost on them.

Then he caught a hint of movement at the door and smiled. "Sylvie!" he called in greeting as he rudely brushed past his two cousins and strode toward the door. His sister walked in with a servant.

"How good to see you," Erik said. The servant quietly stepped aside and Erik took Sylvie's hands and exchanged kisses of greeting.

"Hello, Erik! I was hoping you wouldn't mind my early arrival. I came to..." her voice trailed off as she caught the hum of whispered conversation at the front of the church where the priest stood with Sylvie's two cousins. "Erik, who is here? Those voices sound familiar." She spoke quietly.

Erik's powerful voice carried easily to the front of the church. "Oh, it's Father Arnaud and a couple of interfering gossips."

There was an audible gasp of shock from both Martine and Clémence. Erik chuckled under his breath. In a low voice he explained, "I think they're your two cousins; they look as Christine described, and they're here to try and discredit my claim to the title."

"Oh, are they?" Sylvie muttered. She took Erik's arm. "Take me to them, would you, Erik?"

He obliged.

"Sylvie! What are you doing here?" Clémence demanded.

"Just wanted to have a chat with my brother before the ceremony began," Sylvie replied airily. "Have you been introduced yet?"

"Not yet," Martine replied.

Sylvie smiled graciously and turned to Erik. "Erik, may I present my cousins, Martine La-Frenière and Clémence Bourbeau, née de Chagny?"

Father Arnaud grinned behind his hand. Sylvie had pulled a master stroke by introducing the cousins to Erik, rather than the other way around; it clearly showed that he outranked them both.

"Pleased to meet you," Martine replied politely, while elbowing her sister in the ribs.

"Yes, quite pleased," Clémence managed to get out, surreptitiously rubbing her side.

"Erik tells me you two are here to counter his claim on the count's title," Sylvie dove right to the heart of matters. "Let me assure you that his claim has been proven and verified. Our mother wrote to both the solicitor and me before she died, describing the circumstances of his birth. He is the legitimate firstborn child of Count Erik, my father. Uncle Philibert should never have been made count."

"But why?" Martine asked. "Why did monsieur not claim the title then? Why did we never hear of a cousin Erik before now?"

"Erik was a sickly child," Sylvie lied smoothly, copying Christine's story. "They did not know whether he would live, so they kept his existence a secret. Then when his nurse fell down the stairs and died, Erik became frightened and ran away from home. When my father died, they could not find my brother, and so the title passed to your father."

Erik nodded, impressed with her facile explanation. "Quite so. My apologies, cousins; I had not realized it was you, when my sister came in."

Clémence and Martine were slightly taken aback at seeing the friendly affection between their two cousins. Sylvie had been ostracized for so long they had nearly forgotten about her—and now, to see her on the arm of the new count was disquieting. Would their positions in the family change, now that it was known their father wasn't a true count after all? What would their husbands say?

Ever practical, Martine was the first one to realize that Erik was now the patriarch of the de Chagny family—and therefore, it behooved her to try and get on his good side.

"Our apologies, dear cousin," she effused. "My sister and I never meant to cast any aspersions upon your character. The Chagny name is an old and respected one, however, and I'm sure you can understand our reservations at hearing there was a new member of it." She held out her hand and Erik gave her a long, cool look with his golden eyes before gingerly taking it.

"We know so little of you, you see," Clémence added, obviously fishing for information.

Erik offered nothing. "I am a very private man," he agreed.

"Yes, but now that you're family, you must give us a chance to get to know you!" Clémence exclaimed.

"I must?" Erik responded coldly. "Oh, I don't think so. I feel I already know as much about you as I wish to. I know about how you worshipped your older brother, coddled your younger one until he was useless, insulted his wife, pauperized and ostracized your own cousin. Now I find you here in the church on the morning of my wedding, trying to prove I'm not who I say I am.

"Let me say this: the de Chagny name may be old and respected by some, but never by me. If it makes you feel better, let me assure you that I will not be using it. I would not sully my reputation with it—and if you knew my reputation, you would know what a statement that is! I may be the Count de Chagny in title, but in name I'm reverting back to the old count's surname. I am Erik de Carpentier. My wife will be Christine de Carpentier, and we both consider it an improvement." Erik placed his hand on top of Sylvie's, still resting on his arm. "If you'll excuse us, I have a wedding to prepare for. Good day." He turned abruptly and went back up to the organ with Sylvie.

He watched as Martine and Clémence slunk away speechless into a pew, and grinned. "God, that was fun," he muttered.

Sylvie chuckled. "Bravo, Erik; quite a performance."

"No, my dear; the real performance is yet to come. That was just the overture. Wait till they hear me play and Christine sing. Then they'll understand why she will not be leaving the stage."

"Perhaps you'll start a new trend, of the nobles performing in public," Sylvie suggested with a smile.

Kaveh came in then, smelling of tobacco. He sensed the residual tension in the air and glanced around. "Did I miss something?"

"Yes," Erik told him. "You've missed meeting my sister. Sylvie, this is my good friend, Kaveh Tallis. He'll be standing up with me. Kaveh, my sister, Sylvie de Chagny."

As Sylvie and Kaveh went through hand-kissing and greeting rituals, Erik grinned. "Sylvie is blind," he explained, "And thus is spared the sight of your ugly face."

Kaveh just smiled. "And a good thing, too," he remarked evenly. "If your face is typical of Chagny standards of beauty, I can quite see how mine might prove startling. Madame must be a rare exception."

Erik laughed and agreed, thinking of Clémence and Martine. They were beautiful on the outside, but their spitefulness had ruined his perception of their looks. He much preferred his sister's face with its laugh lines and placid beauty.

Kaveh asked, "So what else did I miss?"

As Sylvie began telling him about the confrontation between Erik and their cousins, Erik's eyes were drawn once again towards the door. The church had slowly begun filling up, but he wanted to make sure he saw Christine's coach when it arrived. He was wearing his life-like rubber mask, and he wanted to cover it with his usual white one so he didn't startle her.

He showed Sylvie to a seat near the front (and far away from their cousins). The priest came over and offered, "If you'd like to make another confession before the ceremony begins, Erik, I'm at your service."

Erik frowned. "No."

"Haven't committed any sins since last time, eh?" Arnaud pressed him easily. "No intimidating elderly priests or corrupting town officials? No impersonating honest policemen? No impure thoughts of your bride?"

Erik's eyes flashed gold. "Any thoughts of my bride are pure by association. She's an angel, unsullied; any thoughts I've had of her have been looking forward to when we are married, and are therefore more of a sacrament than an impurity. I will not confess to what is no sin."

Arnaud had been a priest for decades, but he was pleased with Erik's answer. "Very well, then. So... no more lies lately, then?"

"No."

Kaveh protested. "How about to the managers of the opera? You can hardly claim to have told them the whole truth, Erik!"

Erik shook his head. "Not the whole truth, perhaps, but not once did I tell them anything that was false. No, Father," he said, turning back to Arnaud. "I have nothing to confess."

"Good thing; here comes your bride."

Erik turned swiftly to see the coach slowing down to let out the passengers. He snatched his white mask out of his pocket and tied it on, and then went to meet Christine.

Darius got out first, and offered a gallant hand to Meg and her mother. He turned back to help Christine out as well, but Erik got there first and neatly stepped in front of him to offer his hand to his bride.

She got out and his jaw dropped. Her wedding-dress was beautiful, a pale blue silk that matched her eyes, hugged her torso, and rustled luxuriously as she stepped down. He took both of her hands in his. "You look lovelier than I've ever seen you, my dear."

"You look very handsome too, my love," Christine said with a smile. She stood up on her tiptoes to kiss him, but he backed up a step. She frowned; it looked as if there were something wrong with his white mask. It was oddly shaped, bulging in the center.

"Wait a moment, Christine. Come with me; I have a surprise for you." He led her into the cool darkness of the church; the others followed at a distance, to give them some privacy.

"What is it? It must be important if you won't even accept a kiss first," she teased.

"Not as important as a kiss, but I thought you might like it," Erik replied. He reached back and untied the mask, and pulled it slowly from his face.

Christine gasped. Erik looked like a normal man.

"What—what—" she stuttered in disbelief.

He smiled, the expression taking on a whole new aspect when he wore this mask. "Remember long ago, in my ravings to you beneath the Opera,

I told you I had made a mask which would make me look like any ordinary man? I went back and found it; I thought it might be nice to wear for our wedding. What do you think?"

Christine looked it over very carefully. When she studied it, she could see the edges of it just below his eyes and above the top of his upper lip. The mask did not make him handsome—oh, no—his chin was still too bony and his brow overhung his deep-set, golden eyes—but it made him look ordinary. No one would give Erik a second look if he walked down the street wearing this mask!

"I wish we could be married without your wearing a mask at all, my love, but this one is far and away better than your others." She stood on her tip-toes again. "Now may I get a kiss?"

Smiling, Erik bent down, touched his lips lightly to hers, and then straightened and offered her an arm. "Come, my dear; shall we go and be married?"

"I think that a fine idea, sir—surely one of your best!"

"Well, I thought so," he replied modestly.

Father Arnaud met them both at the front of the church. "Good morning, madame!" he greeted Christine. "Still want to marry this ugly fellow, do you?" He was so full of *bonhomie* that Erik didn't even so much as stiffen at the words; after all, they were true, were they not?

"I certainly do, Father!" she replied, smiling. "And the sooner, the better!"

"Very well, then, let us get started."

The other wedding-guests had arrived while Erik and Christine were talking. He looked out and saw that Anneke, Darius, and a few other servants had followed them in a second carriage. Christine had invited whomever among the household staff wanted to attend.

"Oh, dear," Christine murmured. Erik glanced over to see her eyes trained on Clémence and Martine in the second row. "Raoul's sisters," she explained. "I'd been hoping they would decide not to come."

Erik patted her hand. "I wouldn't worry about them, *ma douce*. They won't cause any trouble. I've seen to that."

"Oh, Erik," Christine exclaimed with dismay. "You didn't threaten them, did you?"

"Threaten them? What kind of a man do you take me for?" Erik protested innocently. "I'll have you know I never threaten." He gave a wolfish grin, white teeth sparkling in his homely, masked face. "I occasionally promise consequences, but I never threaten."

Christine gave him a sharp look. "You didn't promise them any consequences for anything, did you, Erik?"

"No," he admitted. "Our conversation stalled before it reached that point. I think we were all glad."

Christine sighed and shook her head with a smile.

Erik grinned and indicated a new pair of guests who had just come in. Christine smiled and waved at Erik-Daaé and his nurse, a rosy-faced, comfortable-looking woman dressed in black taffeta, with a silent, dark-haired cherub with giant blue eyes.

Christine had talked to her son the day before, and told him that she was going to marry M. Erik—that he would become a part of their family and they would all love each other. Erik-Daaé was a little skeptical of the whole wedding aspect of it (he was not fond of having to go out among other people) but he was eager for M. Erik to be part of the family.

"And after M. Erik and I are married, he'll be your step-father," Christine explained to the little boy. "Your *beau-père*."

"Beau?" Erik asked, pointing to his own face.

"He will become handsome when you are married?"

Christine smiled sadly. She should have foreseen the fact that Erik-Daaé might be confused by the French word for step-father, which was quite similar to the word for handsome. "No, *cheri*. M. Erik will never be handsome. '*Beau-père*' means he's not your real father, but will be married to me and will act like a father to you," Christine explained.

"What's a father?"

Christine blinked in disbelief. She had told her son about his papa, and about his death and all, at least as much as she thought he could understand. He had never met Raoul, though, and had no frame of reference for a father.

"A father is... well, a father is just like a *maman*, only he's a man," she finally explained lamely. "And he's not called *maman*, but *papa*."

"Oh." To her surprise, the explanation seemed to satisfy the little boy. He thought about it for a few minutes and then asked, "M. Erik will become my papa, then?"

"Yes, that's right. When M. Erik and I get married tomorrow, he will be your *papa* just like I am your *maman*."

Erik nodded, satisfied. "And then he will bring me a bull for Escamillo."

Christine chuckled. "Yes, he very well may. Or more likely some soldiers for 'Faust,' if I know Erik," she continued half to herself.

Now, watching them come in and sit down, Christine smiled at her son and waved. He lifted one hand, very solemnly, and waved back—and then tucked his hand back into his lap and looked around to see if anyone had noticed. She felt Erik chuckle beside her.

"And I thought *I* was timid around others," he murmured, amused. "Your son has me beat."

Kaveh came and took his place next to Erik, and Christine touched Erik's arm and went to the back of the church to walk down with Meg. She stopped briefly to speak with Sylvie, and then turned to walk down to the front.

Erik smiled, sitting down at the organ again. He had written this bridal march several years ago for Christine, and his heart filled with a poignant joy at his finally being able to share it with her. She looked so beautiful in her simple gown of pale blue that his eyes filled with tears. She carried the bouquet of flowers that Erik had asked Meg to bring to the church for her.

Father Arnaud began the ceremony with a blessing on the couple, and then went directly into asking whether there were any legal objections to this marriage?

Erik glared at his two cousins, and they refused to meet his eyes. There were no objections.

The priest continued, asking Erik and Christine for their consent to be wed.

He spoke in the Latin of the church, asking Erik if he accepted Christine as his lawful wife in the holy sacrament of matrimony? If he did, reply, "*Volo.*"

Erik locked eyes with Christine and made his answer quietly. "*Volo.*" I will.

Arnaud asked Christine the same thing.

"*Volo,*" Christine replied.

Father Arnaud reached for their hands and joined them together, right hand to right hand. "Now you may make your vow to the lady," he murmured. Erik had told him he didn't want to repeat after the priest, but wanted to make his own vow, himself.

"I, Erik de Carpentier, take thee, Christine Daaé, for my lawful wife, to have and to hold, from this day forward, for better, for worse, for richer, for poorer, in sickness and in health, until death do us part." His voice gained strength as he spoke, until even their servants sitting in the back could hear him easily.

Christine hid her amusement at Erik's forgetting the de Chagny part of her name, and made her own vow to him.

Father Arnaud smiled, and stood up straight, intoning, *"Ego conjugo vos in matrimonium, in nomine Patris, et Filii, et Spiritus Sancti."* I join you together in marriage, in the Name of the Father, and of the Son, and of the Holy Ghost. He sprinkled them both lightly with holy water, grinning at Erik's surprised gasp, who hadn't been expecting it.

Then he held out his hand, and Erik placed the ring in it, a plain gold band that Christine recognized. Her hand flew to her mouth—she had never expected to see that ring again! She had left it in the jewelry box with all of her letters!

Father Arnaud continued in Latin to bless them both, and then he held up the ring. He sprinkled holy water over it and made the sign of the cross. He prayed over it and handed the ring back to Erik, who took Christine's hand in his. He kissed it and reverently slid the ring onto her finger. "With this ring I thee wed," he said in a low, vibrant voice, "and I plight unto thee my troth."

Father Arnaud smiled at Erik's almost worshipful tone, and continued, *"In nomine Patris, et Filii, et Spiritus Sancti. Amen."* He closed his eyes and prayed, again in Latin.

When he got to the *"Kyrie eleison,"* Erik and Christine provided the response in a quiet murmur. *"Christe eleison."*

"Kyrie eleison," Arnaud repeated, and then went on. His voice took on a certain urgency as he implored the Lord, *"Esto eis, Domine, turris fortitudinis a facie enimici."* Be unto them, Lord, a tower of strength, from the face of the enemy. Arnaud thought that life probably still had some unpleasant surprises in store for this unconventional couple; they could use the Lord's protection from the enemy.

"Amen," Erik agreed, and then turned questioning yellow eyes to the priest. "What comes next?"

Arnaud smiled and said, "That's it, Erik. In the sight of God and man, for better or worse... you're married now."

"Even though he forgot to include my previous married name?" Christine asked.

The priest nodded. "It hardly matters at this point, as your name is now his. Yes, you're married. Now then, my boy, are you planning to kiss your bride, or were you waiting around for someone else to do it for you? Because you know, much as I'd like to, I'm not allowed..."

His teasing trailed off as Erik turned toward Christine and gently, tenderly, cupped her face in his hands and lowered his lips to hers.

"That's better," Arnaud muttered. "Don't know how I would have explained it to my bishop."

The kiss lasted several seconds, and then Erik tucked Christine's hand through his arm and led her over to the organ. She stood next to him as he played, and when he nodded to her, she opened her mouth and sang the Gloria. Her beautiful, clear soprano rang out, echoing in the nearly empty church as she effortlessly sang the difficult Latin phrases.

Gloria in excelsis Deo, et in terra pax hominibus bonae voluntatis.
Laudamus te, benedicimus te, adoramus te, glorificamus te, gratias agimus tibi propter magnam gloriam tuam, Domine Deus, Rex caelestis, Deus Pater omnipotens.
Domine Deus, Agnus Dei, Filius Patris,
qui tollis peccata mundi, miserere nobis;

qui tollis peccata mundi, suscipe depreca-
tionem nostram.
Qui sedes ad dexteram Patris, miserere no-
bis.
Quoniam tu solus Sanctus, tu solus Domi-
nus, tu solus Altissimus, Iesu Christe,
cum Sancto Spiritu: in gloria Dei Patris.
Amen.[12]

It was amazing, and quite obviously Erik's own arrangement. Christine closed her eyes and clear, crystal-pure sound issued from her. She reached the highest notes with ease, landing on them flawlessly and without strain. As a priest, Arnaud had never been to the opera. He had nothing to compare Christine's voice to, except perhaps to his imaginings of how an angel sounds when singing glory to God for the pure

---

[12] Glory to God in the highest, and on earth peace to those of good will. We praise You, we bless You, We adore You, We glorify You, We give thanks to You for
your great glory, Lord God, Heavenly King, God the Almighty Father.
Lord Only-begotten Son, Jesus Christ, Lord God, Lamb of God, Son of the Father,
You Who take away the sins of the world, have mercy on us.
You Who take away the sins of the world, hear our prayer.
You Who sit at the right hand of the Father, have mercy on us.
For You alone are holy, You alone are the Lord, You alone are the Most High, Jesus Christ,
With the Holy Spirit in the glory of God the Father. Amen.

joy of it. He was surprised that a fallen human could even make such sounds. That was it: Christine sounded like an angel from heaven.

If Christine sounded like an angel in heaven, Erik sounded like a fallen seraph when he joined her in song. His voice shared the same clarity, resonance and flexibility as Christine's, but held a certain earthy passion that hers lacked. It was somehow ironic, Arnaud thought—it was like listening to Lucifer sing it, directly after being cast out of heaven. Even in his happiness, Erik's voice held a certain poignancy that brought tears to the eyes of the listener.

There was an instrumental bridge, and Arnaud could hear, for the first time, Erik playing solo. He played without even looking at his music, his burning yellow eyes locked onto Christine's face. The complexities of the music escaped the priest, but he could appreciate the skill and astounding talent that was displayed— especially when he remembered that Erik had written every note of this himself.

When it was over and Arnaud was surreptitiously wiping his eyes on the sleeve of his cassock, he went over to congratulate the new bride and groom.

"I knew you wanted to play your own music, but I didn't expect anything like that!" he confessed freely. "But I must ask why you both felt you must perform at your own wedding, though? I would have thought you'd be glad to have someone else take over that task, so that you could both concentrate on being married."

Erik lifted one eyebrow and handed the priest his music. "Do you know anyone else who could sing this?" he asked. "Or play it?"

Arnaud sucked in a breath as he glanced at the complex dissonances and intricate harmonies in Erik's sheet music. Erik had written it for two singers with incredible ranges— specifically for himself and Christine. Finally Arnaud gave in and laughed, handing the folder back to Erik. "I might have known that someone like Erik de Carpentier would have to complicate everything and have it all his own way—even his own wedding!"

"*Especially* my own wedding," Erik clarified with a smile.

They went down then, and began accepting the congratulations of their friends and neighbors (for several of the neighbors and townsfolk had sneaked in after hearing that the new Comte de Chagny was about to marry the widow of the old one!). For once, even Erik smiled and spoke kindly to his wedding-guests. There seemed to be no end of them; many had crept in during their singing at the end, and were now complimenting both bride and bride-groom on their musical talents as well as on their marriage.

It reminded Christine greatly of her success at the opera, and she couldn't stop smiling; it was far better than she ever could have wished, to find Erik alive and still loving her, to marry him, and to have people finally—on their wed-ding-day, no less!—begin to give him the ad-miration and acclaim that had been so long overdue him.

After quite a while of this, Erik began to feel a little uncomfortable. He still wasn't used to so many people around, and even if they were all friendly and wishing him well, he still began to wish himself away. He sent a panicked glance over someone's head toward Kaveh, who stood on the sidelines watching with an indulgent smile.

The Persian knew his friend fairly well. If he didn't get Erik out of there, his temper would soon start to flare up, and that would bode ill for the start of his married life. He began gently but firmly pushing people aside until he could get to Erik. "Had enough of society for a while?" he muttered.

"Oh, God, yes!" was Erik's heartfelt reply.

"No fear; I'll take care of it," Kaveh assured him. He spoke up loudly, to be heard over the congratulatory din. "My friends, it is time for the *comte* to return home with his new bride!" he announced, clapping Erik on one shoulder to help propel him through the crowd. Erik put his arm around Christine, clamping her to his side as he followed Kaveh, watching him cut through the crowd like the prow of a boat in the water.

Kaveh saw them into their coach and was about to turn away when Erik tucked a leather pouch into his hand. He whispered something to Kaveh, who first looked surprised and then shrugged and gestured for the coachman to drive away. He then turned back to address the crowd. "My friend the *Comte* de Chagny wants you to know that he appreciates your good wishes, and wishes to bestow a token of his esteem upon all of you, his new neighbors!" At this, Kaveh reached into the pouch and withdrew a double handful of gold coins. With a smile, he tossed them into the air over the guests, and then began to gather his own party.

He found Sylvie and quietly invited her back to the house, smiling when she assented. He helped Mme. and Mlle. Giry into the servants' coach with the servants and Erik-Daaé, and then he and Darius mounted the two horses that he and Erik had ridden to the church.

Christine was impressed, when they returned to the Chagny estate. The servants had really outdone themselves in preparing the wedding breakfast. Huge plates of ham, cheese, cakes, and bread covered the sideboard, and several ornate pots of various kinds of tea stood on a little table beside it.

"Erik, this is wonderful!" Christine exclaimed. "But why did you allow all those people to watch us be married? I thought you preferred privacy."

He shrugged, his usual spare one-shouldered gesture. "It's the first time I've ever been in a crowd of people without them all either fleeing in terror or wanting to maim me in some way. Perhaps I just wanted to enjoy the novelty."

"Oh, Erik!" Christine shook her head with a mildly disapproving smile.

"Besides," he continued, coming over to take her in his arms, "I want all my neighbors to know what a lucky man I am, with such a beautiful new bride who sings like an angel!" He bent down for a kiss, and then continued, "I wanted to make sure that you got a chance to meet our neighbors, so that you would have people around here to socialize with when we return."

Eyes glistening at his thoughtfulness, Christine smiled at him. Every so often he reminded her, either with a word or a touch, how well he knew her from reading all of her letters. He remembered how unhappy she had been in Sweden, not having any friends to talk to, and not being able to spend much time with her husband. Erik knew that he would not be very social, himself, but he did want to make sure that Christine would have people to befriend even though he didn't much like crowds himself. She rewarded his generosity with another kiss, just as Kaveh arrived with the priest and all the wedding guests.

"Oh, this is just lovely!" Mme. Giry exclaimed.

"Truly, *Maman*," Meg agreed. "And now I wonder why Christine and M. de Carpentier couldn't have got married when they knew each other before! We certainly weren't invited to her wedding with Raoul!"

"It was in Sweden, Meg—it would have been a very long voyage for something that wasn't very exciting," Christine laughed.

Erik, hearing this, shook his head. "If that boy were alive today, I'd strangle him," he remarked.

"Erik," Kaveh said in a warning tone. "Please, no talk of strangling over breakfast. It makes my stomach upset."

Erik looked innocent. "I wasn't talking of strangling over breakfast, my dear sir. I was talking of strangling in Sweden. Luckily, though, there seems to be some legitimacy to the Biblical passage that tells us to leave our vengeance up to the Lord. Certainly I would never have thought of pitching him over the rail of a ship into the North Atlantic—it took the Almighty to do that."

"Erik!" Christine said, shocked.

She was even more shocked when Father Arnaud laughed. "At least you can't be blamed for that one," he said cheerfully.

"That one, perhaps," Kaveh muttered, "But what about—"

"M. Tallis, please," the priest cut in. "Whatever Erik's sins have been, they have also been forgiven. On his wedding-day especially, there is no need to bring up past violence. Let the dead stay buried."

"Yes," Erik agreed. Then, with a wry humor that astonished both his old friend and his new bride, he continued, "Just make sure not to bury the groom along with them; we're hard enough to tell apart as it is."

There was a moment of stunned silence while Kaveh and the priest processed Erik's casual acceptance of his appearance, and then the priest started to chuckle. Erik smiled then, and Kaveh broke out into a startled laugh. Christine exchanged amused glances with Meg, and Mme. Giry grinned broadly. Neither of them had ever seen Erik's true face, but both had heard rumors, and Christine had told them about Erik's rubber mask.

With the tension broken, the guests began talking and laughing together, and that was when the rest of the guests arrived. Not all of them had been invited; Erik eyed Clémence and Martine suspiciously as they descended on the buffet tables like starving locusts. "At least they'll be well fed," he murmured an aside to Father Arnaud, who drifted over to him with a plate piled high with breakfast.

"And we're all grateful to you for that, my

boy," he replied genially. "And don't worry;
M. Tallis and I will make sure they're all out of
your hair by tea-time."

"Tea-time? My thanks," Erik said dryly. It
was then just past noon. He groaned inwardly
and looked around for Christine. She was chatting happily with the Giry women and one of
the neighbors that he remembered seeing from
the church. He caught her eye and she smiled
and excused herself from the group.

"Miss me?" she asked lightly, taking her
husband's arm.

"Dreadfully. Don't desert me in this horde,
please."

Horde? Christine glanced around. Fr. Arnaud was still there, as was Kaveh and the Giry
women. Sylvie was there talking with Martine
and Clémence, and there were a couple of
neighbors. Christine smiled. By Erik's standards, it probably was a crowd.

"I will happily stay with you. You're by far
the most interesting person in the room anyway." Christine stayed near Erik for the rest of
the time, too happy to do much more than smile
and touch him every now and then.

For his part, Erik reveled in the light
touches, and once he politely excused himself

from the middle of a conversation with Kaveh and Sylvie in order to pull Christine from the room so he could kiss her in the corridor outside.

By the time the "breakfast" guests had cleared out, it was the middle of the afternoon. They went into the drawing room where the bride and groom entertained their guests musically. In the middle of a piece, Erik happened to glance up at Meg, who was practically quivering with constrained tension. Instinctively knowing what she was suffering from, he smiled to himself. He knew how she felt; if there was a piano in the room, he had to be sitting at it; likewise, if there was a large floor in a room with music, Meg had to be dancing.

He gave her a small smile and nodded toward the center of the room. Meg had her shoes off in a flash, and was pirouetting in the center of the floor in a heartbeat.

Meg had come a long way since Erik had lumped her in with little Jammes, whom he had said "danced like a calf." She had grown tall and willowy, with an innate grace that showed in her every movement. Erik hadn't had the chance to watch her dance for several years, and he was quite favorably impressed with the progress he now saw. Her movements were the perfect physical expression of his playing and Christine's glorious voice.

He caught Christine's eye and nodded in approval, and Christine smiled and agreed as she went on singing.

Mme. Giry watched her daughter with a fierce light of pride in her eyes. She was only a lowly box-keeper, dowdy and stout, but her tall, black-eyed daughter had risen to one of the highest positions in the dancing world. And she stood to rise still higher, too: Mme. Giry had not yet given up on Erik's old promise that her daughter would someday be Empress.

She noticed that the green-eyed Persian gentleman couldn't take his eyes off her daughter. Kaveh watching with open-mouthed admiration as Meg leaped and twirled with amazing control, grace, and flexibility. Mme. Giry smiled to herself, wishing that her husband Jules could be there right now, to see this—if only for a moment.

# # #

The maid came in and announced dinner, breaking the spell. It was a quiet meal after the excitement of the day, and Erik found it a welcome reprieve from the constant pressure of making conversation with relative strangers.

After dinner, Mme. Giry loudly declared that it was her bedtime. She wished everyone a good night and promptly headed up the stairs, not bothering to stifle her loud yawn. With her gone, the conversation lagged as the remaining four tried to find things in common to talk about. Finally Christine gave up—and she really was rather tired—and excused herself very prettily. She wished them all goodnight and went up, blushing a little when Meg winked at her.

Erik remained with Meg and Kaveh for a little while longer, chatting with Meg about the most recent opera gossip. He drew her out quite skillfully, and soon Meg was talking freely and joking with the man who used to terrify her and her friends when they were younger. Kaveh didn't say much, but offered a quiet comment here and there that surprised Erik with its acuity about the arts. He had never realized that Kaveh attended the opera for pleasure; self-centeredly, he had always simply assumed that Kaveh had been there simply to spy on him.

Meg replied to Kaveh's comment; he answered, and soon Erik was the one who fell silent, listening to the two of them talk. The thought struck him that he could get used to this. Having women in his house was not the horror that he had used to fear. Neither Christine nor Meg were empty-headed fashion-conscious busybodies who were only interested in being seen. Actually, he rather liked Meg, now that he was getting to know her. And she was quite skilled, he thought. He appreciated how beautifully she had danced, earlier when Christine was singing.

Christine, who was waiting for him upstairs. He rose swiftly and bid a hasty goodnight to the pair.

He didn't hear the indulgent chuckles of his friends as he left.

Chapter 19

"A Consummation Devoutly to be Wish'd"

When Erik got to his room, the first thing he noticed was that the connecting door was open. The second thing he noticed was that Christine was in his room, reading by the gaslights. The warm yellow light turned her blonde hair into spun gold and made her blue eyes look deep and mysterious when she glanced up at him with a smile.

"My love," Erik breathed, nearly overcome by the sight of his wife—his wife!—sitting there in his room, waiting for him on their wedding night.

Christine didn't say anything; she put down her book and came close to him. Reaching up, she carefully undid the ties that held on his rubber mask, and pulled it away. "This was a lovely surprise," she told him quietly, "and for your sake I'm glad you have it. But I wish I could have married you with your real face showing." She placed one hand gently against his sunken cheek, her thumb caressing the prominent cheekbone.

He shrugged. "If it were only us, I would have. I just don't want word to get out that the new *Comte de* Chagny is a living corpse. And you know that others have not been as... accepting... of my looks as you are."

"Well, at least you look like you, now, and I can kiss my husband the way he was meant to be kissed by his wife." So saying, she pulled his head down and met his lips with hers.

The kiss went on for several minutes, and finally Christine was forced to put her head down on his shoulder to catch her breath.

"Oh, Christine," Erik murmured. "Do you have any idea how much I love you?"

She nodded. "I'm just sorry I didn't always love you so well as I do now," she murmured. "When I think of all the time we've missed with each other..." She shook her head, lifting her face to gaze apologetically into his burning yellow eyes.

"We needed the time," he consoled. "We needed the time apart to become who we are now, and learn to love each other properly." His hands roamed down her back, pressing her close to him as he brought his mouth to hers again. Their lips met and clung, as he felt her warm mouth open to him and he nearly cried when he tasted Christine on his tongue. His breath came sharply, almost like sobs, and his hands began to tremble where they rested on her lower back.

He backed away; he had to. Insecurity reared its head and he wasn't even aware of the single tear that slid down his gaunt cheek as he stared at her.

"Erik? Erik, what's wrong?" Christine asked, coming closer.

He held up a hand to keep her away. "Christine... oh, Christine, I'm so unworthy of you," he said brokenly. "You shouldn't have to put up with my beastly desires, my love. You don't have to go through with this; no woman should have to bed a corpse."

"What?" Christine cried. "What 'beastly desires'? Erik, haven't we been through all this before?" She sighed, her breath rattling in her chest as she exhaled her frustration. Taking another deep breath to calm herself, she had a sudden epiphany: Erik was afraid. He had never done this before, and he was practically grasping at straws to keep himself from drowning in uncertainty.

He had never before been anything but completely confident and masterful when he was with her; even that time he had knelt at her feet and kissed her skirt, he had still retained control of the situation. She knew he must be humiliated by having to admit to her, the woman he loved beyond reason, that the most personal and intimate expression of love was something of which he knew nothing.

Christine placed her palm against Erik's hand that he'd put up to separate them. She folded her fingers, intertwining them with his long, cool, slender ones. "Erik," she said softly. "I know that until now, you have been the teacher and I, the student. But for right now, I have a few things to teach you. Are you listening?"

He nodded mutely, slowly closing his hand on hers.

"You are not a corpse. You are a warm and living man who happens to have an unfortunate-looking face."

"Delicately put," he remarked.

"Hush, and listen. Don't interrupt the teacher." Christine adjusted her grip on his hand, so that he wasn't keeping her at arms' length; as she spoke, she took a step closer. He didn't notice; his eyes were locked on hers.

"I love you more than anything," she went on. "More than my career, more than my memory of my father, more than I even loved Raoul," she finished with a blush. "For you understand me, and he never did. Really, my dearest, I'm the one who is unworthy of you after how I treated you." She came closer but without touching him yet, until she could feel the heat of his body against the front of her dress. "And lastly, whatever 'beastly desires' you may feel for me... well, they're not exactly one-sided."

Erik looked startled. Christine went a little pink, but smiled up into his eyes. "Not remotely," she clarified, standing on tiptoe to kiss him again briefly.

Erik lengthened the kiss, and then smiled at her pleased expression. His voice low and husky as he slipped off his shoes and took out his cufflinks, he said, "Then, *Madame* de Carpentier, I shall humbly submit to your tutelage."

One of Erik's greatest skills was the way he could make his magical, angelic voice express every single nuance of what he was feeling at any given time. At the moment he was nearly overcome by desire and love, and the combination of the tone of his voice and the intimate gesture of his beginning to undress sent shivers down the spine of his new bride. She closed her eyes. He touched her cheek briefly, and then ran his graceful hand smoothly down the side of her neck until her breath caught in her throat. "What is your first lesson, then?" he whispered. "For I assure you, the pupil is most willing."

Fighting to control her reactions to him, she opened her eyes. "I dismissed Anneke for the night," she said.

The seeming *non sequitur* made him blink in confusion until he noticed that she was still wearing her wedding-dress—the one with the intricate draping and bustle in back, and the ninety-nine tiny hooks that she couldn't reach by herself. She gave him an impish grin. "Your first lesson is how to be a lady's maid." She turned her back to him and glanced back over her shoulder. "My dearest, would you mind helping me with my dress?"

A sharp intake of breath was her only answer, but after a startled moment, she felt his deft fingers at the nape of her neck as he unfastened the top hook. Then she felt his lips brush her skin there as he went on to the next one. Another few hooks opened the dress wider, and he kissed her shoulder where the dress gaped. Another few hooks, and he was able to press his lips to the middle of her back, just above where her corset covered. Christine shivered.

The rest of the hooks went quickly, and soon the dress was all unfastened. She turned back to face him, with the dress sagging off her shoulders. Her eyes were large and dark blue; she gazed at him for a moment before placing her hands flat against his chest. She slid them up toward his shoulders, nudging his coat off. She touched her lips to his neck, paying no attention to her dress that was nearly falling off. It was his turn to shiver now, as her small, neat fingers went to the buttons of his waistcoat. Next came his silk cravat, which soon went the way of the coat, and her husband stood there in his shirt-sleeves, braces, and trousers.

Unable to stop himself, Erik reached out with both hands and laid them gently on Christine's shoulders. He caressed them gently, stroking down to her upper arms, before repeating the motion. With each stroke, her dress fell a little further down, until finally she pushed it down and stepped out of the pool of lacy pale blue fabric.

She was left in her white silk chemise, beaded corset, and rosebud-embroidered crinolette with its padded *tournure*. Erik, his eyes alight, took a step back to admire the way her skin gleamed ivory in the candlelight. "You are truly lovely," he whispered as he leaned down to taste the skin on her shoulder; she gasped as his teeth scraped over the spot where her neck and shoulder met. She took his hands and brought them around behind her waist. "Untie it, love," she whispered as he fumbled briefly with the ties of her crinolette. Then she stepped out of that as well, and kissed him rapturously as she began undoing his shirt-buttons. She copied him, kissing his chest as she unbuttoned, and his trembling hands made a couple of nervous feints before landing gently in her hair. Then all at once, she pushed shirt and braces together off over his shoulders.

Then she was in his arms again, being kissed with such ardor she felt like she was about to burst into flames. His strong pianists' fingers were gentle, tangling in her hair as he held her face up to his. She stroked his bare shoulders over and over, absently noting the textures of his flesh as she touched, smelled, and tasted Erik.

When the kiss ended, he rested his forehead against hers. "What next, *ma professeur?*" he inquired with a breathless chuckle.

"You're taking my breath away," she accused. "I'm finding it hard to breathe now, and it's all your fault." She gave him a tender smile, eyes twinkling.

"My apologies, my dear. What can I do to make amends?"

"Well, I think getting out of my stays will help me breathe better."

"Say no more. Anything to assist my dearest of teachers." Erik turned her around and pulled her back to lean against him, his hands going around her waist in front. She let her head fall back on his shoulder as he unhooked the bottom hook on her corset-busk. His teeth grazed her ear as he did the next one, and she gasped. The corset only had five hooks, and when he reached the top one and she felt his fingers brush her breast, she shivered. He held her away from him long enough for the corset to fall to the floor between them, and then he tightened his arms again. His hands swooped up to her breasts, her collarbone, back down to her waist, her hips.

"Oh, love," she breathed, turning in his arms to cover his mouth with hungry kisses. "Methinks the pupil is surpassing the teacher now!"

Overcome with emotion, Erik took refuge—as always—in opera. He was a little nervous, though, and decided to keep things light. He substituted his own spur-of-the-moment libretto for Faust's. Softly he sang, *"Ne me permets-tu pas, ma belle professeur, que j'enlève les bras de ta chemise de soie?"*[13]

Christine's jaw dropped and she let out a startled giggle. "Erik!" she exclaimed in mixed amusement and shock. Thinking quickly, she

---

[13] Faust: *"Ne permettez-vous pas, ma belle demoiselle, Qu'on vous offre le bras pour faire le chemin?"*
(Won't you permit me, my beautiful young lady, to offer my arm to help you down the street?)
Erik: *Ne me permets-tu pas, ma belle professeur, que j'enlève les bras de ta chemise de soie?*
(Won't you permit me, my beautiful teacher, to remove your arms from your silken chemise?

gave him a mischievous smile and sang her response. *"Oui, monsieur, quoique tu n'es pas jeune ni beau... n'es pas jeune, ni beau. Et j'ai beaucoup besoin qu'on me donne les mains."*[14]

Erik chuckled in appreciation for her quick wit, and bent suddenly to scoop her up in his arms. "Where shall we go, then, *ma belle professeur?*"

Christine pointed through the door, and Erik somehow managed to squeeze both of them through it sideways. As though she weighed nothing, he carried her over to the bed in the mistress' chamber and laid her carefully on it as though she were made of glass.

She lifted her arms to him and he joined her, raising himself up on one elbow to kiss her some more. He ran one finger down around the low neckline of her shift. "Does this come next, then, my pretty teacher?" he asked, referring to

---

[14] Marguerite: *"Non Monsieur, Je ne suis demoiselle ni belle, demoiselle ni belle, Et je n'ai pas besoin qu'on me donne la main."*
(No, sir, I am not young nor beautiful, young nor beautiful, and I have no need of your proffered hand.)
Christine: *"Oui, Monsieur, quoique tu n'es pas jeune ni beau... n'es pas jeune, ni beau.*
Et j'ai vraiment besoin qu'on me donne la main."
(Yes, sir, though you are neither young nor handsome (be neither young nor handsome), and I have a great need for your proffered hands.)

his playful question about removing her arms from it.

Christine shook her head, her eyes sparkling. "No. Those do," she said, tugging at the waist-band of his trousers.

Erik hesitated. At her encouraging expression, he stood up again and pushed off his shoes. "Very well; a moment, though." He went back into his room and turned off the gas-lights, and then came back into Christine's room and lowered hers to a dim flicker. Then he unbuttoned his trousers and pushed them off. He returned to the bed quickly, too quickly for Christine to be able to see very much of him.

"Erik, why did you lower the lights?"

"It's better this way, trust me," was his quiet reply. "My body is... not all that pleasant to look upon. I would spare you the sight of it."

Christine stroked down his chest to his stomach, where the muscles tightened and quivered under her fingers. "Please, Erik. Your body can't look any worse than your face, and I love your face as if it were mine. Please, I would like to see you."

Erik froze in fear, and then, with a sigh, swung his legs over the side of the bed and stood up with his back to her. He crossed the room to turn up the lights, first one and then the other. He heard a rustling noise, and when he turned back to face Christine, he discovered she had removed her shift. She stood beside the bed in nothing but her skin, which was rapidly turning pink as he gaped at her.

"I hope you don't mind," she whispered. "It seemed only fair, after all."

"You're..." he had to stop and clear his throat, which was threatening to close up. "You're so very, very lovely. My wife."

She took a few steps toward him, her eyes appraising his form frankly. "Erik, you're so..." her eyes swept up to meet his, looking startled. "You're so beautiful!"

He was. His body was long and lean, still slender, but more like whipcord now than a skeleton as it used to be. She could see the contours of his wiry muscles, outlined by the lamplight. He approached her with his natural grace and fluidity, usually obscured by his clothing, that made her knees go weak.

As he drew near, she finally saw why he hadn't wanted her to see him: he was scarred. Horribly, dreadfully scarred, all over. There were lines across his back and shoulders that might have come from a whip; there was a burned mark across his belly shaped like the links of a chain; there was a puckered scar under his breastbone that might have been from an unsuccessful stabbing. There were many more, lower down, that she dared not even think about how they got there.

"Oh, my love," Christine cried, tears springing to her eyes. "What are they all from?"

He lifted one shoulder in a shrug; Christine smiled suddenly, to see his favorite gesture performed *au naturale* when she was used to seeing it translated through all his clothes. "From my enemies," he said simply. "I did say—did I not?—that not everyone has been as accepting of my face as you are." He stepped closer and his voice lowered, with an added edge of sarcasm. "I warned you, my dear, that I was not all that attractive to look upon. You've already seen my face; why should my body be any *more* attractive?" He stopped a few feet away.

Christine went closer, close enough to touch. "If you think these scars make you unattractive to me, Erik, then you're quite wrong," she told him softly. She smiled up at him, her hands moving to rest on his slim hips. "They just point to where I need to kiss you first."

Erik hesitated only a moment before crushing her to him, burying his face in her hair. The shock of feeling Christine's warm, supple skin pressed nakedly against his own was enough to completely take his mind off his scarring and fill it with a whole different sort of images. "Christine, are you sure? Are you very sure?" he demanded in a broken whisper.

She nodded, tipping her head back to face him. "Very sure," she promised. "Please, Erik. You're my husband now. Come and make me your wife."

In a single smooth motion, he scooped her up in his arms and claimed her mouth; his lips never left hers as he lowered her back to the bed and stretched out beside her. And in the next infinite span of time, they lost track of who was the student and who was the teacher, until they finally separated to lie together side-by-side—sated and shattered and very, very much in love.

"I love you," Erik whispered when he could breathe again, with tears wetting his cheeks. "Oh, Christine! I never knew it could be like this. I had dreamed, but in all my years of wanting you, I never dared hope for you to be able to see me as a man."

She rolled over to nestle her head on his shoulder. "We have been a long time getting to this point, that is certain—but my love," she said, stroking his chest, "you've been a man to me ever since that last day when we kissed and cried together. You called yourself a corpse, a dog, a monster, but that was the first time I truly saw you as a man! It was a man that I fell in love with over the years, even when I thought you were dead. It was a man that I wrote all those letters to, when I missed you so much. It was a man that I married this morning, and vowed to spend my life with. And it was a definitely a man with whom I've just consummated it!"

She smiled impishly, and then sobered and shook her head in wonder. "I just never knew it could feel like that, though!" She pressed a kiss to the underside of his jaw. "It has never been like that before, Erik; that was amazing!"

"Was it all right, then?" he asked gravely.

"All right?" she gave a breathless laugh. "That was the single most wonderful experience of my life."

Erik had no reply but to kiss her. His eyes closed as he gathered her in close to him, and soon they were both asleep.

Christine awoke the next morning in Erik's arms. His body was pressed full-length against her back, and one leg was tossed carelessly over hers. She smiled, nestling in closer—this was what she had always wanted to do with her husband, to embrace him in bed, to sleep with him, to wake with him. She rolled a little and turned her head to face Erik. His grotesque face looked peaceful, even happy, and she realized that with all the time they had spent together in his house under the opera, this was the first time she had ever seen him asleep. She smiled tenderly, closing her eyes again and tucking her head under his chin to go back to sleep.

Sleep would not come, however; her bodily needs soon made themselves known. She got up carefully so as not to jostle the bed and wake her husband, slid on her dressing gown, and went into Erik's room to ring for Anneke.

She found and used the chamber pot, and then washed her face. The water in Erik's basin was cold, and she pulled her dressing-gown around her more tightly. Anneke came to the door and Christine gave her orders in a whisper: fresh water, fresh flowers, towels, tea, and breakfast. She closed the connecting door, leaving it just barely ajar while she waited for Anneke's return. She tidied up a little, picked up the clothing they had strewn around the room, and fished into the pocket of Erik's fallen waistcoat for his watch. It was still early.

In less time than she expected, her maid returned with three other housemaids in tow, who were carrying the water, the flowers, and the breakfast trays. Anneke had the towels draped over her arm. Christine directed the others in a whisper where to put the things, and then ushered them toward the door. "The train does not leave for another two hours," she told her maid. "Come up in an hour to help me dress, and we shall join the others for the trip to the station."

Anneke curtseyed, smiling to see how happy her mistress was, and went out. Christine went back into her room, where Erik had rolled onto his back, still sleeping. She got an impish gleam in her eye and took off her dressing gown. She stole back into the bed next to Erik, sliding her naked skin against his, and leaning up on one elbow to kiss him.

His deep-set eyes blinked open sleepily. She bent her head to kiss him again. A ghost of a smile began to quirk his lips, and he pulled her head back down. "*Madame*," he whispered. "This is, without a doubt, the nicest awakening I have ever had."

Christine grinned. "Now, my love," she teased. "*Now*, you have tasted all the happiness the world has to offer."

Erik, remembering his own words to her last week after she had cried with him and kissed him for the first time, laughed freely for the first time he could remember. Was this what Christine had meant when she'd told him "No, you haven't," with such an enigmatic smile? Somehow, he knew it was. What a minx!

"I have tasted it now, it's true," he replied, smiling. "But I haven't had time yet to truly savor it, so if you'll permit me…" he clasped her in his arms and rolled them both so he lay half on top of her. "…I'd like to taste it again."

"I'll permit you," Christine assured him, stroking down along his scarred back, his lean hips, his thighs. "I'll permit you whenever you wish, my dearest. You do have a few years to make up for—and I am yours now, after all."

Erik bent his head to run his tongue along the edge of her bottom lip. "Then perhaps I'll have a longer draught this time," he muttered, swallowing her response with his mouth.

The tea, breakfast, and hot water had all cooled by the time they got to them... but neither one minded the delay.

Chapter 20
Fulfilling a Promise

T he train ride from Rouen back to Paris was rather enjoyable; they rode with the Girys in a private compartment, and Christine enjoyed seeing the cheerfully deferential way in which the older lady addressed Erik. They had a good-natured argument about the man that Meg was to marry, while Meg sat there blushing and interjecting a half-hearted protest from time to time. Christine stifled her giggle more than once.

"No, *Monsieur* Ghost, it won't do for you to go back on your word. You promised me that my little Marguerite would be Empress, and we shan't settle for anything less."

"But *madame*, when I made that promise I was severely overstepping my capabilities. For that I apologize, and beg you to release me from that promise."

"Are you saying that my daughter doesn't deserve to be Empress?"

"No, *madame*. I am sure she is much more deserving than most of those who have held the title; however, I have no way to bring it about. When I initially made that promise with you it was for the sole purpose of gaining your good-will so that I could more easily manipulate you. I have already apologized for that, as I do re-gret trying to deceive such a good woman."

Mme. Giry shook her finger at him. "Oh, *Monsieur* Ghost, you know that is not true! You are far too good a man to want to hood-wink an old woman. No, I trust you, and I trust your capabilities—much more than you do yourself, apparently."

"*Maman*," Meg began. "You know that *Monsieur* de Carpentier has no power to make me Empress! And I wouldn't want to be, any-way. And besides…" Her voice trailed off into a mutter. "We live in a republic."

Her mother spoke up stridently. "Ah, now, I

never said anything about marrying a *French* emperor," Mme. Giry said with a twinkle. "Bonaparte is dead, after all. But someone as well-traveled as M. Ghost surely must know emperors in other countries."

"And I do, but I would never wish the young lady married to those tyrants. Those Turks and Persians can be cruel to their women."

"Are you sure you're not just saying that to sneak in an insult at M. Tallis?" Christine teased him.

The corners of his mouth quirked slightly in acknowledgement, but he sobered. "Kaveh is far and away the best man I have ever known, police officer or otherwise. Although others of his nationality can be violent and callous towards women, he has always been compassionate and respectful of the fairer sex."

"He's not exactly an emperor, though," Christine pointed out with a sly grin at Meg. She had noticed the open-mouthed admiration with which Kaveh had watched Meg's impromptu dance the day before, and Erik had told her about leaving the two of them in a *tète-á-tète* when he came up the night of their wedding. She knew that nothing would ever come of such an attraction even if they did share one, but it was fun to tease her friend.

Meg just sighed and shook her head at all this foolishness. "Christine! Don't encourage them, I beg you," the dancer entreated. "It's bad enough, the way your husband provokes and torments poor M. Tallis, without getting me involved as well!"

Christine laughed. "I assure you, 'poor' M. Tallis gives Erik back as good as he gets from him, Meg."

"You think so, do you?" Erik asked his wife good-naturedly.

She only smiled at him and squeezed his hand. He returned the squeeze and then turned his attention back to Mme. Giry. "*Madame*, I give you my word that such emperors as I become acquainted with, I shall surely send your way. But I must ask whether a nobleman would suffice?"

"M. de Carpentier, it's really not necessary!" Meg spoke before her mother could. "I would really rather just continue dancing!"

"Ah, but you can't dance forever, my girl," her mother pointed out. "Another few years and you'll have to quit anyway. It will be far easier to give up if you have a rich, adoring husband by then."

"*Maman*!" Meg cried, scandalized.

Erik laughed. "Don't be so down on your mother, little Giry," he said, lightly using her old nickname from the opera. "She's a very astute woman. And, to hold up my end of the bargain I made with her, I promise I shall do my best to see you settled with a rich, adoring husband long before you get too old to dance. And do not worry, my dear," he winked at Meg. "We shall make sure that he is someone you'll adore as well, even if he is not an emperor. Will that do, *madame*?" he addressed Mme. Giry.

"Very well, *monsieur*, very well, and I thank you!" The old woman sat there beaming toothlessly. With her old friend the Opera Ghost now a nobleman and out in society, he was sure to come in contact with far more members of the nobility than she ever could. Now that she had extracted his promise to keep her marriageable daughter in mind, she was content.

Mme. Giry was no fool.

They left the Girys off in Paris and as the train chugged southward, Christine fell into a doze with her head against Erik's shoulder. They were the only ones in their compartment as the sun began to set, and the clacking of the wheels had a soporific effect on her.

Chapter 21
Provence

Erik woke her when the train pulled into Sète. "Christine, my love. We are here." She stirred and lifted her head from his shoulder, stretching her neck.

"Where is 'here'?" she asked, peering out the window.

Erik swung the door open and Christine caught a whiff of tangy salty air. "Sète." He handed their bags out to the porter, who lugged them over to the carriage and grunted a syllable or two to the sleepy driver. Erik helped his wife into the carriage, the driver snapped his whip, and they lurched into motion.

Christine was suddenly no longer sleepy.

The cool, salt-scented air acted like a tonic on her, reminding her of happier times when she was young. "Oh, Erik, this is wonderful!" she exclaimed, leaning her face out the window to let the night air blow on her. "Is it like this all the time?"

He put his arm around her and leaned in to brush a kiss against her neck under her ear. "The air? Yes. Breathing this air is one of the main reasons I regained my health, living here. Well, that, and Kaveh stubbornly refused to allow me to die."

"Good of him," Christine remarked tartly. Then, "How far is it to the cottage?" she asked.

"Not far. The town isn't very large."

There was a meal laid out for them on the table when they got there. "Erik, where did the dinner come from?" Christine wanted to know.

He smirked. She was slowly getting used to actually seeing his facial expressions; for so long she'd had to depend on learning his emotions through his voice alone, or from the expression in his glowing yellow eyes, or from the slump of his shoulders. It was odd and a little exciting to see his feelings actually show up on the irregular skin of his unmasked face, for he had taken off the rubber mask as soon as they had come into the house.

"I sent ahead for our housekeeper to prepare the house for our return. She lives down in the village. We should probably dine quickly and get to bed, because I'd wager she'll be up here first thing in the morning to gawk at the masked man's bride."

Christine chuckled and gave him a flirtatious look. "Well, let's hope she has the decency not to come up too early, or else she might see something she wasn't looking for!"

Erik's eyebrows went up at his new wife's comment, and his smirk turned into a genuine smile of mirth. "Christine! I had no idea you were such a vixen."

She reddened a little as she sat down to the meal. "Neither did I. It must be something you bring out in me."

"Then I'm flattered," he replied with a grin, before leaning over to kiss her.

After dinner Erik had to act as lady's maid again, helping Christine out of her travelling clothes. Neither one minded, though, because she then got to act as valet and help him out of his own. And afterward, Christine fell asleep in the arms of the man she loved, with his lean, naked body pressed up against her own, and she was content.

Thus began the most blissful month either of them had ever known. The housekeeper, Mme. Blaine, came up from the village every day to clean and prepare meals for them (and sure enough, she had come up especially early the first morning!), but otherwise left them alone. Erik delighted in showing Christine the small but comfortable cottage where he had lived for the last five years. Christine especially liked the music room, as she recognized many of its furnishings from his house below the opera.

Erik took her out sea-bathing with him, and was surprised to find she could swim like a fish. He could swim well, too, after having lived on a lake for all those years, and the two of them frequently spent whole afternoons in the water. The cottage was located next to a long stretch of sandy beach, where, Erik explained, hardly anyone but themselves ever went.

He donned his old white silk mask for their forays into the village, where Mme. Blaine had told everyone all about the masked man's lovely new bride. Christine soon won their hearts by her warmth, her friendly smile, and (best of all, according to the curious townsfolk) sharing a little of the story of how she knew Erik.

It was such a romantic story that soon everyone in the town knew it, and delighted in whispering pieces of it among themselves whenever Erik and Christine came to the market. "She was a singer, she said, and he was her teacher. He was sick—remember how he was, when the Persian fellow first moved here with him? —and she thought he had died, so she married someone else. Her husband died in the navy, and she only recently discovered her teacher was still alive!"

Christine heard the whispers and smiled to herself. If they only knew the whole story, instead of the watered-down version she had made public!

But Erik was so different from the man she had known beneath the opera house, that she was drawn to spend hours at a time—whole days, even, just talking with him and getting to know him. Erik enjoyed the attention... especially on those days when they didn't leave the bedchamber.

He reflected that Mme. Blaine probably told the rest of the village about that, too, but for once he didn't really care. He was pleased to think that finally, after almost half a century, he was getting to live like any other man with his wife.

Christine sent semi-weekly letters back to Paris, to the Girys, to Sorelli, to her own household to see how Erik-Daaé was doing. She missed her little son dreadfully, and made Erik promise to bring her son along the next time they traveled.

Erik spent his spare time that month drawing up plans for an expansion to the cottage so that his entire household could winter there, and he had the contractor hired a week later. "By the time we return in the winter, it will look like a whole different cottage," he said, rubbing his hands with anticipation.

"Pity," Christine said with a wistful smile. "I'll have very fond memories of honeymooning here in this one."

Erik embraced her. "And honeymooning here with you has helped to heal some memories of mine, so that was helpful." At Christine's puzzled glance, he explained only, "I was very ill here, for a very long time."

He sobered. He had never told Christine how Kaveh and Darius had had to keep watch on him day and night for several weeks, to keep him from suicide. He had been lucky, really, that he'd been too physically weak to fight Kaveh when his friend had forced him out of bed and dragged him, quite literally, into the sea.

The first time Kaveh brought him into the sea, he had tried to drown Erik. Kaveh had held his head under water for what seemed like hours, but Erik's sense of self-preservation had kicked in. He had pushed Kaveh away and fought his way back to the surface, glaring daggers at him.

Dripping and panting, Kaveh had nodded at him. "There, I thought so. You haven't lost your will to live or else you would have let me kill you, Erik. So now that you know you still want to live, how about starting to?"

That night Erik had taken some food for the first time in over a week, and the next morning he got out of bed and dressed himself of his own volition. The effort exhausted him so much he had immediately gone back to sleep, but the next day he did it again and stayed up longer. The next day, even longer.

Kaveh was not a cruel man. He had merely done what needed to be done. It had been a hard lesson, but now Erik was grateful for it.

He had already told Christine about the

other times that Kaveh had saved his life; someday he would tell her about this one as well... but not yet. Their happiness was still too new, too fragile and exquisitely delicate. He didn't want to risk it yet.

And he had other things to think about now, anyway. It was almost time for Christine to audition for the Company at the opera. He worked with her several hours a day now, and once her voice had got back into shape, it had become better than ever. He breathed a big sigh of contentment as he heard her singing scales on her own as she puttered about the cottage. She was better than she had ever been before, even when she had brought Paris to its knees. He nodded. She would get in. He told her so, and she smiled.

Then the smile faded. "Um, Erik? What... what about my students?"

"What about them?"

"Well, if I'm singing leads as we hope I do, I shall be involved too much in rehearsals to have time to continue teaching my students."

Erik frowned. Her students were really the least of his worries. "They'll have to find someone else."

"But there is no one else," she said. "No one

who's any good. Remember my writing to you about how abysmal the vocal coaches were? I wished I could have found one like you..." She stopped speaking suddenly, cocking her head to the side as she gazed at her husband thoughtfully.

"What are you thinking in that lovely blonde head of yours, my dear?" Erik asked playfully, twirling one of her curls around his finger.

"Erik... why don't you take over my students?"

"Me?"

"Yes! You're a wonderful teacher. Look what you did with my voice!"

"Your voice was exceptional to begin with, and besides, what I did for your voice was mostly for love of my student," he reminded her.

She melted into his arms and pressed her mouth to his. "And every time I sing now, I do it for love of my teacher," she admitted quietly.

But her idea had her too excited to be distracted by kisses and caresses. "Think, then, about the fact that you would be training the future opera singers, both the leads and the chorus. For the sake of the quality of the music itself, at least promise me you'll think about it?"

"For the quality of the music itself, eh?" he mused. "Might have known you'd choose one of the two arguments that I couldn't resist. All right, *ma douce,* I'll think about it."

"Wonderful! Just think of what you did for Jean-Michel's voice in just one lesson when he didn't even know you were there! I know you could train the best company in all of Europe if you wanted to!" She paused a moment, and then slid one hand up behind his head to toy with his thin black hair. "Just out of curiosity, my love... what was the other argument that you couldn't resist?"

He lowered his head and touched his lips to her forehead. "When you allow me to kiss you, my dear," he said humbly, "it completely melts my heart. You can do anything you like with me, then." He kissed her again, his lips lingering against her warm, smooth skin. "Oh, it is so good to kiss someone on the forehead, Christine!" he rejoiced. "You just cannot know how good it is."

Christine brought his head down further, and captured his lips in a searing kiss. "You may kiss me anywhere you like," she whispered. "I'm yours, Erik. All yours."

At that, the subject of Christine's students seemed to pale into insignificance.

Chapter 22
Home Again

The month came to an end all too soon, and it was time for them to return to Paris for the auditions. They moved back into Christine's flat only two days before auditions were scheduled to begin. The next day, the rest of the household arrived from Rouen.

"Maman! Maman!" Erik-Daaé shouted as he raced through the door into the flat. His nurse followed at a distance, looking exhausted.

Christine knelt down in the entryway, laughing. "Hello, *cheri*! Did you miss us?"

Erik, standing behind her, could have kissed

her for the easy way she said "us" instead of just "me."

"Ouiiiiiiiii!" the little boy affirmed as he leaped into his mother's arms. He remained there for a brief span of seconds and then wriggled down to the floor again. He went over to Erik and looked up at him. He had to tip his head back as far as he could; Erik towered over him.

"Bonjour," Erik greeted the small boy gravely.

"Bonjour. Maman says you are my *papa* now."

Erik inclined his head. "Did she."

"Oui! And she says that a *papa* is just like a *maman*, only he's a man."

"That is essentially correct. Both are parents."

"She says you will be my *beau-père.*"

Erik's lips twitched at the sobriquet. "Yes, I am now your *beau-père*, even if I am far from *beau*. You'll be my handsome stepson, though, Erik-Daaé."

"Yes." Erik-Daaé agreed. "You are just like my *maman*, now, *monsieur?*"

"In a manner of speaking, yes."

Erik-Daaé nodded, and with determined and

serious intent, he went closer to Erik and hugged him tightly around the thighs. Then, overcome with his usual sudden shyness, he ran away up the stairs.

Erik watched him go, bemused.

Christine chuckled. "Don't worry, my love; he was just welcoming you the way he knows parents are supposed to be welcomed."

"Ah." Erik continued gazing up the stairs, lost in thought. He loved Christine more than life, and would happily give her anything she ever wanted... but in finding her and marrying her so fast, he had not really given much thought to his new role as a stepparent. He knew nothing of children, save that they usually shrieked and ran away in fear when they saw him. He still was not used to Erik-Daaé's matter-of-fact acceptance.

Being Erik-Daaé's *beau-père* was definitely going to be an experience.

Kaveh and Darius had stayed in the Rouen house while Erik and Christine took over their Provence cottage, but with the couple's return to Paris, they returned as well. Supper that night was a jolly event, with every member of the new household present for the first time. Christine ate her meal with her eyes sparkling in amusement as she listened to Kaveh and Erik argue and bait each other. The discussion heated up in a matter of moments.

When Darius offered her a refill of her wine, she touched his arm lightly and asked in a low voice, "Is this how they've been for the last five years, Darius?"

Not quite smiling, the manservant shook his head. "No, *madame*. During our first year all together, they used to fight quite a lot."

"As opposed to now?" Christine asked dryly, watching Erik lean across the table to shake a furious finger in Kaveh's face as he replied to him through gritted teeth. Kaveh's color rose as he leaned forward and retorted just as sharply.

Darius gave another almost-smile. "Yes, *madame*," he said. "As opposed to now."

"I see," she murmured. "Thank you, Darius."

Next morning, the two men greeted each other with cordial smiles, and Christine just shook her head.

Richard and Moncharmin were holding open auditions that day, and after spending a leisurely morning warming up and getting reacquainted with Erik-Daaé after a month's absence, Christine and Erik walked over to the Opera. For her audition, Christine brought a new piece that Erik had written for her over a three-day stretch during their honeymoon. It matched her more mature voice splendidly, and instead of leaving her drained and fainting, as she used to feel when she sang, this piece seemed to infuse her with new energy.

It was a joyful, triumphant, almost religious piece, which stirred the blood and made the heart race with happiness. Erik had told her this particular piece had come to him, nearly in its entirety, during their wedding as he listened to Christine make her vows to him. He said it described his mood at that moment quite perfectly.

Moncharmin and Richard had tried to curry favor with Erik when they thought he was just the *Comte de* Chagny, but now that they knew he was also the former Opera Ghost, they virtually abased themselves before him. Erik had to come out and tell them quite plainly that he was retired from his former employment as a phantom, and that he was there that day solely in the role of loyal and supportive husband for the future diva.

Which is not to say that he made no veiled

threats of what "accidents" might occur if they hired anyone of a lesser talent than he felt "his" opera house deserved. He did have a reputation to uphold, after all.

When Christine sang, Erik played her accompaniment, and the managers and the audience could not even respond for several seconds after the piece was finished. Christine stood up and made her curtsey to them, and Erik a stiff, shallow bow, and they had made their way completely across the stage before both managers leaped to their feet applauding wildly. Then the cleaning staff, the other auditioners, and the rest of the staff who had happened to be within listening distance, also joined in and applauded them both.

So five years after she had deserted the Opera, Christine was re-hired by the same managers and offered the lead in *La Juive*, which would be the opera's season opener.

Erik was contented. Christine had finally reached the heights for which he had trained her. Best of all, she was *his* now. Since he had been hers from the very beginning of their acquaintance, the imbalance of their relationship had finally been corrected. Life was good.

He was slowly getting more comfortable

with his new stepson, also, even playing with him sometimes. Their favorite game was to act out the operas with Erik-Daaé's toy animals, but Erik—hoping that the boy's obsession with Bizet would fade—still had not provided him with a bull for Carmen.

The shy little boy eventually got used to the two strangers who moved into "his" house. He accepted Erik more or less right away, due to Erik's music and magical tricks, but it took him far longer to get used to Kaveh and Darius. Kaveh finally won him over by bringing a piece of wood and a penknife with him one day, when the little boy was playing outside with his nurse. He did not speak or look at the boy, but seated himself on a highly visible rock and began carving.

Intrigued, Erik-Daaé drifted closer, where he watched for nearly forty minutes before his curiosity finally got the best of him and he asked, "What are you doing, *monsieur?*"

Kaveh did not look up from what he was doing. "Carving."

"Why?"

"I like to carve, and to make things."

This piqued the child's interest, and he thought it over for several silent minutes before asking the crucial question. "What are you making?"

"A bull."

"Why?"

"I like bulls. Don't you?"

"Oh, yes, *monsieur*!" Erik-Daaé replied, his excitement finally getting the better of his shyness. "I wish to fight them, when I am big."

"I'll bet you sometimes pretend to fight them even now, while you're little. Don't you?"

"Oh, yes, *monsieur*!"

Kaveh finally dared to look up and smile at the small boy. "When my bull is finished, would you like to play with him with me?"

Erik-Daaé bounced a little in his excitement. "Oh, yes, *monsieur!*" His tiny face was all smiles.

Kaveh grinned. "I'll wager your papa will like my bull, as well."

Erik's dry, quiet voice drifted over from around the corner. "I'll wager you're right." As he hadn't yet obtained a toy bull, he had once been pressed into performing the bull's part himself. It had made him feel ridiculous. He could never get used to the unself-conscious way that Christine played with her son, pretending things right along with him. It always made him feel foolish. He was beginning to love young Erik-Daaé on his own merits, but still had no idea how to relate to the child when music was not part of the equation.

By the end of the day, the new wooden bull had been finished, christened in play, and Kaveh was no longer a stranger to Christine's son. Indeed, all it took was a carved horse a week later before he was "Uncle Kaveh" instead of *"monsieur."*

Chapter 23
Gossip

With the opera season well underway, Christine was frequently away evenings. Erik always attended performances; he found it amusing and ironic to purchase his old box for the entire opera season. He never tired of hearing his Christine's crystalline, angelic soprano; the regular attendees soon became used to seeing his bony and unattractive (rubber-masked) visage watching from box five whenever La Carpentier performed.

He was frequently accompanied by a distinguished-looking foreign gentleman with jade-green eyes, and once or twice he had been seen walking down the street accompanied by a tiny, dark-haired, blue-eyed boy, rumored to be the son of the late *Comte de* Chagny, La Carpentier's first husband. The present *Comte de* Chagny, M. Carpentier, looked to be treating the boy well, though, the rumor-mongers whispered. He always spoke to the boy affectionately and referred to him as "my son."

Christine was so wrapped up with her singing and her new marriage that she had no idea of the magnitude of the rumors that surrounded her new life, until the final night of the season. She'd had a triumphant finale as Aïda, where her anguish during the final scene had been most affecting. As the stone rolled shut, burying Aïda alive with her lover Radames, Christine had imagined how Erik must have felt to see her going away with Raoul and knowing that he would die alone there beneath the opera. Her agony at the thought came through clearly in her song and brought most of the audience members to tears.

Still somewhat emotional, not only because of the scene but also the tumultuous applause when she had taken her curtain call, Christine went down to the Rotunda. She stopped for a moment to admire the sculpture of the Pythea in the fountain, as she always did. After her years with Raoul when she had been unable to express the true vivacity of her nature, she found something appealing about the Pythea's windblown locks and the wildness of her pose.

The Rotunda was empty of people, the majority of the audience having already left while she had changed and removed her stage makeup. She made her way to the entrance to wait for Erik to pull up in their family coach. Leaning against a pillar near the doorway, she went unnoticed by the two chorus members who strolled chattering through the Rotunda. The great round stone room had even better acoustics than the stage did, and their idle conversation echoed around the room until it reached Christine's ears.

"You'll never believe what I found out about La Carpentier," the girl said. Christine recognized her voice; she was a small, swarthy girl named Euphrasie, with an earthy sense of humor and a rich, vibrant contralto.

"You're such a gossip, 'Phrasie! All right, what did you hear?" the young man replied. Christine recognized his voice; it was her former student, Jean-Michel, whose lessons Erik had taken over when they'd returned to Paris after their honeymoon. Christine and Erik had been quite gratified when the young man had made it into the chorus only a few months after beginning his lessons with Erik.

"I heard that La Carpentier is really a countess!" Euphrasie intimated.

Jean-Michel laughed, the sound echoing in the great mirrored room. "You've just now learned that?" he teased. "I've known that for ages."

"Have you?" the girl exclaimed. "So you knew that she's married to the ugly man—you know, the one who sits in box five?"

Jean-Michel's voice sounded pained. "Please don't call him that, 'Phrasie. I know he's not handsome, but le Comte de Chagny deserves nothing but respect from any person who aspires to be a singer!"

"I'm sorry, Jean-Michel. I didn't mean anything by it. Do you know the *comte*, then?"

"Yes," the boy said shortly. "He is my teacher, and before that, *Madame la Comtesse* tutored me herself."

Euphrasie paused; Christine amused herself picturing the girl's jaw dropping in shock. She changed the subject, her voice once again taking on that sly quality that told Christine more gossip was in the offing. "Speaking of *Madame la Comtesse*, rumor has it that she was married to the previous *Comte de Chagny* as well. How on earth did that happen?"

"I overheard her talking to La Giry one time," Jean-Michel said. "About when she disappeared right off the stage. Apparently, she married Comte Raoul de Chagny soon afterwards, and retired from the stage."

"I heard that too!" cried Euphrasie. "Of course, she was La Daaé then. It was right in the middle of the prison scene in Faust—she called for the angels to take her away, and then the stage went dark. And when the lights came back on, she was gone!"

"Well, she seems to have returned from her trip to heaven no worse for wear," quipped Jean-Michel. "And you never know—maybe she was part of the estate, and got passed along to the next *comte* along with the title and lands."

Euphrasie let out a shocked giggle at her friend's irreverence. "Jean-Michel, you're awful! It's odd, though, isn't it? To think of her being married to a *comte*, and to go on singing on the stage anyway."

Christine glanced around the other side of

the pillar she leaned against; the two were standing out of sight, and all she could see were the shadows the two chorus members cast on the wall. Jean-Michel's shadow shrugged. "The present *comte* is such a great musician that it is no great surprise that his wife continues to perform. As to her previous marriage, I have no idea, and I don't care. She certainly seems fortunate in her current one, whether it was her idea or not."

Euphrasie laughed. "You must admit, though, that theirs does not *seem* like an arranged marriage."

"No indeed; she is very devoted to him."

"And he is so attentive to her! So tender, kind and respectful. He gives her roses every week. No, it must be a love match. You should hear the other girls sighing after him, whenever he brings flowers or sweets to her dressing room! Most of them are quite enamored of the man."

"Even you?" Jean-Michel teased.

Euphrasie's voice sounded embarrassed. "Perhaps. We all agree that for all he's so ugly, La Carpentier is still one of the luckiest women in Paris."

Jean-Michel laughed. "He sometimes brings

a friend with him to the opera, a Persian gentleman."

"Yes, and his friend is *very* handsome! But we all still prefer M. de Carpentier. He's much more romantic!"

"Richer, too," Jean-Michel added practically.

"True—but riches and looks don't matter so much, when a man is as talented and devoted as the count is."

"And as influential," Jean-Michel replied. "They say the managers do whatever the count says. Shall I tell the count what you've said about the chorus girls?"

Euphrasie's response was a shriek and a splash, presumably from the fountain. "Don't you *dare*!"

Christine, listening, smiled a little to herself as the two young singers headed back up the stairs. Christine couldn't decide whether she was amused or chagrined at the idea that she had been "passed along with the title," but Jean-Michel's loyalty to Erik pleased her. Public recognition for Erik's genius was long overdue. She also liked hearing the opinions of the chorus girls, as represented by the little contralto.

So Erik's wealth and looks were equally un-important to them—they were all in love with him because he loved his wife so much! She was still chuckling when Erik pulled up outside in their coach. He helped her in and pulled the door shut, leaning out the window to tell the coachman to "Drive on!"

As the coach lurched into motion, he took one of Christine's hands and kissed the inside of her wrist at the top of her glove. "And what has happened to bring that delightfully mis-chievous little smile to your face, *ma douce*?" he asked in a low voice. "Besides your marvel-ous, yet unsurprising triumph this evening?"

"I've just overheard some extremely enter-taining gossip about us," Christine replied.

He tugged off her glove. "Oh?" He pressed her fingers to his lips.

"Oh, yes," Christine said. "Did you know, for example, that you only married me because I got passed along as part of the count's es-tate?"

Erik huffed out a startled laugh. "What?"

Christine nodded. "Yes, but you've made such a noble attempt to fall in love with me that you've become known throughout the opera as a most devoted husband."

- Letters to Erik -

Erik paused in his nibbling of his wife's fingers to say, "I should hope so."

"In fact, you're so devoted to me that half
the girls in the chorus have fallen in love with
you," Christine went on with a grin.

Erik, in the middle of reaching for Christine's other hand, stopped dead. "Good God!"
He studied her face in the dim moonlight.
"You're serious?" He finished removing her
other glove and proceeded to unbutton her cuffs
so he could kiss further up her wrists.

"Completely. According to one of the chorus girls, you leave a train of swooning girls
behind you in the corridors every time you
bring me flowers."

Erik glanced up sharply. His expression of
utter shock, unmistakable even through his
rubber mask, made her giggle. At the sound, he
closed his mouth sharply and grunted. "Mmph.
I might have to start traveling through the walls
again." He shook his head in disbelief as he
moved closer, beginning to kiss her neck. He
whispered in her ear, "What else did these wor-
thy souls mention?"

Christine shivered at the sensation of his
warm breath against her ear. "Simply that
you're the best catch in Paris, and I'm the

luckiest woman," she replied, a little breathless. "And I knew that already."

Erik smiled and moved closer. "It's an odd opinion," he remarked, beginning to kiss her neck. "However I doubt I shall have much success talking you out of the notion."

"None at all," Christine confirmed, tilting her face up for his kiss.

They had reached their Paris flat by this time, and Erik handed his wife's gloves back to her and helped her out of the coach. He opened the door of their flat for her, but then apparently lost patience and swept her up in his arms.

Kaveh and Darius, quietly playing chess in the sitting room, looked up to see Erik carrying Christine past the doorway; her arms were locked tight around his neck, and he was just bending his head to kiss her. They did not stop until Kaveh and Darius heard the master bedroom door kicked shut.

Kaveh moved his queen. They grinned at each other. "Checkmate," Kaveh said.

Darius tipped his king, jerking his head in the direction their friends had gone. "So it would seem."

Chapter 24
Epilogue

1909

The late afternoon sun shone in the music room at the top of the house. In one corner at the desk, a serious young man toiled over a set of blueprints while his father bent over behind him to peer over his shoulder. In another corner was a tall, black-haired girl about seventeen years old, playing the violin.

She came to a difficult passage in the piece, and slowed the tempo a little. Both men tensed slightly, shoulders set in an attitude of waiting. She got through the passage and sped up, and both men relaxed, exchanging a quick smile before focusing on the blueprints again.

The girl played on, oblivious to the reactions of her father and brother. When she reached another intricate passage and hit two sour notes, though, she stopped playing and glanced up guiltily. Both men were watching her.

"Try again, Darice," her father suggested gently.

She applied her bow again, but missed the same two notes. Scowling, she tried again, but that time and the next, she hit three wrong notes. She stomped her foot in frustration.

Erik-Daaé at twenty-four had developed a dry and satirical sense of humor. He raised his eyebrows and told her innocently, "Well, you're certainly getting a lot of expression into the music. That's the angriest *Pax et Requiem* I've heard ever since I was learning to play it myself."

Darice, still irritated, smiled in spite of herself at the irony. "Come and show me how to do it, then."

He brushed a lock of hair out of his dark blue eyes and rose. "Certainly, unless Papa wants to..?"

Erik shook his head. "No, son, go ahead. I'll

just look this over one last time." He sat down at the desk. He would never admit it, but his stepson could play this piece much better than he himself could—now that his joints had begun to stiffen with arthritis.

Erik-Daaé went and took the proffered violin. Setting it under his chin, he closed his eyes and took a deep breath before starting to play.

The piece, which had seemed to drag in the girl's skilled but inexperienced hands, came to life when played by its master. Erik-Daaé had no need of sheet-music; he kept his eyes closed while he played and his upper body swayed slightly in time with the music.

He fairly flew through the difficult passage that had stumped his sister, and her eyes narrowed.

"Again, please," she interrupted. He obligingly started at the beginning of the difficult phrase. She watched avidly, eyes and ears completely focused on Erik-Daaé's playing.

Erik sat at the desk and watched them both with a little smile quirking his malformed lips. Twenty-five years ago if someone had told him that he would someday watch his and Christine's daughter play the violin, or that he would be just as proud of Raoul de Chagny's son as if he'd fathered him himself, he would have thought them mad. Now, though, it seemed the most natural thing in the world.

"All right, I think I have it now," Darice reached for the bow again. Taking the violin, she tucked it into her neck and began playing. The tempo was slower and the notes more deliberate, but when she got to the passage that had defeated her, she locked her golden eyes onto Erik-Daaé's dark blue ones and played through the entire passage.

He nodded his approval, and she lowered the bow with a smile.

Their father spoke up. "Very much improved, Darice. You may play as well as your brother yet." He smiled, his skin stretched tightly across his unmasked, skull-like face.

She returned the smile with a mischievous glint. "Actually, I plan to surpass him. It shouldn't be too hard—now that you have him building churches, he'll be neglecting his practice in favor of his plans... just as now."

Erik-Daaé gave her a stern look. "You know all the bids for the new church are due next week. I wanted to show them to Papa for comments before I turn them in. I do not make a habit of neglecting my practice, sister dear."

"No, but you will," Darice teased. "And then I'll play better than you do, and I shall become first violin, and be the most sought-after woman in Paris. I shall have suitors lining the corridors at the Opera, all fighting each other for the chance to speak to me!"

"Papa and I shall likely save them the trouble of fighting, by killing off all the unworthy ones before they even come near you," Erik-Daaé's expression was completely deadpan. Darice glanced at her father, to see whether Erik-Daaé was joking, but he merely nodded in agreement.

"You wouldn't dare!" Darice exclaimed, mostly sure they were teasing her, but not completely convinced of it.

Erik smirked, the expression slightly incongruous on his skeletal face. "Never, ever say that to me," he advised.

"To either of us, really," his son chimed in. "You must understand that we will dare anything, anything at all, to guarantee your safety."

"*Vraiment!*" Erik agreed.

"Oh, how nice," Darice replied sarcastically. "I suppose you won't be happy unless I marry Louis de Castelot-Barbezac, or someone like that?"

"He does at least enjoy music for its own

sake," her brother pointed out, "And since he's the son of a dancer just as we're the children of an opera singer, he'll never be snobbish." Louis was the son of "Little Meg" Giry, who had married *le baron de* Castelot-Barbezac—much to the delight of her mother, who had continued robust and vigorous until her sudden death in a carriage accident at age ninety-four.

"That's true," Darice conceded. "I do despise snobs. Aunt Clémence and her family have never liked us, even though our branch of the family was the noble one and not hers. She always acts like she is better than we are."

"Luckily, we need not pay any attention to Clémence," Erik remarked. "And your Aunt Sylvie has more than enough graciousness and nobility to make up for both Clémence and Martine."

The young siblings both laughed and agreed. Sylvie had always been their favorite aunt. Martine had mellowed eventually and become a real member of the family, but Clémence had never forgiven Erik for being the true Comte de Chagny.

"I think Aunt Sylvie got all the looks of the family, too," Erik-Daaé remarked. "Martine and Clémence think they're beauties, but they're nothing to Aunt Sylvie."

Erik nodded. "Your mother says you look more like a Daaé than a Chagny—which is to your advantage, considering the Chagnys produced me! Darice takes after the Chagnys, but she looks more like Sylvie than like her other aunts. God forbid she should look like her father!"

"She doesn't have your face, Papa, but she has your hair and build. She also got her musical talents from you, and therefore has the advantage over me," his son replied with a fond smile for his sister.

"True," Darice agreed with a smug look. "And music is far more important than looks, anyway. *Maman* says so."

Erik smiled. "And I'll be eternally grateful that she chose to see it that way," he replied. "But remember, *ma cherie*, that all the natural talent in the world will never take the place of sufficient practice. Erik-Daaé did not inherit much musical talent from his father's side, it is true—but he practices more than enough to make up for it. Mind you don't let pride in your talent take the place of practice."

"I won't, Papa."

"All right, then. We should pack up and go

down; your mother should be home from Aunt Sylvie's in time for dinner, and she was going to stop at the station and pick up Kaveh on the way home."

Erik-Daaé rolled up his plans while Darice put her music away. As they did so, she asked him, "Why do you always work on your architecture here in the music room, anyway?"

Erik-Daaé had not quite lost his reserve and thoughtfulness from childhood. He gave the offhand question serious consideration before answering. "Music is essentially mathematics, filtered through human passion and creativity. Architecture is human creativity expressed through mathematics. Working on one in the presence of the other helps me with both."

"Oh! Is that why you usually do your practicing at the Opera?"

He nodded. "The Opera is a prime example of creativity and mathematics combined with beauty. It is the best of both worlds."

"Flattery will get you nowhere," Erik told his son mildly. "Although I appreciate the compliment. Now then, hurry down. I want to see your mother when they come in, and if Kaveh is home he will probably want to see me, and he will gripe if he has to climb all the way up here to do it."

With Erik's full support, Kaveh occasionally acted as a volunteer consultant to the Paris police force. Not only did this allow the gendarmes to have access to his decades' worth of police experience, but it enabled him to keep his hand in. Best of all, if anyone in Paris started inquiring about the opera phantom, Kaveh would be the first to hear of it and warn Erik. That was part of the agreement the two men had come to, years before when Kaveh had joined their household.

Darice, lighter on her feet than the two men, skimmed down the stairs swiftly. They heard her greeting Kaveh as he came through the door.

"Hello, Uncle Kaveh!" they heard her say. "How was Paris?"

They exchanged kisses before Kaveh responded, "Cold and overpopulated as always, my dear."

"Wonderful," Erik muttered sarcastically. "He *is* home; we may as well forget about getting anything useful done this evening."

Erik-Daaé laughed. "On the bright side, though, if Kaveh is home, that means Mother is, too."

"True." Erik's face brightened as he swiftly fastened his mask back on. Although comfortable unmasked among his family, he still preferred to go masked among others, even his best friend.

Christine was just coming in when they met her at the bottom of the stairs. Her husband and son greeted her, and then Christine took the two young people aside for a moment to convey Aunt Sylvie's greetings. Erik and Kaveh were left alone in the entry hall, and Kaveh spoke in a low voice. "I believe it is almost time for dinner, Erik; afterwards, I need to speak to you on a matter of some urgency."

"Police business?" Erik asked, and was surprised when Kaveh shook his head.

"No, not exactly. You'll see."

The maid came to announce dinner just then, and Erik swallowed his next question. Kaveh smiled at him and mouthed, "Later!"

The meal was something of a celebration: it was the first time the whole family had been together in months. With Erik-Daaé living in Paris and Kaveh spending so much time there working with the police there, neither one had the time to come home as often as any of them would like.

The dinner went quite late as they all caught up with each other's doings, and simply enjoyed being together after so long. Afterwards, Christine wanted to hear the new piece that Darice had composed, and Erik-Daaé was going to accompany her. They all headed up to the music room, while Erik and Kaveh went upstairs to the study.

Kaveh was panting. "I will never know why the whole lot of you choose to congregate in the tallest part in the entire house! Can't you have some pity on the elderly and infirm?"

"We're the same age, daroga," Erik reminded him, amused.

"More or less, damn you," Kaveh growled. "But you're a wizard, as you know; I should think you could take pity on us mere mortals, and move the study and the music room to a lower story!"

Erik shook his head gravely. "That would never do. Then I'd have to associate with *you* more often." Erik poured out two glasses of cognac, handed one to Kaveh, and sat down opposite him. "So," he began. "What news do you have for me that is not 'exactly' police business?"

Kaveh took a sip. "It is… it is a matter of

some delicacy, Erik. It does have to do with the phantom of the Opera. It isn't exactly police news, but if handled incorrectly it might well could be." He handed Erik a letter, addressed to "The Daroga, Rue de Rivoli 206."

"It's from a journalist," he began. "He has somehow learned some of the story of the ghost in the opera house, and is collecting information to write a book about it. He wants to know the rest of the story."

Erik's eyes widened, so that Kaveh could see them flash under his overhanging brow. His voice lowered. "Oh? The *rest* of the story?"

Kaveh nodded. "This is his third letter. His first two were filled with inaccuracies, but there has been more than a kernel of truth in them. If he should happen to find out who the Opera Ghost really was, then—" he shrugged expressively.

Erik brooded over his cognac. "I see what you mean."

"I think I should meet with him, Erik."

Suspicious yellow eyes swept up to meet his. "What?"

Kaveh spread out his hands. "I think we need to find out how much he knows."

Erik hesitated a moment, frowning, and then

said, "Perhaps you should meet with him, at that. But what do you plan to tell him?"

Kaveh shrugged. "The truth, mostly."

"Explain." Erik demanded.

"Simply that you and I decide ahead of time how much of the truth I should tell him. You know that the truth is easier to remember than a lie."

Erik thought about it for several long minutes, and then looked up. "Why not tell the whole truth, but end the story in the middle?" Erik suggested.

"How so?" Kaveh asked.

Erik gave his one-shouldered shrug. "When I sent Christine away to marry that young puppy, I expected to die. It was only due to your intervention that you did not. We could simply end the story there, before the intervention."

Kaveh looked thoughtful. "That could work," he said. "That could very well work. I could just end the story with Christine and Raoul getting onto the train to go to Sweden, and then just tell him that as far as I know, they are still there."

"Yes; instead of having him poke his nose around Paris, we'll send him on a wild goose chase all through Scandinavia. He won't find a thing; there is nothing to connect the Chagny family with the opera ghost except for my cousins, and they're all either dead or ignorant of the ghost's story."

Kaveh nodded. "I'll do it. But one final problem is—"

"You're just full of problems today, *daroga*," Erik observed, deadpan.

"Just today?" Kaveh asked with a grin. He went on. "The letters were sent to my old flat on the Rue de Rivoli. The owners are gone to Italy for the winter months; my old neighbor took their mail and gave me the letters. I believe the journalist thinks I still reside there. I'm fairly certain none of us want him knowing where I really do reside, and a café won't give us enough privacy. I'm not sure where to meet him."

Erik grinned. "Oh, that's not a problem," he said airily. "You'll meet him in your flat, of course."

"But it's not mine anymore. And it's all locked up for the season!"

Erik smiled and spread out his fingers, stretching them. "Am I, or am I not, the lover of trap-doors? Have you ever seen a lock I can't open?"

Kaveh started to chuckle. "We're going to break into my old flat, meet the journalist, and then leave?"

"Can you think of a better plan?"

"Dozens. But none, I must confess, with as high an entertainment value. All right, I shall write to *Monsieur le journaliste* tomorrow and make arrangements. You get me into the flat, and then I'll let you know what happens."

"Oh, no," Erik denied. "I'm coming in with you. I want to see this journalist."

Kaveh blinked. "How do you plan to manage that?"

"Do you still have some of Darius' old clothes?"

"Why, are you going to dress up as my servant?"

"You know I'm good at impersonating Persians, *daroga*."

Kaveh, began to smile as he caught on to Erik's plan. "It's a pity he's passed on; he'd think it quite a lark, I'm sure. Let me go find something for you; we can get it tailored tomorrow if necessary, and then I'll arrange for the journalist to meet me the next day."

By the time they had finished working out the details, everyone else had retired for the night. Erik bid his friend good night, and headed downstairs to his room.

Christine was there, sitting in front of the mirror at her dressing table, taking off her jewelry.

She wore only jewels that Erik had bought for her, Erik noticed with satisfaction. Although she'd had a perfect right as Raoul's widow to wear all the jewels the young pup had obtained for her, she had done so only rarely during his life and never after his death. She had begun giving them away shortly after she married Erik. Clémence and Martine had been quite happy to receive them.

Now Erik was pleased to see her wearing the delicate strand of pearls he had given her on one of their early anniversaries, and the matching set of tiny pearl earrings he'd given her later that year for no special occasion except he thought she should have them.

Erik waited until she'd removed the pieces and laid them carefully inside the wooden jewelry box that he'd made for her so long ago, and that she had once filled with letters. He came up behind her and slid his arms around her. He placed a kiss on her neck. "What did you think of Darice's new piece?" he asked.

She stood up and leaned her head back against his shoulder. "A bit simplistic, perhaps, but a lovely melody. Interesting chord progression as well. I think she has potential."

"Mm-hm," Erik agreed, nuzzling her neck. "Much like another young singer I once knew."

Christine chuckled and turned in his arms to face him. "She's only a few years younger than I was when we first met, Erik," she reminded him as she reached up to untie his cravat. "What will you do if, three years from now, Darice meets up with some older musical genius with a dark past, who takes her to his house and promises her stardom in return for her love?" She gave him a teasing smile.

Erik dropped his gaze. Somehow, having a daughter of his own had shed a new light on some of his more precipitous actions with Christine when he'd first known her. He swallowed. Then he looked up and met Christine's gaze with a rueful shrug. "Hunt him down and strangle the life from his body," he answered honestly. He looked down and added, "Just as your father would have wanted to do to me, had he still lived. As he'd have had every right to."

Christine took advantage of Erik's downcast

look and reached up to untie his mask. She laid it on the dressing table and gave him a kiss. "There, that's better," she remarked, stroking gentle fingers over the marks the mask had made on his pale flesh. "No masks in the bedroom, my love; remember our agreement?"

Erik nodded, his eyes closing in contentment at her facial massage.

Christine smiled at Erik's paternal protective urges surging to the fore at the mere thought of his daughter meeting someone like him. She cupped his face in her hands and brought it down to her level so she could kiss him. "You must admit, it all worked out for the best for us," she said.

He smiled and returned her kiss. "It did," he agreed. "Here, now; it's my turn." He gestured for her to resume her seat before the mirror, and he began removing her hairpins. He dropped them into the bowl on the table until her tailbone-length hair tumbled in waves down her back. He picked up her silver hairbrush and brushed the hair out slowly, admiring the silver sparkles in the blonde waves as they slipped through his fingers.

Christine sighed in pleasure. "Truly it was one of your best decisions, Erik, having me reassign my lady's maid. She never did brush my hair as nicely as you do."

Erik shrugged. "Well, I had to reassign her, didn't I, when you declared our bedroom a mask-free area? Besides, she was conducting a romance with Darius as I recall. I did what I could to help them out."

The thought of Darius reminded him of his plan with Kaveh, to impersonate Darius for the journalist. He smiled to himself as he began plaiting her hair.

Christine noticed his faraway expression in the mirror. It was accompanied by a small and mysterious smile.

"Erik?" she got his attention.

His deep-set golden eyes met her blue ones in the mirror. "Hmm?"

"You're looking exceptionally mischievous this evening. What did you do to Kaveh?"

Erik smiled wider. "Nothing at all, my dear. Do I have to have done something *to* Kaveh, to look mischievous?"

He tied off her braid and bent down to whisper in her ear. "Sometimes we get up to mischief together, you know."

"Oh, dear," Christine said with mock dread. "What are the two of you up to now?"

Erik chuckled. "Oh, it's not that bad. We're just playing a trick on a nosy journalist."

Something in his tone caught Christine's attention, and she stood up and faced him again. She started undoing his coat buttons as she asked, "What nosy journalist is this?"

Erik caught her trepidation and closed his hands around hers, stilling them. "It's nothing to worry about, love, honestly. Some journalist has contacted Kaveh, wanting to know about the ghost who used to haunt the opera. We have worked out what to tell him, and we shall be going to Paris on Wednesday so he can meet with him." He stroked his knuckles down her cheek. "I'm going along to get a look at the journalist, but he won't even see me." He released her hands.

"Are you sure, my dear?" Christine asked, her eyes searching his as her hands returned to his buttons.

"I am." He reached around behind her to unfasten her dress, and when that was done he simply kept his arms around her as she finished unfastening his clothing for him.

"And no one will get hurt?" she pressed, knowing the bloody history that he and Kaveh shared.

"No one," Erik promised, bending to kiss her. He kissed her again, lingering there to taste her lips.

"Why, M. de Carpentier," Christine said teasingly. "You certainly don't kiss like a man who's almost seventy!"

"Don't rush me into aging, *madame*," Erik warned, curling a lock of her hair around his long, slender fingers. "There are many enjoyable aspects to *soixante-neuf,* you know."

Christine gave him a demure smile as she tied the ribbons on her silk nightgown. "I expect you'll show me each and every one at some point," she said.

"In particular detail," Erik promised as he took his wife's hand and kissed it, pulling her after him. "Come to bed, Christine."

# # #

Two days later, around 8:30 in the morning, Erik neatly picked the lock of Kaveh's old flat on Rue de Rivoli. Wearing his rubber mask and Darius' old suit, Erik helped Kaveh get settled into a chair with a blanket over his legs like an invalid. The doorbell rang, and the two men stopped just for an instant to grin at each other.

Erik went down the stairs and opened the door. The caller was a heavy-set, bearded fellow with thick brown hair and little round silver spectacles. "Gaston Leroux," he announced. He handed Erik his card. "I am here to see M. Tallis."

"Very good, sir," Erik said deferentially. He ushered the caller upstairs and knocked on the door. "M. Gaston Leroux to see you, sir," he called.

"Ah, excellent!" Kaveh replied. "Go and make us some tea, would you, Darius? M. Leroux must be frozen solid, or nearly."

The two men made small talk as the water heated, then as Erik busied himself in the corner pouring out the tea for his friend and the portly journalist, Kaveh opened the subject of the Opera Ghost. "Now, then, M. Leroux, what would you like to know about the opera phantom?"

His visitor looked uncertainly in Erik's direction, no doubt surprised by the Persian's bringing up the topic in front of his servant.

"Ah, please do not concern yourself about my man Darius, *monsieur*. In fact, I was going to have him remain here while we talk, so he could jog my memory if necessary. It isn't what it once was, is it, Darius?"

Erik said nothing, but his eyes sparkled with amusement as he served the two men their tea and took his place standing behind Kaveh's chair.

Kaveh took a sip of tea. "After all," he continued, "we must both try our very best to make sure M. Leroux has the true and complete story for his book, mustn't we?"

"I would appreciate that, sirs," Leroux replied, adding some lemon to his own tea. "With this book I intend to prove, once and for all, that the opera ghost really existed."

FIN

CPSIA information can be obtained at www.ICGtesting.com
Printed in the USA
LVOW090723030712

288673LV00001B/26/P